D0388968

BOOK FOUR

QUARANTINE

theGIANT

LEX THOMAS

QUARANTINE

the GIANT

BOOK FOUR

Carolrhoda LAB

MINNEAPOLIS

Carolrhoda Lab™ is a trademark of Lerner Publishing Group, Inc.

Carolrhoda Lab™
An imprint of Carolrhoda Books
A division of Lerner Publishing Group, Inc.
241 First Avenue North
Minneapolis, MN 55401 USA

For reading levels and more information, look up this title at www.lernerbooks.com.

Cover and interior images: © iStockphoto.com/Charles Mann (road). © iStockphoto.com/windujedi (man); © iStockphoto.com/picture (cracked asphalt).

Main body text set in Ommegaand 11.5/18.

Library of Congress Cataloging-in-Publication Data

The Cataloging-in-Publication Data for *The Giant* is on file at the Library of Congress.
ISBN 978-1-5124-0103-5 (trade hardcover)
ISBN 978-1-5124-0159-2 (EB pdf)

LC record available at https://lccn.loc.gov/2015043911

Manufactured in the United States of America
1-38937-20911-3/18/2016

To the Quarantine fans

1

GONZALO STARED INTO THE EYES OF THE
mountain lion. It had emerged from the woods under the
purple light of dusk, slunk into the middle of the road, and
stopped. Now the animal gazed at him unblinking and completely still. Not even a twitch of a whisker. This was bad. Gonzalo had no weapon, and no car.

The lion seemed to be thinking. Sizing him up. Deciding
whether to pounce.

Gonzalo was big, and that tended to keep him out of fights.
If things ever got as far as Gonzalo making a fist, the other
guy would see that Gonzalo's fist was the size of a car battery
and lose his nerve.

Gonzalo made his hands into fists. The mountain lion took
a step toward him.

This wasn't a person—this was an animal. It was born knowing how to rip the flesh out of another animal's neck with its

mouth. It had no more inner conflict over the morality of the act than Gonzalo did about grocery shopping.

The lion lowered its head below its shoulders. Its round, green eyes were buried inside a heavy brow and massive cheekbones. Little black pupils like bullet holes remained aimed at Gonzalo's eyes.

No human could outrun a mountain lion, especially not Gonzalo. Running was something he could do for about five minutes before the effort of propelling his two hundred and ninety pounds forward would have him gagging for air.

Gonzalo glanced behind himself. There was a bicycle within reach in the tall grass, next to a human skeleton wearing a bicycle helmet. A neon spandex shirt was loose over the ribcage, and black spandex shorts sagged between the hip bones.

The mountain lion growled from deep in its belly. Gonzalo looked back at those tight black pupils as he edged toward the bicycle. The lion watched.

Gonzalo bent down slowly with his eyes on the animal, and grasped hold of the bicycle's curved handlebar. The mountain lion took three steps toward him. Its legs moved gracefully, its muscles bulging like rocks under its fur. Its head stayed low. Gonzalo pulled the bicycle up off the ground, and the long grass that was tangled in its spokes and gears tore with a dry, raspy rip. Each grass blade snapping seemed enough to provoke an attack. The animal's advance was unhurried, its front paws stretched far out in front with each step, ready to spring forward at any moment.

Gonzalo went for the bike. He ripped it up, threw his leg over, got his butt on the tiny seat, and pounced on the pedals. He was wobbling on the pitted asphalt a second later, and he could feel on his skin that sharp claws were about to dig canals down his back and mighty fangs were going to clamp down on his neck. He pumped his feet in a frenzy, weaving down the road, willing himself to go faster and faster, the forest on either side whipping past in his peripheral vision, until his legs were about to quit.

The bite never came. When Gonzalo finally looked back, the mountain lion wasn't chasing him. It wasn't watching him either. It wasn't there at all. The beast had lost interest and wandered off. Gonzalo allowed his pace to slow. The bike seat was the size of a child's sneaker. It felt like a medieval torture device trying to split him in half. Gonzalo spat out a slew of curses. He couldn't believe he was in this situation. Just two days before, on his nineteenth birthday, he'd had wheels, weapons, a gas mask—he'd had an entire van full of supplies. His search for Sasha had already gone on for six months, and it'd taken him exactly that long to assemble all that gear. He'd had one ax and three sledgehammers. Weeks of food that he'd stockpiled, fishing gear, galoshes, hiking boots. It had taken him months to find boots that fit his enormous feet. The same was true of the van. It was one of the only cars he'd been able to find that he could fit inside. And someone had gone and stolen it when he was bathing in a creek. The notes he'd been keeping on his search for Sasha, six months of clues, gone. The phone he'd had since before the quarantine, the one that contained every picture he had ever taken of Sasha, lost forever. If he failed in his mission to find her out here in the infected zone, he would never see her face again.

Gonzalo slowed to a coast and pulled a pack of cigarettes and a lighter out of his pocket. At least he still had his smokes. He fished one out with his lips and lit it, his hands still shaking from the rush of the lion encounter. He'd picked up a little habit since graduation. Hadn't really intended to, but there wasn't much in the infected zone that made you feel good anymore. Cigarettes, though, you could still find around. His mom would have killed him if she knew. He took a deep drag and relaxed a little. He never felt safe in the infected zone, but his smokes helped take the edge off. He was going to quit as soon as he found Sasha and got back to the real world. Gonzalo put the pack and lighter in his pocket and pedaled back up to a respectable speed.

The sun had sunk below the horizon, and the purple sky had darkened to a deep violet. It would be dark soon. The road up ahead was getting harder to see. He needed new wheels, preferably a vehicle like the van, big enough for him to sleep inside. If he couldn't find something soon, abandoned by the side of the road, he'd need to find some other kind of shelter.

He needed a weapon. He didn't care what it was, but he'd go for the most frightening one he could find. His favorite kind of fight was the one that never started, the kind that was about to start until you pulled out a chainsaw splattered with red paint and the guy thought better of it and ran. He needed water and food. He needed more clothes than the shorts and T-shirt he was wearing. Thank God he had his high-tops. If he were barefoot, he'd probably step on a rusty nail, get gangrene and—

Something caught his eye in the dark woods to the left. A pair of luminescent green eyes in the darkness, staring at him and matching his pace.

Before Gonzalo could react, the mountain lion burst from the forest, cut across the road, and launched into the air. The lion swatted him off the bike with a heavy paw. It felt like he'd been hit by a telephone pole. Gonzalo's back smacked against the asphalt, and instantly the monster was on him, jaws open, rows of sharp teeth bared. It lowered its head to chomp down on the soft flesh of his throat, but Gonzalo threw his arm up. The lion's fangs sank into the meat of his forearm instead. He tried to yank his arm away, but the lion's jaws only clamped down harder. The strength of its bite was terrifying. Like a pickup truck parked on his forearm. Its brow was twisted in a knot, its snout bunched into rolls of bristling fur. Its eyeballs glistened in the fading light, spherical and green and furious.

It opened its jaws wide, and its fangs withdrew from Gonzalo's flesh. It went for his neck again. Gonzalo sacrificed his arm once more, except this time, the lion's fangs buried into his bicep. He didn't have long. The beast was stronger—it would be digging into his neck soon.

Gonzalo shoved his fingers into the lion's right eye socket until he could feel the rope of optic nerve. He gripped the eyeball. It felt like an oiled plum. The lion yowled, unclamped its jaws, and whipped its head away from Gonzalo. The eye, however, stayed with Gonzalo. The maimed lion thrashed around, violently shaking its head, then bounded off into the woods.

Gonzalo panted in the steadily growing darkness. The lion's eyeball slid off his palm. He lifted himself up and stumbled sideways. He had a lot of holes in his arm. Blood poured down to his fingertips and dripped onto the road. He made sure that his muscles still worked and that all of his fingers could flex and extend, but the effort made the pain swell. He'd have to treat his wounds soon, or they might get infected.

He plucked the pack of cigarettes from his pocket and shook one out. It took him a while to light up, his hands were shaking so badly. Maybe the nicotine buzz would make his arms hurt less, he thought. Cool wind shook the trees like pompoms as the smoke kissed his lungs.

Gonzalo leaned over and picked up his bike. He'd learned not to dwell on near-death experiences. It was best to just soldier on like it'd never happened. The bike didn't seem too damaged. After a few more puffs, he got back on and pedaled to a shaky start. The bicycle wobbled underneath him at this low speed, and he had to crank the handlebars back and forth to keep from tipping over. Stupid tiny bike. He probably looked like a circus bear riding this thing. He pedaled faster, his knees nearly striking his chest, and the bike picked up enough speed to steady him. The rear wheel squeaked with every rotation.

He thought of Sasha.

2

THE QUAD WAS AN OCEAN OF VIOLENCE.

Hair colors smashed into each other. The pile of packaged food and supplies in the center of the quad would be completely gone soon. Gonzalo clutched a can of corn in his hand like it was a gold brick. He'd scooped the can up when another kid had dropped it. A can of corn was way more than Gonzalo thought he'd get today. Now, it was just a matter of getting off the battlefield alive.

Gonzalo ran as fast as his runty legs could carry him. He was sixteen, but he looked twelve. Everything about him was tiny compared to the other kids. The other boys his age didn't just have bigger bodies—they had deeper voices too. Gonzalo was still the hairless boy he'd been when he started junior high, and he was beginning to think that puberty would never strike. The Freak mob in front of him towered over him by at least a foot. As they slowed down, he slowed down. He dodged a Nerd who lunged for his can, and kept running. Gonzalo glanced back to see if the Nerd was still chasing him and saw the kid get flattened by the entire Varsity defensive line, which was charging right for Gonzalo.

He tried to run faster. Those yellow-haired monsters were set to bulldoze him in seconds. Gonzalo cut right in the hope that he could get out of their path. Ahead of him, a trio of Geeks dragged a pallet of gallon-sized water jugs back to the sidelines. When they saw the Varsity wall of death behind Gonzalo, they abandoned the pallet and fled. Gonzalo tried to turn and avoid the water jugs, but someone tackled him from behind. His face hit the plastic jugs, and another heavy Varsity guy landed on top of him, crushing his chest into the wooden pallet.

Varsity hollered as they dove on top of each other to pile onto Gonzalo. The weight of this mound of muscle and bone squeezed all the air out of his lungs. Gonzalo began to panic. He was going to suffocate. He felt the wood splintering underneath him. His ribcage was going to cave in. His skull was about to pop. Muffled voices yelled and cheered and laughed above him.

When the Varsity pile finally climbed off him and started collecting the water jugs, one of them picked Gonzalo up by the arm pits and threw him to another Varsity, who threw him to another. The Varsity guys played catch with him like he was a ball. They thought it was hilarious. Gonzalo didn't. He still clutched the can of soup. Despite everything, he'd held onto it. The next guy trying to catch him fumbled the catch, and Gonzalo was able to scurry away.

He wove through a crowd of Geeks and Freaks who were fighting. He dove between people's legs, he hunched over as he ran, all to make Varsity lose track of him. Ahead, Gonzalo saw a guy twice his size get two teeth knocked out in a fight over powdered pancakes. He saw a Nerd girl get dragged to the ground by three Skater girls who wanted her pants. He saw a mason jar full of batteries shatter over a Freak's head.

Gonzalo dashed in the direction of the nearest hallway, desperate to get away from the whirling elbows, the gnashing teeth, the packs of kids who hunted together like wolves, but something caught his eye. A tiny Slut, with her red hair in a high ponytail. She was smaller than him, which was rare, and she was carrying a bag of rice away from the Slut food pile, toward the hall. She turned and looked right at him, and she was smoking hot. His pace slowed to a jog. For a moment, he forgot where he was. She had definitely stared right at him, from across the quad. And nobody stared at him. Nobody even glanced at him, especially not a pretty girl. He watched her disappear into the hall.

Gonzalo snapped out of his trance and broke into a sprint. The open doors of the hallway were twenty feet ahead. Once he got there, he could hide. He could eat. He was going to enjoy prying open that can and filling his stomach with corn in some dark, hidden corner of the school. Two tall guys were fighting up ahead to his left, and just as Gonzalo tried to zip past them, one guy's wild punch clocked Gonzalo in the side of the jaw.

When Gonzalo opened his eyes again, he was on his stomach in the dirt and people were stomping on him. No, not stomping on him—people were running over him, stepping on his back like he was the ground. He blinked to clear his vision and pushed himself up to his hands and knees. His can of corn was gone. The two guys who'd been fighting, gone too. A flood of Sluts ran past. He didn't know how long he'd been out, but the food drop was still going strong.

Gonzalo crawled toward the hallway, coughing and sputtering, with a sore jaw, a thumping head, blurred vision, and no food. When he finally hit the linoleum floor of the hallway, he wanted to kiss it.

He couldn't keep running in the drops like this. He knew he'd starve if he tried to keep going it alone. If he had other people looking out for him, he'd be okay. He needed to join a gang. Any gang. It was the only way he'd be able to survive. There was only one problem.

He didn't like people.

Gonzalo had never been a big talker, he'd always been the quiet kid. In the three months since McKinley had been quarantined, Gonzalo had barely spoken to anyone. He would've liked to go it alone, but that was becoming impossible. He was terrified every day now. Terrified of running in the drops, of starving, of the bigger kids in the halls—which was pretty much everyone. He was terrified of this virus they all had. He was terrified about the fact that they had no idea what was happening outside. But as scared as he was of all these things, Gonzalo never let it show. That was his one strength—he could remain stoic in the face of anything. He had always been like that. His father was like that, and so was his grandfather.

They were giant, barrel-chested men. Biggest guys in the neighborhood. They were real proud of that. Gonzalo was too. His father's face seemed chiseled out of stone. His grandfather's was the same, except his was a giant stone on a rocky shore that had been eroded over time and covered in salt deposits and barnacles. Neither of their faces ever moved. And they barely ever spoke. Even if Gonzalo wasn't big like them, he could be tough like them. He could keep his face still, his mouth in a frown, and his eyes mean no matter what was happening around him.

Thinking about this now, all he wanted was to be back home on the living room couch, watching TV with his father and grandfather in their easy chairs, and not saying a word, while his mom and sister zipped around the house like whirling tops, chatting endlessly with each other, or on the phone, or at them.

Gonzalo made his way to the administrative offices, where the Skaters lived. When he got there, a group of them were prying the linoleum tiles off the floor of the hallway, while the rest of them seemed to be goofing off. He'd join any gang that would have him at this point, but the Skaters looked like they knew how to have a good time. Their leader, a kid who called himself P-Nut, launched through the air on a skateboard and landed it on a wooden desk in the middle of the hall. He tried to kick-flip off it but totally biffed the landing and fell laughing into a gaggle of Skater girls. They looked eager to catch him. When P-Nut threw one leg forward, grabbed a doe-thin girl in a belly shirt, dipped her like Zorro, and kissed her, Gonzalo wanted to be him.

Gonzalo approached one of the Skaters. The guy's head was shaved except for a round patch of hair on each side, which he'd tinted gray and gelled into bull horns. Gonzalo wanted to ask Bull Horns if he could join. He tried to talk, but his face didn't move. He was nervous.

"Can I help you with something?" the Skater said, looking down at him.

Gonzalo tried to summon the right words. He didn't want to mess this up.

"Why are you looking at me like that, shrimp?" the Skater said.

Now it was getting awkward. He really needed to say something, but he was drawing a blank.

"Check out how this kid's fuckin' lookin' at me. I asked you what you want, kid."

It's probably better this way, Gonzalo thought. They'll hear the fear in your voice if you talk. They'll know they can mess with you.

Gonzalo's mouth remained in a frown, his eyes mean and unflinching. Other Skaters gathered at the doorway, behind the bull-horned kid. Gonzalo didn't know what to do. The seconds ticked away.

"I think you better get the fuck out of here, shrimp. How 'bout that?" the Skater said.

Gonzalo didn't like this guy. He was mad at Gonzalo for nothing. Gonzalo didn't like his friends either. All of their hairstyles were stupid. Still, for the sake of food and protection—and a chance to be around girls—he tried to put his feelings aside. He just had to open his mouth and ask one question: Can I be in your gang? But all that happened was that his scowl deepened.

"I said get out of here!"

An altercation between some other Skaters and a Scrap boy down the hall distracted Gonzalo. The Scrap boy was on the ground on his back. The Skaters were shouting at the Scrap, accusing him of trying to dye his hair black to look like a Skater. The Scrap boy pleaded that his white hair was only dark because it was dirty.

"Are you deaf, kid?" the bull-horned Skater shouted in Gonzalo's face.

Gonzalo ignored the Skater and rushed toward the Scrap,

who had been forced into a corner and was getting kicked. Gonzalo wedged himself between the Skaters and the Scrap and held his hand out like a traffic cop, signaling stop. The Skaters were momentarily struck dumb. He could understand how they'd be confused because even he didn't know what the hell he was doing. He wished he was the kind of person who could look the other way, because these Skaters were all bigger than him by a large margin. Even the Scrap on the ground was bigger.

"You think you're gonna stop us?" a Skater in dirty clothes with filth-covered hands said. He walked forward, like he was going to brush Gonzalo off. Gonzalo shoved him. It took all of his strength to force the guy back, but he tried not to let the effort show. He never looked away from the filthy Skater's eyes, and he didn't blink.

The Skaters were truly confused now. They examined Gonzalo from head to toe, probably wondering whether he was some sort of MMA whiz or had a bottle of hydrochloric acid from the chemistry lab in his back pocket, or if he was flat-out bluffing, which he was. The Scrap boy bolted away, and Gonzalo got a fist in the mouth at the same time. He stumbled with the blow but managed to stay on his feet. He ran.

The Skaters chased. With each heaving breath, red spit blew from Gonzalo's split lip. The Skaters' gleeful laughter grew louder behind him. At a junction with another hall, the Scrap boy went left and Gonzalo went right. The hallway ahead dead-ended. There weren't any staircases, or other hallways to turn down. He'd trapped himself. Gonzalo skidded to a stop at the next classroom and found the door open. He ran inside and slammed the door shut behind him. He grabbed the nearest classroom chair and wedged its back under the door's handle. It was a good trick, but it wouldn't work forever.

The door handle swiveled. The door opened half an inch, but the chair wedge stopped it.

BOOM. The door rattled with the impact. They were going to get in. Gonzalo scanned the empty classroom for a weapon. A shard of glass. A hunk of cinderblock. Hell, he'd take a ruler at this point. There was nothing but four other chairs, gray plates of steel where the windows should have been, and a white projector screen spread out on the crud-covered floor like a picnic blanket with ghosts of dingy shoe prints across it.

BOOM. One of the metal legs of the wedged chair bent under the force. This was gonna be bad. The effort they were putting into bashing this door down meant they weren't gonna let him go. They were going to hurt him. He tried to make his hands into fists, but he couldn't stop them from shaking.

BOOM! The wood of the door splintered.

"Hey," he heard a voice whisper.

Gonzalo looked around the room like he was losing his mind. He swore he'd just heard a voice. And then he saw her. The Slut girl who'd stared at him in the quad—except now she was dressed like a Freak. Her hair was blue now, and she'd painted black all around her eyes so that they looked like empty sockets. She was leaning out of an air vent in the wall. She held herself in the push-up position with her hands on the floor. Her forearms were dirty, but her lipstick was hot pink and glossy. Her crop-top hung down, her olive skin was glazed in sweat, and she held his stare. This had to be some sort of mirage.

BOOM! He heard the door crack. The Skaters were about to get in.

"Quick, come with me," she said and pushed herself backwards into the air duct with surprising speed.

The dark hole beckoned, the vent cover hanging open below it. Gonzalo ran and dove into the wall. His skin slid across the metal floor of the dark duct, and it hurt, but he'd made it all the way inside.

"Pull the string!" she whispered from the dark.

Gonzalo looked down and saw a white string running next to him along the floor of the vent. He grasped it and pulled it taut. He saw that the string ran through an O-ring screw at the opening of the vent. Pulling the string lifted the air vent grille cover back up into place, like it had never been dislodged at all.

The next BOOM was more of a CRASH, although muffled, and Gonzalo heard the Skaters rush into the classroom. Then it got quiet. After a minute he heard them leave. As their voices faded, they started joking around about something else.

The metal walls around Gonzalo were cool to the touch. The sound of the school was now muted and distant.

A flame sparked to life right in front of his face and illuminated the area around them. The Slut/Freak, who had just saved his ass, was right in front of him, holding a lighter. Their faces were inches apart, separated by a steady flame.

"Why'd you help me?" Gonzalo blurted out.

Her jaw dropped, and her mouth stretched into an O. "You talked!" she said.

"So?" Gonzalo said.

"I didn't know you could."

"You didn't answer my question."

"They were going to kill you."

"I probably could have handled them."

She burst out in laughter, but at a whisper's volume.

"They were chasing me 'cause I'd already kicked their ass last week," Gonzalo said. "They wanted a rematch."

She only whisper-laughed harder. Her teeth twinkled in the light of the butane flame.

"They were after you 'cause you helped that Scrap," she said. Her laughter trickled away, but her smile remained.

"Have you been watching me?"

She broke eye contact. "Just that thing now in the hall."

Her face got soap opera serious. He wondered if she'd been watching him from the vents for longer than she was letting on.

"So what's with the hair? Are you in one gang or two?" he said.

"Something like that."

"You guys have food?"

He was trying to sound practical about it, but the truth was he was ready to follow this girl into a gas chamber. It felt so good to be talking to someone again. Maybe it was just the her-saving-his-life thing, but she actually seemed like someone he could trust. He was also dying to gently mess up her lipstick.

She started inching backwards, away from him.

"Trust me, it's not for you," she said.

"What does that mean?"

"You're a good guy, Gonzalo."

"Wait, don't leave."

She retreated from him faster, the glow of her lighter going with her.

"Don't follow me," she said, before the little flame by her face winked out.

He followed anyway.

3

THE NIGHT HAD ALREADY BEEN COLD, BUT
the rain made it colder. Gonzalo shivered by the side of the
road. He shuffled forward. The sky was just beginning to
lighten. Cold pellets of water splattered against the back of
his neck. Rain sprayed off his shoulders and the crown of his
head. It ran pink down his arm when it mixed with the blood
from his seeping bite wounds. His socks were soaked. His
waterlogged high-tops hung on him like ankle weights.

His bicycle's tires had gone flat within an hour of riding,
and he'd been on foot ever since. He'd tried to get some sleep
under a fallen tree right off the road, but the wet ground
had sucked the heat from his body, so he'd stayed on the
move. The rain had only been coming down for maybe fifteen minutes, but it had already washed all the heat from
his skin. The cold was seeping into the meat of him. And his
body still hadn't recovered from the strain of fighting off a

wild, hungry animal. He wanted to fall to the ground, but he kept walking.

Gonzalo had followed the road out of the forest, and now an oil field stretched out to his left. Giant steel hammers balancing on pivots were silhouetted against the graphite sky. There had to be fifty of them that he could see, frozen like an army of tin men. He tried to imagine them all pumping at the same time. He remembered liking to watch the motion when he was a kid, on family road trips, as they dipped and swung their hammer-heads fast on the way down, then slow on the rise back up. On the other side of the road was a peach orchard, and he wondered which had come first. He shuffled down off the road to where the ground was overgrown with weeds and smothered in decomposing peaches. Here and there, peaches still hung from the trees and looked perfect and ready to eat, slick and wet.

Gonzalo ate peaches in the rain. Seventeen of them. His hunger mattered more than the cold. He pulled off his T-shirt and cinched the sleeves and the bottom with knots to make a sack. He picked as many ripe or near-ripe peaches as his sack could carry and hit the road again, shirtless this time. The food in his stomach reinvigorated him and gave him the energy to keep walking. He almost felt good, but the awareness of how vulnerable he was with no gas mask or weapon kept him wary.

After an hour's walk, Gonzalo's feet felt like two big blisters.

He arrived at a gas station on the outskirts of a town called Monroe. The station sat next to a tiny, red brick strip mall, which had a liquor store, an injury lawyer's office, and a ski rental place. A boxcar diner sat in an empty lot across the road. All of the businesses had been picked clean. Not a ski pole in sight. No food, no clothes to be found, but the stop wasn't a complete wash. There was an abandoned car at the gas station—a lime-green Honda Fit. Its lustrous green paint remained dry underneath the gas station's canopy. The car looked new. Too good to be true. Gonzalo approached it cautiously, like a fox circling a bucket of fried chicken.

He tried the door. It was unlocked. Gonzalo tried to get into the driver's seat, but the little car didn't accommodate his size. His knee bashed up against the steering wheel as he fumbled to adjust the seat. The seat slid back, but not far enough for him to fit. His chin was crunched down on his chest, and the top of his head mashed against the ceiling. His left leg hung out of the car.

Gonzalo thought he heard something odd through the pouring rain—the crackle of multiple engines revving. He tried to lean back out of the car but found he was stuck. He twisted himself toward the passenger seat and looked out the rear window of the car. A few hundred feet back, by the liquor store, a man and a woman were running in the street. They wore gas masks. The man was carrying someone over his shoulder, slumped like he was dead or unconscious. The slumped body's head swung with the man's gait, and Gonzalo saw that his hair was white. Infected. The couple was running full-blast, and Gonzalo saw why. Four dune buggies came ripping around the liquor store, driven by white-haired teenagers wearing amber-vision ski goggles and chrome hubcap chest plates. The vehicles were steel pipe skeletons with buzzing engines. One buggy spun out in the middle of its turn. The driver was pissed and she smashed her fist into the steering wheel. The other three buggies gained on the man and woman, who continued running toward the gas station.

Gonzalo panicked. All that madness was racing his way, and fast. There was no time and nowhere to run. He pulled the rest of himself into the Honda and yanked on the door. It barely clicked shut with all of Gonzalo stuffed inside. The sound of the rain outside went dull and quiet. He hit the power locks and they worked. He twisted the rearview mirror until it reflected the adults in the road behind him.

They weren't running anymore. The woman was face down in the street, underneath one of the buggies. She'd been run over. The unconscious boy the man had been carrying was lying in the mud nearby. The three infected kids held the man. Rain spattered off their chest plates. The man writhed, and for a second, he nearly slipped away, but the infected squeezed him tight. They pulled the man's arms behind him and yanked off his mask. He looked about fifty and more scared than he'd probably ever been in his life. His lips were clenched tight. He was trying to keep his mouth shut, trying to hold his breath, but the infected weren't having it. They clawed at his lips. He lost that fight. The wet, dirty teen fingers managed to pry his mouth open. They bent his head back like a sword swallower. One of them kicked him in the stomach and he coughed out all his air. The man held on for as long as he could, staring up at the sky, but he knew it was all over. He sucked in the inevitable breath. With his head held back and his mouth wide open, the blood shot three feet into the air. It gathered into one wobbling globule in the air for a moment before splashing back down onto his face. Satisfied, the teens let go, and the man crumpled to the street.

Time to leave. Gonzalo felt around for car keys in the ignition, under the sun visors, glove box. Nothing. He could hear his own breathing speeding up. No keys. *Goddamn it.* His uncle had taught him how to hot-wire old cars, and that had come in handy out here, but he knew this new Honda would be too complicated. Besides, he couldn't reach under the dash unless he cut off his own legs first. Gonzalo slapped shut the plastic air vents in the dash. He didn't know what else to do.

The windows were fogging up from his body heat. He was sure the infected would notice it. The rain was easing up, the sky filling with a flat, colorless light. The scene of the dead adults was getting clearer, easier to see. Which had to mean the same about him. If they looked over, what would they see?

The lightening sky reflected in the rear window or the silhouette of a humongous nineteen-year-old stuffed into a subcompact car?

The infected hoisted the unconscious teen up from the mud. Gonzalo noticed that the kid had a hubcap strapped to his chest, just like the others did. One of the infected, with his goggles pushed up on his head, smacked the boy's cheek until he woke up. When his eyes opened, he saw the bodies of the dead adults and started to scream. He tried to hug the dead man and woman. Gonzalo was pretty sure now that they'd been his parents.

Gonzalo'd heard of infected tribes out here in the zone, extreme ones like this, but he'd never seen them for himself. There were the Greaseballs, who lived in the sewers in some town. There was a rumor that a group of infected lived in an abandoned Sears somewhere and called it The Mountain. No one seemed to know which Sears it was, or in which town. He'd once eavesdropped on a group of hunters who'd said The Mountain was actually a Home Depot. He'd heard other tribe names over the months too, like Burnsquad; the Cervixens; the High Valley Titans, who lived in some ski lodge; the Batshit Battalion, who lived in a mental hospital; and the Gravediggers, who hid in a gold mine. These killers had to be the ones called the Buggy Boys. Gonzalo didn't know what they were about—only that they were ruthless, and they didn't take kindly to one of their own trying to leave with his parents.

The Buggy Boys pressed in on the screaming boy. They grabbed his head and stared into his eyes. They handed him a flask and made him drink it. They talked to him calmly. He thrashed against their grip, but the longer they spoke to him, the more docile he became until finally he nodded quietly and even hugged them.

Sweat dripped off Gonzalo's nose. He'd steamed the windows halfway up. The sky was getting brighter. The rain was nearly done. What could he do? He could try to make a run for it now, but it was already getting too bright. He was too big for them not to see him running in a crouch across the street. He could try to get around to the back of the gas station, but then where would he go? If they saw him, he couldn't outrun those dune buggies.

He looked into the rearview again, and the biggest of the kids, the one who had slapped the unconscious kid awake, looked at Gonzalo. Gonzalo didn't dare move. He prayed that the guy was just looking at the car. The big kid left the others behind, walked to his dune buggy, and reached into it.

Gonzalo had to make a break for it *now*. He fumbled around for the door handle but froze. The kid stepped into the frame of the rearview again. He held a rifle, which he raised and pointed toward the car.

No.

I should've run for it, Gonzalo thought and closed his eyes.

A gunshot silenced his thoughts. Gonzalo's whole body jerked, but he felt no pain. He hadn't been hit. He glanced back through the mirror. The rear window was intact. The kid was putting his rifle away. He hopped into his buggy and drove it past the gas station to the road, where he stopped. Gonzalo watched through the front windshield now as the kid walked to a deer lying in the road. Its legs flickered with a last bit of life, and blood still pumped from its gunshot wound. The kid dragged the deer up over the front end of his buggy, got back in, and drove away. The others followed. Gonzalo watched them roar off, in shock that they'd never bothered to take a hard look at the lime-green Honda Fit sitting at the gas station.

He waited a while. Long enough to be sure their poison was gone from the air. When he unlatched the door, Gonzalo's bulk popped out of the cramped car like biscuit dough from a cardboard tube. He couldn't believe it, but it seemed he was safe for now. He should've been lying dead on the ground with that kid's parents.

Gonzalo walked toward the unlucky duo. He didn't want to have to look at them up close, but he had to see if their gas masks were operational or if there was anything else on them he could use. The infected hadn't wasted any time searching the bodies for valuable items. They'd seemed more concerned with reclaiming the boy. Gonzalo had never seen anything like that. He'd never seen people that vicious, infected or not.

The remains of the man and woman were gruesome. Her head had been run over and her mask crushed. His mask had a broken face shield. His face was glazed in blood. From the way his eyes bulged from their sockets, there was no doubt that how he'd died had been a hellish way to go. Gonzalo had to look away.

"Sorry, my man," he said and proceeded to dig through the guy's pockets. The right front pocket had car keys in it. Gonzalo pressed the lock button on the bloody key fob and heard the Honda Fit chirp.

The sound put things in perspective. He was still alive, and now he had a car.

4

IT WASN'T EASY TO FOLLOW THE GIRL THROUGH
the aluminum air ducts in total darkness, without her noticing, but Gonzalo managed. The ducts were dusty, riddled with
dead bugs and what he assumed were cobwebs collecting on
his face and hands. A constant breeze of refrigerated air blew
down his body. He would have thought the tight ducts would
be claustrophobic, with the walls crowding in on all sides,
but bugs and webs aside, he found them oddly comforting,
like he was swaddled in metal. He followed by listening to the
sound of her body shuffling across the duct floor and the
pop of the metal warping under her weight. Her sounds were
so much louder than the murmur of the school. He almost got
lost at a few of the junctions with other ducts, but eventually he saw her ahead of him in the darkness, climbing out
of a vent that led to a bright hall. Gonzalo followed at his
fastest crawl.

He crawled out of an open, low vent and emerged at the edge of the Market. He closed the cover behind him and pressed himself against the wall. The hallway before him bustled with a major crowd, made up of every gang, fresh from fighting on the quad. Here, the fighting had turned to haggling over items for trade, with each gang running its own store in separate classrooms. The teeming crowd of different hair colors looked like a bowl of Easter candy. He saw the same Geek he remembered from the drop getting his cheek sewn shut by a Nerd medic. A scuffle between a Freak and a Varsity started up beside them. He watched as bits of gossip spread through the crowd like viruses, like they always did. He watched people boasting over what they'd gotten in the drop or bitching about what they lost. There were clandestine conversations happening within gangs as they traveled through the hall, carrying their items for trade from one store to the next.

"I told you not to follow me."

Gonzalo had to squint to see her standing in the shadow of the lockers, only three feet from him, blue hair and black eye sockets like a raccoon. She was wearing a black, frumpy men's trench coat now.

"Did you?" Gonzalo said.

"Well, don't just stand there where everyone can see you," she said and waved him over.

He joined her in the shadows. He was taller than her—not by much, but still taller. He still wanted to kiss her. He really didn't know anything about her, but what did that have to do with anything? She looked up at him with a grumpy expression that was almost as cute as her smile.

"What?" she said, and Gonzalo realized that he'd been staring.

"I'm trying to figure out who I want to get to know more—Slut you or Freak you."

She laughed, and he thought she blushed a little. Or maybe it was that he just hadn't noticed the natural rosiness of her cheeks until now.

"Listen, you don't want any of what I'm involved in," she said.

"How do you know that?"

"I can tell."

"You don't think I can handle your gang? I can handle anything." He crossed his arms and let his face sink into a scowl. He couldn't stop acting cocky. It was just flowing out of him. His Uncle George would have been proud. He always told Gonzalo that girls this hot could sniff fear, like how a bear can smell the food at a campsite twenty miles upwind. "Give me a chance."

She shook her head. "Gonzalo, you're a nice guy . . ."

"You keep saying that."

She shrugged. "It's not a bad thing. You just seem a little innocent, that's all."

"You obviously haven't been watching me for very long."

She laughed again. "Oh, you turn into Batman or something?"

Maybe she *had* actually been watching him for a long time. What if she was completely obsessed with him? That would be great. Unless she wasn't. He didn't even know what she was talking about, what innocence had to do with anything, or what it was she thought he couldn't handle.

"Look, I want to hang out with you. Tell me what I gotta do to make that happen," he said.

His directness seemed to catch her off guard. He couldn't read her reaction.

"Would you join a gang just to hang out with me?" she said.

The question felt like a trick. It sounded a little pathetic when she said it like that. Was he going to lie and deny it?

"Yeah, why not," Gonzalo said with as much bass in his voice as he could muster.

"And you'd be willing to do whatever it takes?"

How bad could it be? he thought.

"Whatever it takes."

"I need to see you pickpocket. Something valuable."

"Are you serious?"

"Uh huh."

"What, out there in the Market?"

"Yeah. I thought you could handle anything."

"I can, but . . ." Gonzalo guessed it didn't seem much worse than beating someone up for food in the drop, but what did he know about pickpocketing? He'd get caught for sure. "Which gang is this again?"

She rolled her eyes. "Forget it. I knew this was a bad idea—"

"Wait." He reached out and grabbed her. She looked down at his hand on hers, but he didn't let go. She met his eyes. "I'll do it."

She smiled. There was a devilish quality to how low her eyelids hung. She pulled him into the crowd, and Gonzalo's pulse quickened. She spoke quickly and softly as they wove through gang traffic.

"Picking pockets is all about distraction. It helps that you're a Scrap, which is good, 'cause people are already ignoring you."

"Thanks."

She laughed.

"What's my distraction?"

She pointed at herself as her eyes flicked across the moving crowd.

"So, you do this all the time?" Gonzalo asked.

"I'm pretty good, yeah, if that's what you're asking."

"I think that's cool."

"Are you going to tell me next that it's always been your dream?"

"No, I'm telling you the truth. I'm out there getting beaten to death for food, and I'm still not getting anything to eat. You've found another solution. A smarter one."

She scrutinized him.

"But it's high-risk," she said.

"What isn't around here? I can handle risk."

"'Cause you can handle anything, right?"

"That's right."

"Great. You see that Nerd?"

She pointed at a Nerd boy standing outside the door to the Pretty Ones's store. He was wearing a full backpack and reading a paperback, most likely waiting for his Nerd girlfriend to finish browsing the Pretty Ones's homemade beauty products.

"This is almost too easy," she said. "I should really give you something harder."

"What are you talking about?"

"See the loop of white cord coming out of the front pocket of his backpack?"

"I see it."

"That's a phone cord. Not cheap."

She walked toward the Nerd, and Gonzalo followed. This was actually happening. Part of him had been hoping that she might be joking about the whole thing, but she was serious. His palms got sweaty.

"You walk into the Pretty Ones' store and hang by the entrance just behind him," she said, "like you're looking for someone inside. I'll distract him, and you snag it."

"Then what do I do with it?"

"Stuff it down your pants, I don't know. Just get it out of sight quick."

They were almost to the Nerd.

"Okay," she said. "Here we go—"

"Hold up. Don't I need more tips? Isn't there more to it?"

"It's not calculus. You see something you want, and you grab it."

"This is nuts."

"Or you let it pass you by."

"All right, I get it. I'm not backing down."

"Perf. It's showtime."

She stopped just sort of the Nerd. Gonzalo wanted to stop with her but he knew he had to continue. He did everything she'd told him to do. He walked just past the Nerd and stood behind him in the doorway to the Pretty Ones's store. Beauties in matching white dresses drifted through the room, offering condescending advice to their customers and modeling their various wigs for sale—Scrap hair dyed in various colors that had no gang affiliation, like lilac, hot pink, pistachio, and gray, which they called diamond. Gonzalo acted like he was looking for someone in the room. He was sure everybody knew he was an imposter. People entered and left in streams beside him, and he pretended to inspect them, like he was looking for someone in particular. He was just stalling. He turned around to face the Nerd's back.

She was still there, in front of the Nerd, but she'd taken off the frumpy coat and was bent over at the waist, tying her shoes with barely a bend in her knees. The Nerd ogled her butt, in her black jean cutoff shorts, which were connected to her black thigh-high soccer socks by paperclip garters. Gonzalo lost himself in the sight of her, forgetting that he was supposed to be dipping into this guy's backpack. It was only when the Nerd adjusted his shoulder strap that Gonzalo remembered the loop of white cord and saw it waggle below him. The zipper was closed, pinching it. Gonzalo checked that the Nerd's gaze hadn't wavered, then hooked his finger through the loop and pulled. The cord came freely for about a foot before getting caught on the zipper. Gonzalo was sure someone was going to see him.

Over the Nerd's shoulder, he saw her drop to one knee and start stretching her hip flexor. Gonzalo took it as a sign he was taking too long. A girl could only tie her shoes for so long. Gonzalo grabbed the zipper tab with his other hand and slowly eased the zipper open. It sounded like nylon fabric slowly ripping in two.

The Nerd kept leering. Gonzalo kept pulling. Finally, the rest of the cord came up, half of it tangled in a large knot. He bunched it up in one hand, just as the Nerd turned around. As soon as he saw Gonzalo, he took a quick step back and stared, like it was sketchy for Gonzalo to be standing so close to him, and he was right. It was weird. It was suspicious. And the guy had a sense something was wrong, because he started to slip off his backpack.

"Are you looking at my sister?" Gonzalo said.

The Nerd's suspicion fell away and he became flustered. "No."

Gonzalo let his scowl deepen.

"I—I don't know what you mean," the Nerd stammered. "I was just staring off, lost in thought, y'know?" He looked around. "Oh. Is that your sister there? She's very lovely, yes. I mean, I'm just noticing that now. But I wasn't . . ."

"Pfff," Gonzalo said and walked back to her, shaking his head like he was disgusted. The Nerd retreated into the Pretty Ones' store.

"You got it?" she said.

Gonzalo let her see the coiled cord in his hand for a second before shoving it in his pocket. She raised her eyebrows.

"I really didn't think you'd go through with it. How do you feel?"

Gonzalo's pulse filled his ears. He felt out of breath even though he'd expended no energy. He'd expected a hand to clamp down on his shoulder from behind, for someone to catch him, but it didn't seem like it was going to happen. He felt a little bad for the Nerd, but his relief at not getting caught was euphoric.

"I wouldn't tell my granny, but that was a rush," he said.

"Right?"

"So?"

"So what?"

"Do I get to hang out with you or not?"

She tried not to smile. "I gotta talk to the others, see what they think," she said, then turned to leave.

"You don't have to check with the others to give me your name, do you?"

She smiled back over her shoulder as she shrugged the trench coat back on.

"It's Sasha."

Gonzalo stood in the middle of the Market and waited for Sasha to return. His heart rate calmed. The sweat on his brow dried cool. He never could have guessed when he'd woken up that morning that this would be where his day would lead. That said, he'd never expected his high school to blow up either.

He saw a low head of blue hair weaving through the taller crowd. The hairs on his arms stood up. Was it her? He suddenly felt worried about what response she would bring from the gang when she returned. He couldn't take a no.

Sasha stepped into view and sauntered over. She leaned in close and whispered into his ear.

"Welcome to the Mice."

5

GONZALO HAD A CRICK IN HIS NECK. HIS HEAD had been bent left and jammed up against the ceiling of the Honda Fit for all of the two-hour drive to Loveland. He didn't fit into the car any other way, even with the seat pushed back. Maybe he could have looked for a bigger vehicle that would start, but when you turn over rocks, you tend to find snakes. He'd found a flannel shirt in the backseat, so at least he was warm. What he really needed was a gas mask.

He'd been lucky. The stretch of road down through the foothills of the Rockies had been relatively desolate. The pavement ahead of him was scattered with debris, fallen tree limbs, battered lumps of roadkill, and broken-down cars. He hadn't seen any signs of life. Infected tended to stay away from the roads, and although adults were fewer and farther between, he'd seen their numbers grow over the last six months.

Six months. Gonzalo couldn't believe it'd been that long since he'd "graduated" from McKinley. The military had trucked him out of Colorado that day to Chapel, a border town in New Mexico, where some parents had taken up residence to wait for their kids. His parents had been there, and the reunion had been wonderful, but a month later he'd heard that everyone in McKinley had died. He couldn't just accept it as true. He had to see for himself. Against his family's wishes, he'd traveled back into the infected zone and found out that Sasha had escaped.

His arm felt like an old chew toy. He looked at the dirty gauze wrapped around it. Dense orange circles of crust had seeped to the surface where the mountain lion had bitten him. He wondered if he needed a shot. The answer was probably yes, not that he was likely to find one.

A warm breeze eased down the street. Loveland was still. All this emptiness was eerie. If he closed his eyes, he could picture all the old bustle of business. The stores should have been teeming with customers. There should have been people hurrying across the street, kids on bicycles, car horns honking. There should have been mailmen and UPS trucks and big rigs on their routes. Church services, traffic infractions, and phone-gazers. Instead, the streets were filled with dried puddles of dead leaves and animal dung that had melted into the blacktop after last night's rain. Streetlights were inhabited by squirrels, and parked cars had been carpet-bombed by the local birdlife.

Almost every town in the infected zone was like this, and Gonzalo had poked through a lot of them. It'd only been two years since the state had been evacuated, so most buildings hadn't had time to fall into major disrepair. Things needed to be fixed here and there—broken windows, fallen gutters—but for the most part, everything just needed a good cleaning. Colorado wasn't dead. It was just in a coma.

Gonzalo parked the car in front of a boarded-up Army Surplus store that his grandparents had once owned. He squeezed out of the lime-green Honda Fit and took in the sight of the familiar building, its windows now boarded up. It had always loomed large in his memory. He remembered the display cases of decorative knives. The camo parachute pants and winter jackets on hangers. The dangling dog tags and the barbed-wire-imprinted bandanas. And of course, the mannequin up front, dressed in army greens, a flak jacket, and a gas mask. He hoped it was still there, or one like it.

Gonzalo clicked the button on the door handle and pushed. It opened easily, and that made him nervous. The inside of the store was a dark void. He didn't know what he might be walking into. This might be someone's home. Someone toxic, waiting silently and watching, until the moment when Gonzalo would hack up blood and die. A crow squawked half a mile away. It made him flinch.

"This is some bullshit," he said.

He took a deep breath and held it, just in case, and walked

into the dark of the store. Gonzalo strained his eyes, but there wasn't much to see. The glass display case was there, the front cash register, toppled retail displays—they were all there, but they were all bare. A few T-shirts were scattered on the floor, a few saggy, empty boxes, but everything he would have wanted was gone. He wondered if it had all been scavenged, or whether his grandfather had kept the store open during the evacuation and sold out his entire inventory. He hadn't thought to ask back in New Mexico. Gonzalo blew out his used breath and stepped outside. He squinted as his eyes adjusted to the glaring noonday sun.

"Not bad," a voice said.

Gonzalo turned toward the sound of the voice and sank into a defensive crouch. A guy was sniffing around his Honda Fit. He was dressed like a teenager. Big hoodie with loud street art designs printed across the front, skateboard shoes, low-hanging book bag. The illusion was shattered when Gonzalo saw his face. The man's skin had apparently been in a long-term abusive relationship with the sun. His hands rested on the push bar of a shopping cart full of junk. He had to be in his forties.

The man grinned at him, which didn't make Gonzalo feel any better. A grin out here usually meant you were two seconds away from getting jumped. Gonzalo was starting to get fed up with not having a weapon on hand. Who knew what this guy had in that shopping cart?

"She yours?" the man said, gesturing toward the car.

Gonzalo didn't give the guy the benefit of a response. He tried to knock him over with the intensity of his scowl. Gonzalo drew back his shoulders, rising to his full height, and balled his fists. The man seemed oblivious.

"What's this, a 2012?" he said. "I knew a guy that had one of these. Cherry."

Gonzalo took sturdy but cautious steps toward the man, and finally Gonzalo's size seemed to register with him.

"Whoa, you're a big fucker, huh?"

Not the response Gonzalo was hoping for, but he held his scowl.

"You're not gonna break my neck, are you?" he said and laughed. Gonzalo didn't. "What are you, an Indian? You got kinda that look to you. You from that reservation down by Durango?"

Gonzalo shook his head slowly.

"I heard the army couldn't do nothing about making them go. Good for them, I guess, right? You sure you're not one'a them?"

Gonzalo shook his head again. He was tracking every move this guy made, every word he said. He couldn't figure out what this guy's angle was. The man seemed a little stupid, but Gonzalo couldn't be sure it wasn't an act. He might be trying to get Gonzalo to let his guard down so he could steal the car.

"I'm Dan," the man said and stuck his hand out for a shake. Gonzalo made no move to make him comfortable. "Hey, no problem. You don't know me. I don't know you. I get it. 'Nuff said."

They both stood in silence. Dan didn't leave. Gonzalo wasn't going to make a move until he knew whether this guy was a threat. Dan started tapping his fingers on the handle of his shopping cart, like the silence was unbearable.

"Have you seen any women?" Dan said. Gonzalo thought of the woman lying face down in the road with a dune buggy on her back.

"No," Gonzalo said.

"There's gotta be some somewhere, am I right? I'm losing it, boy. Gonna stick my crank in a hole in the ground if I don't find one soon. I met a dude the other day that said when he came over the wall, he found a watermelon and a drill and that watermelon became his wife for a week." He burst out in laughter and looked at Gonzalo through grinning eyes. "How you like that?"

This wasn't how people talked to each other out here. Life didn't get casual. People didn't joke around. If you got close enough to someone to talk, your only goal was to find out if you were dealing with friend or foe. If it was foe, you got the hell away as fast as you could. If it was friend, you found out what you could do for each other, and if it was nothing, you got the hell away as fast as you could.

"What are you doing here?" Gonzalo asked. Dan's laughter dried up quick.

"Just giving you props on your car is all. She sure is a nice one," Dan said, this time dragging his hand softly across the hood. "I drove in on an ATV. It up and died on me. And I haven't found anything since that'll start. They're all missing parts. People already picked them clean of every useful thing under the hood. Or sometimes they've just been shit in, or the dead driver's still inside. I'm not used to seeing a shiny, green apple like you got."

This guy really wasn't letting up about the car. He was practically drooling. He might be thinking of taking a shot. Maybe he had a knife somewhere in that baggy sweatshirt.

"What I'm asking is, why are you in Colorado?"

Dan twisted a little in his oversized sweatshirt. "We all got our reasons."

"Yeah, what's yours?" Gonzalo said, deadpan.

The man's expression sank into a frown that rivaled Gonzalo's. His chin dipped and he looked at Gonzalo from underneath his brow.

"It ain't prison," he said.

Gonzalo held his stare.

Dan shrugged. "Hey, it's not like I broke out of maximum security or something. I just skipped bail. And no bond is worth following me in here. At least not to them. Me, I don't mind it here. So . . . it all works out in the end."

"You're not looking to hunt infected?"

Dan laughed again. Gonzalo was starting not to mind the way he laughed. "Are you kidding? Keep them the fuck away from me. That's what you're doing? You're one of those types?"

Gonzalo shook his head. "I'm looking for someone."

"Family?" he said.

Gonzalo was about to tell him who, but he kept his mouth shut.

"You seen anybody?" Gonzalo said.

"Nah, brother. Like I said, only person I seen since I been here, 'cept for the watermelon man, is you."

"How long you been here?"

"Three weeks."

Finally, it all made sense to Gonzalo. If Dan had been in Colorado for less than a month, then he didn't know anything about survival here. He was basically a babe in the woods, which jibed with how naive he acted. It almost made Gonzalo nervous for the guy, even though Dan was over twice his age.

"Can't wait till I got a car like you," he said. "Where'd you find it at?"

"At a gas station . . . So, you're telling me, you haven't seen any infected? Not one?"

"Naw, thank God. I haven't seen a one. That other dude did say to stay away from the brewery in Greeley though."

"Because there were infected there?"

"Sounded that way."

Gonzalo felt a little rush. It wasn't much of a lead, but it was something. Once he found a gas mask, he would head to Greeley and find this brewery. His uncle had lived in Greeley and had worked in a slaughterhouse there. Maybe he would check in on his uncle's apartment again. He'd found it felt good to stop in on familiar places, just for the sake of reminiscing. The same had been true of his family's house in Pale Ridge. In all this ugliness, it felt good for the soul to remember what life before the virus had been like.

"Hey, you wanna come over?" Dan said.

"Say what?"

"I got a place a few blocks over I've been stayin' at."

"No, I really got to get going."

"Come on, man, I never get to see anybody."

Gonzalo shook his head and walked around Dan to the driver's side. "Sorry. I got things to do."

"Like what? You're going to Greeley, aren't you?"

Gonzalo glanced at Dan, who nodded and pointed at him.

"A-ha, yeah, you liked hearing that, huh? Who you're looking for is infected, huh?"

Gonzalo pulled out the keys and unlocked the driver's-side door.

"You got a gas mask?" Dan said.

Gonzalo swung the door open.

"'Cause I got a spare. I'll give it to you."

Gonzalo paused and narrowed his eyes at Dan. "You got a mask?"

"Yep, another one just like this one." Dan reached into the piled junk in his shopping cart and pulled out a full-face gas mask with what appeared to be a fresh filter on the front. The impulse to knock Dan out, snatch that mask, and drive off was nearly overpowering. But that would make Gonzalo no different than the shits who stole his van in the mountains.

"If you've got one at home, why don't you just give me that one?" Gonzalo said.

"Nah."

"I need that mask."

"And I need somebody to split a bottle of gin with. Whaddaya say? That's win-win for you. You get a mask and a buzz."

"What do *you* get?"

"Some conver-fuckin-sation, bro! Just come on."

Dan pushed his cart down the street. Gonzalo held a debate in his head while Dan got further and further away. In the end, his desperate side won. No matter how much trouble this could lead to, Gonzalo was bound to have worse trouble without a gas mask. He got in his car and followed Dan at four miles per hour. There was no way Gonzalo was leaving his car unattended. Two blocks over and one down, he pulled into the driveway of a townhouse while Dan fiddled at the front door with a key.

Dan left the door open and Gonzalo walked into a drab front room, decorated with yellow and brown paintings of flowers. The paint was globbed on thick, like spackle. The carpets were dirty, and molding in spots. Gonzalo stood by the window, where he could keep an eye on his car.

"I got no power, but there's still a little bit of gas," Dan said.

"Figure this is a special occasion." Dan started up the gas fireplace with the push of a button. "Sit down," he said and moved to a rolling drink cart across the room.

Gonzalo settled into a La-Z-Boy recliner next to the window. He switched his attention from the window to Dan, who was fixing up two drinks. Both drinks were poured from the same bottle, which helped Gonzalo relax, if only slightly. He kept a close watch on both gin-and-tonics until one was in his hand.

"Cheers . . . ," Dan said and clinked his glass to Gonzalo's, then frowned. "I don't even know your name."

"About that mask . . ."

Dan smiled and waved it off. "Ah, forget it. I'm Dan, you're Stan, who gives a stink, right?"

Dan sat down on the couch next to the recliner. He downed half his drink in one gulp.

"How's yours?" he said. "I make 'em stiff."

Gonzalo sipped his drink. It was stiff, all right. The gin burned. He wanted to cough but he held it back, along with asking again about the gas mask. For now, it seemed like Dan actually was just excited to talk. Maybe the guy had no ulterior motive. Maybe all Gonzalo had to do was be gracious. Dan talked for what seemed like hours, though it couldn't have been that long. He never let there be a moment's silence. He told Gonzalo story after story. He kept talking about when he was Gonzalo's age. How great things were then. How it sucked to get old. He told Gonzalo about girlfriends he'd had in the past, before the infection, before he got in trouble with the law. About glory days when he was in high school. About how he was sure there were more people like the two of them out here, and if they could just find them, they could all live together. They'd have it made. Dan refilled both their drinks constantly until the bottle was finished. When Gonzalo was starting to feel a little buzz, Dan was already bombed.

"This's our world now," Dan slurred. "That's whus so great. We can do anything."

"Yeah, but if people are starting to move back here, aren't you gonna be in trouble? I mean, with your bail situation or whatever? It's gotta go back to normal sometime, right?"

"You're thinkin' small time. I'm thinkin' . . . fwoosh."

"What?"

"Ughhhh, I am feeling this shit," Dan said. He was sprawled across the couch, head tilted back. "I han't drank anything in a while. Guess my torelance—tolerance—went away."

"Yeah, tell me about it," Gonzalo said, even though it wasn't affecting him nearly as much. He hadn't had too much experience with booze, but with his body mass, it'd never done much to him.

"You know what?" Dan said. "You're cool, man. You're one of the coolest people I've met so far."

"Thanks, Dan," Gonzalo said and let a half-grin slip. His belly was warm, his mind was nicely fuzzy, and the La-Z-Boy's cushions were the softest thing he'd felt in a while.

"You like to have fun?" Dan said. His tone had shifted for some reason. He stared at Gonzalo like his answer to this question was important.

"I guess so."

"No. No, I'm saying . . . do you *really* like to have fun?"

"I don't know what the hell you're saying, Dan."

"I'm talking about females!"

"Girls? You're asking if I like girls?"

"Exactly."

"I do, but you know there's none around, right? If you're looking to meet women, you shouldn't be in the infected zone."

Dan swatted the air in front of him and shook his head. "Forget it. I never should'a even asked."

"I'm still not sure what you asked."

Dan sat up in his chair. His gregarious mood suddenly evaporated.

"Maybe you should leave," Dan growled. "Whatever the fuck your name is."

"Okay . . . but I'm gonna need that mask," Gonzalo said.

"Yeah, yeah, yeah," Dan said. He rose to his feet and nearly fell over. He careened toward the fireplace like the room had tipped on him. He caught himself on the mantel and knocked a painting off the wall. "I'm fine."

Dan pushed off the mantel on a zigzag path across the room to a door in the front. He whipped the door open with too much energy, and it slammed against the wall.

"Sonofabitch," he muttered. Dan steadied himself against the doorframe. Beyond the open door was a staircase that led down to a basement. "I'll get you your goddamn mask."

Dan was angry, and the sudden change in his attitude sobered Gonzalo. Who said there was actually a gas mask down in that basement? Could be a shotgun. Gonzalo stood up. Forget the mask, he thought. I should leave.

Dan clomped down the stairs out of view.

Gonzalo strode toward the front door but froze when he heard a thump and then a loud crash from the basement. He glanced toward the front door, but his curiosity pulled him toward the open door to the basement stairs.

He peeked his head into the doorway. At the foot of the stairs was Dan. Blood pulsed out of his ear. He'd tripped somewhere on the stairs and now his skull was cracked open. His body spasmed with several jolts, and frothy spit sputtered out of his lips. Then it all stopped. Gonzalo descended the stairs to Dan, knelt down, and placed his fingers on the side of his neck. He was dead.

Gonzalo was in shock, but not from Dan's death. In the middle of the room, on top of a ripped-up pool table, was a white-haired teenage girl curled up inside a large fish tank. She looked scared.

HE WANTED TO LEAN IN AND KISS SASHA

while they were still alone. Gonzalo was standing in front of her, in the middle of a small classroom packed full of piles of shoes and backpacks. She was explaining to him that the room was called The Hole and that it was the Mice's hideout, but all he could do was stare at her lips.

"The door's boarded up from the inside, and the only way in here is through the vents. Cool, right?" she said.

Her voice sounded light and carefree, but her face started to pinch with worry. She eyed the high vent in the far wall. Under it was a makeshift staircase of stacked classroom desks. She blew out a breath through pursed lips and her cheeks ballooned.

"Ugh, I hope this goes okay," she said.

Gonzalo leaned back. "What do you mean 'goes okay'? You said you talked to them."

Sasha crinkled her nose. "I was going to."

"You said I was in!"

"Yeah . . . well . . . I got halfway to the vents, and I realized that it's just as much my gang as it is theirs. So, if I say you're in, then they'll just have to deal with it."

Deal with it? Gonzalo thought. That meant they definitely weren't going to like it. A wave of worry crashed over him. What exactly had she gotten him into?

The soft scrape of bodies sliding across metal emanated from the high vent in the wall. Gonzalo stared at it. Someone was coming. Maybe a lot of someones. Anxiety knotted his stomach. He had no idea what to expect, and when he flicked his eyes back Sasha's way, he didn't get much reassurance. She looked a little paler than before, and she was picking nervously at her bottom lip.

A girl, thin as a pool stick, with shoulder-length black hair, wriggled out of the vent like a worm. When she could stand, she sashayed coolly down the desk stairs. As soon as she saw Gonzalo, she jolted to a stop. Her eyelids peeled back, and she covered her mouth with one hand. A hand that looked too big for a girl. With a limp wave, Gonzalo tried to reassure her that he was harmless.

"Uh oh," the girl said, and Gonzalo was surprised by how low her voice was. She wore lipstick of some sort, and her eyebrows were painted on in elegant swoops, but her shoulders were very broad. When he spotted what had to be an Adam's apple, Gonzalo began to realize that *she* might be a *he*.

"Wiggles, this is Gonzalo," Sasha said.

"Ooh, girl, what did you do?" Wiggles said, dropping her hand and revealing a shocked smile.

"What the fuck!" a scratchy voice whisper-screamed from behind Wiggles. A squat kid crawled out of the duct. He was short, like everyone else in the room and had big ears that stuck out like a monkey's. "You brought someone here?! To The Hole?!"

"Calm down, Kent," Sasha said.

"What part of secret don't you get, Sash?" another voice said. A girl in a thermal long-sleeve shirt and sweatpants popped out of the vent behind the monkey-eared boy. Her clothes clung to the curves of her body in a pleasing way, but her angry face made Gonzalo uneasy. Kent led her down the desk stairs by the hand like she was descending the front steps of a palace. The three Mice stood in a row, Wiggles, Kent, and the girl, all in various degrees of upset.

Sasha cleared her throat. "Kent and Mona, this is Gonzalo. He—"

"Who cares about his name? He knows where we live now, Sash. He's seen our faces!" Kent said, still in a furious whisper.

Gonzalo was glad to be out of the McKinley halls, but he wasn't sure this was an improvement. He raised his voice over the others. "Look, I can just—"

"Shhh!" Wiggles went bug-eyed again and put her fingers to her lips.

Gonzalo dropped into a whisper. "I can just leave if it's this much trouble."

Sasha elbowed Gonzalo and looked up at him with a fierce stare. "No. I want you here."

Kent let out a shocked laugh. "Are you kidding me, bro? You can't leave. Not after you've been here. The only way you're leaving is if—"

"He's not leaving," Sasha said, cutting Kent short. "I wanted him in the gang, and what's done is done."

Gonzalo was starting to wonder what they'd do if he tried to leave.

The girl in the thermal shirt, Mona, narrowed her eyes at Sasha. "Does Baxter know?"

Whump.

Another boy had entered the room. He'd jumped down from the top of the desk stairs. This boy was even shorter than everybody else. He had a handsome face that almost looked like an adult's face on a little boy's body.

"I do now," the new arrival said.

Gonzalo recognized him. A couple months back, Baxter had gained a reputation for taking nude photos of people without them knowing and then trying to sell the photos. He finally got busted for it, and his victims ended up tying him to a tree in the quad, naked, as punishment. They hung a sign around his neck detailing exactly what he'd done and encouraging passersby to take humiliating photos of him. Gonzalo would never forget it.

Baxter had stayed tied up there for three days, and some of the things people did to him in those photos were disgusting. Some were violent. By the morning of the fourth day, he'd managed to escape, and no one had ever heard from him again. Gonzalo, probably like a lot of people, had assumed that he'd died.

Baxter strode up to Gonzalo, standing as tall as he was able and staring at him as if Gonzalo had just insulted his mother.

"The Mice don't exist, Sasha. Did you forget that? There are no people watching the rest of the school from the vents. But now that this lump's laid his eyes on us—"

"Don't get in my face about this, Baxter. I know we have to be secret, but what, we can't ever add any members? We can't ever talk to anyone but each other?"

"What's wrong with that? We're not good enough for you?" Baxter said, like he was spitting a poison dart.

Sasha rolled her eyes. "I don't think any of us can stand being in a five-person gang forever. It's just not natural."

Baxter ground his teeth together hard enough for Gonzalo to hear the muffled creak through his closed mouth. The other three Mice seemed more agreeable to what Sasha was saying, but evidently not enough to speak up. Wiggles grimaced at Sasha in sympathy.

"I can vouch for Gonzalo," Sasha said. "If it doesn't work out, it's on me."

Gonzalo took his eyes off Baxter's menacing scowl and looked at Sasha. She'd definitely dropped him into the boil without warning, and she'd never said anything about this "you can't leave the Mice once you join" business. But it was clear she was really putting herself on the line for him. She must've liked him a lot more than he'd first thought. And that actually made Gonzalo excited to back up her play.

"You won't regret having me in your gang," he said. "I'll do my best to prove it."

Baxter started to shake his head, but Wiggles stepped forward.

"Have him fish," Wiggles said. "See if he's got what it takes."

"He'll have to do a whole lot more than fish to prove he's worthy of being in the Mice," Baxter said.

"Well, we gotta start somewhere," Wiggles said. "What Sasha said is right. It's already done. We might as well make the best of it."

"He's probably twice the fisherman you are anyway," Sasha said to Baxter. It was an unnecessary jab, but Gonzalo was starting to understand that sometimes Sasha couldn't help herself.

Baxter scoffed, but his face flushed red. "Fine. Let's go. We'll see about that."

Sasha looped her arm through Gonzalo's. Baxter looked like he'd just swallowed a fly.

"We'll get the gear and meet you there," Sasha said.

"I don't think so. This guy's not laying eyes on our valuables," Baxter said.

"Look, man, I'm not going to tell any of your secrets," Gonzalo said. "I don't know anybody else to tell."

Wiggles giggled. "I love this guy. I'm coming too."

Baxter gave them all a sour look and walked across the room to an opening near the floor. "I'll get the gear. Don't be late."

When Baxter was gone, everyone seemed to breathe a little easier. Kent and Mona started making out a few seconds later.

Wiggles gave Sasha a look. "Why don't we give them some space?"

Sasha and Gonzalo followed Wiggles up the desk stairs.

As Gonzalo entered the duct system, he heard one of Mona's soft groans echo after him. It wasn't hard to understand why Baxter had given him so much attitude. If Baxter wanted a girlfriend, it had to be either Wiggles or Sasha. Based on the way Baxter'd clearly felt so burned by Gonzalo's sudden arrival, Gonzalo guessed Baxter had his eyes on Sasha. He had probably assumed that it was just a matter of time before Sasha gave in to his advances because she had no other options. But Gonzalo had just shown up and dumped a bag of salt in his cookie batter.

Crawling through air ducts was slow going. Most of the ducts in the school ran down the hallways like a spine, with branching ducts like ribs leading to the rooms on either side of the hall. Whenever they heard people in the halls—which was often—they had to stop moving. It took over twenty minutes to travel the length of one hall. But it was definitely safer.

Ahead, Wiggles stopped at the slats of a vent. Sasha squeezed up to her, half on top of her, and peered down onto the hallway. She put her hand on Wiggles' shoulder.

"Is that him?" she whispered.

"Yeah," Wiggles whispered back.

"He's handsome," she said.

"I know."

"So?"

"What?"

"Get out there."

"I can't do that."

"Yes, you can."

"I'm not ready."

"Well, there's no chance it'll ever happen if you don't try."

Wiggles glanced back Gonzalo's way, then back to the vent. "I don't know." She nibbled her nails and stared into the bright hall. "You guys go 'head, I'm gonna hang here a while."

Going ahead meant Wiggles had to lie flat while Sasha and Gonzalo squirmed over her. The shoulder-width of the ducts didn't allow for passing any other way.

"Get it, girl," Sasha whispered as she passed over Wiggles.

Squeezing over Wiggles was weird. It hadn't seemed weird for Sasha since they were girlfriends . . . or friends . . . or . . . Gonzalo still wasn't sure whether he was supposed to use "he" or "she" with Wiggles. Wiggles definitely tried to look like a girl, so "she" was probably the way to go.

As he passed over Wiggles, Gonzalo was able to peer through the vent slats and catch a glimpse of a six-foot Skater guy with an athlete's physique. He was sitting in a chair in a classroom, using a cafeteria knife to whittle a sawed-off tree branch from the quad into a sharp wooden hook. He had a heavy beard for a teenager, bushy and white, and thick wavy hair dyed orange and black. He looked like an angry candy corn. He also seemed like the kind of dude that would beat up someone like Wiggles, not kiss her, and it made Gonzalo feel his first bit of worry for his new gang-mate.

"Good luck," Gonzalo whispered as he passed.

Sasha and Gonzalo crawled on in silence. Absolute quiet seemed to be the number-one rule in the ducts. It was how the Mice stayed secret, but it wasn't exactly conducive to flirting with Sasha. All Gonzalo really wanted was some quality time with her—but with her face, not her feet. After stopping and starting and waiting every two minutes or so, they finally reached a rope ladder in a vertical duct and began to climb up to the third floor. He was beginning to feel that this trip would never end when Sasha finally whispered that they were close.

"This is the vent. I'm gonna keep going a little bit so I can turn around and face you," Sasha said.

She crawled on ahead as Gonzalo approached the vent. The grille cover was off, and he poked his head through. The world spiraled. Gonzalo was looking down three stories to the basketball court floor. He was only a foot from the ceiling of the gym.

Varsity teemed below, getting ready to turn in for the night. Bedtime was rowdy in the gym as Varsity boys tried to talk their Pretty One girlfriends into spending the night with them in the gym instead of sleeping in the girls' locker room. Bedsheet partitions were strung up across the basketball court, turning it into a grid of hanging laundry. The boys told the girls that no one would hear anything through those cotton walls, and some of the girls let themselves be convinced.

Every conversation, whispered or loud, drifted up to Gonzalo, beyond the hanging lights and the banners celebrating McKinley High athletic victories.

"Hey," a voice whispered. "Gonzo. What are you, deaf?"

Gonzalo looked over to see Baxter, sitting cross-legged atop a steel I-beam only a few feet below the vent.

"What took you so long?" Baxter said. "Get down here."

Gonzalo glanced down at the drop to the gym floor again and got woozy.

"Uh, is it safe?" Gonzalo said.

"I knew you didn't have the nerve."

Sasha slithered toward him in the duct. He didn't want to let her down, but he was scared. He hoped she couldn't tell. When Sasha reached him, she grabbed his hand.

"Look, I get that I sort of threw you into the fire back there, but I know you can do this. And I want you to know that I'm really, really glad you're here."

Gonzalo smiled despite his fear. He lowered himself onto

the foot-wide I-beam and straddled it. Baxter held an empty can of house paint. Coiled around his torso, armpits to belt, was an extension cord that used to be orange but had been blackened with a marker. It had to be a hundred feet long, at least.

"Sasha'll stay here and hold onto the goods. This way," Baxter said, and he stood. On the I-beam. Gonzalo couldn't believe it. Baxter turned on his heels and walked across the beam as though a deadly fall didn't await him on either side.

Gonzalo looked back up at the vent and saw Sasha's excited face.

"You'll do great," she said.

Gonzalo cleared his throat. He didn't want to move, but he wasn't going to let her know he was scared. He scooted forward, still straddling the beam like a saddle, and the farther he scooted away from the wall, the more he became sure that somehow, someway, he'd fall. He pictured himself landing feet first and his shinbones spearing out through his kneecaps.

Baxter had already walked clear across the gym until he stood over the immense Varsity food pile that cascaded down the extended bleachers. Gonzalo scooted as fast as he could while Baxter made exasperated gestures at him. There was no way Gonzalo was going to stand up. The gray dust on the beam piled up in front of his crotch as he went, and clumps of it spilled off the sides. He hoped no one would see the clumps fluttering down in the dark gym. Ahead of him, Baxter uncoiled the extension cord from his torso and tied one end to the wire handle of the paint can. He dropped the can off the side of the beam, letting the cord slide through his fingers, and when the can was just about to hit the food pile, Baxter tightened his grip on the cord and slowed its descent so that when the can came down on a twelve-pack of toilet paper, it barely made a sound. Then Baxter pulled cord back up, and to Gonzalo's surprise, the package of toilet paper rose with the can, like the plastic wrapper was attached to the can's bottom. Baxter coiled the cord around his forearm and upper arm as he pulled it up. Gonzalo continued to scoot at his slow pace, and by the time he'd scooted all the way over, Baxter had repeated the process two more times, although neither attempt succeeded in bringing anything up.

"Run this TP back to Sasha," Baxter said with a sour face.

Gonzalo peered back to the other end of the long crossbeam, to Sasha's little head.

"Uh, it's gonna take me a while."

"Not if you stand."

"I'm not going to stand."

"Well, I'm not fishing and running the stuff back while you just sit here."

"Isn't it my turn to fish? I thought you wanted to see what I could do."

"Yeah, well, I changed my mind. Glue is precious. We can't waste it on a rookie."

"You just missed twice in a row," Gonzalo said. "Lemme go. Just once. If I can't snag anything, I'll tell the others I lost my nerve and you're way better at everything."

That seemed to sway Baxter. He glanced over to Sasha and grinned. He pushed the coil of extension cord into Gonzalo's hands. He held up a thin tube of Super Glue and drew a faint line of glue across the bottom of the can.

"A little more than that," Gonzalo said.

"Can't waste any," Baxter said.

Before Gonzalo had a chance to protest, Baxter dropped the can off the beam with a ton of slack. The cord unspooled from Gonzalo's arm and rushed through his fingers. The can hurtled down toward the pile until Gonzalo crushed down on the zipping cord. It slowed, just before landing soft on top of a loaf of bread. He scanned the gym, but no one seemed to notice. He should've reeled the cord back up, but he waited.

"Arms too tired?" Baxter said with a smirk.

"I'm waiting for the glue to dry."

"Really?" Baxter whispered, getting right up next to Gonzalo's ear. "'Cause I think you're scared of losing. So, listen, when you tell everybody else how I beat you, be sure and really sell the part about you being impressed by me . . ."

Gonzalo started pulling up the can, and the bread rose with it. Baxter never stopped talking shit, trying to unnerve him. Gonzalo breathed through the taunting, keeping his focus on pulling it up smoothly. Baxter's whispers faded when Gonzalo finally lifted the bucket up into his lap. He tore the bread from the can, ripping a hole in the plastic wrapper, and handed it to Baxter.

"Here, you can take both at the same time," Gonzalo said.

Baxter had no words to volley back. He took the two items and left. Gonzalo grinned. It looked like it'd actually hurt Baxter to lose, which only made the victory sweeter. Baxter watched with a sneer as Gonzalo's next three fishing attempts were successful. A box of new toothbrushes, a tub of oatmeal, and a jumbo bottle of aspirin. He had Baxter doing wind sprints back and forth until the glue was gone.

Baxter returned to Gonzalo just as he was finishing wrapping up the cord. He'd gotten more comfortable on the beam with each cast of the paint can. Gonzalo swiveled to face Baxter.

"That's the last of the—"

But he had moved too quickly and felt his ass slip off the side of the I-beam. He waved his arms in a herky-jerky frenzy but couldn't reverse his momentum. He fell.

Baxter's hands clamped down on Gonzalo's wrist. The momentum halted, and Gonzalo hung by Baxter's grip. He kicked at the air, but Baxter held strong, and before hoisting Gonzalo back up onto the beam, he stared into Gonzalo's eyes and whispered a single sentence.

"If you try to date Sasha, I'll kill you."

7

THE GIRL FROM THE FISH TANK WAS NAMED
Janine. At the moment, she was backed up into the basement corner and swinging a broken pool cue at Gonzalo, even though he'd been the one to let her out.

"Keep away from me, you sick asshole!" she screamed.

This wasn't exactly how Gonzalo'd hoped his afternoon would shape up, but at least he was wearing a gas mask now. That was an improvement.

"Just calm down," he said. His voice was canned and heavy, now that he was breathing through a filter. He'd forgotten how much he'd actually hated wearing gas masks. This was the tried-and-true kind, the kind from History Channel documentaries and horror movies, with the circular lenses and the hanging filter that looked like a horse snout. He probably looked like a serial killer, but he had to try to get through to Janine. He almost never got a chance to speak with an infected without them running away or trying to attack him, and he couldn't waste this opportunity. "Why would I let you out if I wanted to hurt you?"

"How should I know?" she said. Her face was red with fury and fear. "Get out of my way!"

There was something about people getting crazy that made Gonzalo get calm.

"Janine," Gonzalo said. "Listen to me, I'm gonna say it again. I didn't know this dude, okay? Never met him before today. I don't know what he did down here, but by the looks of him, he isn't gonna be doing it anymore. Now, I will get outta your way, but not till you tell me what I want to know."

Janine slowed her pool cue-swinging and held it out like a spear instead. The heat of her panicked anger was starting to cool, and it looked to Gonzalo like she was finally hearing him.

"What do you wanna know?" she said.

"I'm looking for a girl. About five foot. She's infected, like you. Her name is—"

"That turn you on?" she said.

"That—what?"

Janine looked him up and down. She was buzzing with energy. Teeth bared. She was wearing an oversized Colorado Rockies jersey as if it were a nightshirt.

"You into that too? That sick shit? Like him?"

"What are you talking about?" Gonzalo said.

"I'm not gonna lick your gas mask."

"Uh . . ."

"That's what he made me do," Janine pointed to Dan's dead body, then tightened up on the pool cue. "'Lick all around the seam,' he'd say. He couldn't get off unless he might die. If you think I'm doing that again, I'll kill you. I swear I will."

Gonzalo put his hands to his forehead.

"First of all, ughhh, motherfucker," Gonzalo said. "That's the weirdest shit I ever heard. How am I supposed to know there's people that are horny to die? What the fuck? Are you okay? I wanna kill this guy."

"Yeah, well, if he was alive, you'd be getting in line."

Gonzalo looked over at Dan. His skin was already waxy and his tongue hung out of the corner of his mouth.

"I used to be infected," Gonzalo said and pulled his rat tail out from the back of his shirt collar. It was braided and about five inches long. When Gonzalo graduated, he'd shaved all of his white hair off, but he'd been clever enough to keep a small tuft of it on the back of his neck, in case of a situation just like this. "Trust me. No part of me thinks being infected is hot. And I definitely don't want to die. I'm just looking for my girl, and once I find her, we're getting the fuck out of the zone."

Janine cooled a little, and Gonzalo thought that if he could keep her talking, he could get to asking about Sasha and get some honest answers.

"Look, I got a car," Gonzalo said. "I'm headed to Greeley. I heard there's infected there. Maybe you want to come with?"

"You have a car?"

Gonzalo nodded. Her right eyebrow arched.

"Prove it," she said.

Gonzalo pulled the car keys from his pocket and jangled them. Janine swung her pool cue as fast as a cobra strike and cracked Gonzalo across the head. He fell back, tripped over Dan, and crashed to the floor. He heard the scrape of his keys sliding across the floor.

"Shit," Gonzalo said as he tried to get back up.

Janine was already springing up the steps, his keys jingling in her hand. Gonzalo wobbled on his feet, his head still woozy. He careened up the stairs, leaving dents in the drywall where his shoulders hit. When he got to the top of the stairs, she was already out the front door, and as his feet hit the welcome mat outside, she was unlocking the driver's-side door of the Honda.

"Stop!" Gonzalo shouted.

She hopped into the car and started the engine. Gonzalo charged the car and hooked his hand under the door handle, but she peeled out of the driveway in reverse, almost taking Gonzalo's fingers with her. With a whole lot of noise and burning rubber, Janine spun the car around and took off down the street. Gonzalo clomped out onto the pavement, out of breath and nauseous. He watched his lime-green car grow smaller in the distance before turning a corner and disappearing from view.

"This is some bullshit," Gonzalo muttered.

Now, more than ever, Gonzalo regretted drinking half a bottle of gin in a townhouse with a lonely fugitive. He walked around Dan's neighborhood checking garages and backyards for operational vehicles. He didn't find any cars that would start, but he did find a riding mower with keys still in the ignition and a full tank of gas. He found a stack of moving blankets in the shed nearby and strapped them down over the engine with bungees so that when he started it up, it didn't roar. Riding a mower didn't just look stupid—it *was* stupid. It left him exposed and it was loud enough to be a beacon for trouble, but it was a long way to Greeley on foot. If one tank of gas got him halfway there, it was worth the risk.

Gonzalo maxed out the mower at fifteen miles per hour, and it took him about forty-five minutes to get to the interstate. The engine struggled with the incline of the on-ramp, but eventually he was clocking steady miles to Greeley. On a riding mower. Wearing a gas mask. He was trying to have a good attitude at least, but there was no getting around feeling like a dumbass who'd just gotten his car stolen by a high-school girl.

"I'm gonna tell people she was a gang of seven-foot bikers," he muttered.

The ride got less irritating as he went. He let his mind wander to pleasant things, like the way Sasha used to drape herself over him and run her fingers through his hair when it was long. When a black pickup truck crept up beside him, his body jolted. Between the road noise, the vibration of the mower, and the daydream, Gonzalo hadn't noticed the truck's approach. He maintained his speed and slowly turned his head to look.

The driver was an old man—late sixties—with a big bushy, white mustache. He wore a straw cowboy hat pushed back on his head and had big, sorrowful eyes, accented by dark circles underneath. His face was about as harmless as an old hick could look, but the black bulletproof vest he wore, along with the black leather gloves with reinforced hard caps over the knuckles, made Gonzalo wary. The man had a radio receiver clipped to the front of his vest, like a cop. He pressed the button on the receiver, and his voice squawked good and loud over a PA hidden somewhere under the truck's hood.

"Need a ride?"

A day ago, Gonzalo couldn't get a break to save his life. Now he had Good Samaritans falling out of his pockets—although Dan's status as a friendly stranger had dropped a few ticks when you factored in the captive in his basement and his desire for lethal licks.

"How 'bout it, son? Yes or no?"

If he didn't already look like a fool, he was about to look like a bigger one, turning down a ride in the middle of nowhere. Gonzalo considered the old man and the truck as they both rode forward at ten miles per hour. Unless the guy was a lawnmower thief, or was going to harvest Gonzalo's organs, he couldn't think of why the guy would want to hurt him. He knew what this guy was. He'd seen his type before—a guy heading through the infected zone to exact some revenge for what the virus had done to him. Gonzalo glanced down at the lawnmower's fuel gauge. It hung dangerously close to E. He stopped the mower and turned off the engine. The old man hit the brakes, leaned over, and pushed the truck door open.

Gonzalo scanned the open plains around him to make sure the coast was clear, then pulled off his gas mask.

"Appreciate it," Gonzalo said and pulled himself onto the bench seat of the pickup.

"We can load that mower into the back if you want."

"I'll pass."

Gonzalo paused before pulling the door shut, The man had an Uzi in his left hand, resting in his lap. It was angled toward the dash, but it would only take a flick of the wrist for the barrel to be pointed at Gonzalo.

"Necessary precaution," the old man said. "I'd really rather not have to use it."

"No shit."

Gonzalo pulled the door shut.

"Where you headed?"

"Greeley'll do."

"That's on my way."

The old man stepped on the gas and turned up the radio, a welcome sign that they didn't have to make small talk. An old honky-tonk song helped keep Gonzalo's mind off the fact that the old man was still driving with one hand on his Uzi. A cowboy boot air freshener dangled from the rearview mirror, swinging in time with the music. When the song ended, Gonzalo was surprised to hear a DJ's voice.

"Just a little bit of classic country for you troopers out there, doing your duty. I'm thinking about you, and want you to radio in if there's something—heck, anything you wanna hear—"

"Is this a recording?" Gonzalo said.

"Nope, we got KQOC up and running in Lehman."

"Oh," Gonzalo said. "Who's 'we'?"

"The CNC—Citizens for a New Colorado. We're taking back this state one town at a time, and doing a damn good job of it, if you ask me."

"You got Lehman, sounds like," Gonzalo said, his curiosity piqued. Lehman was between Greeley and the border. It was a small town, but a nice one, the way Gonzalo remembered it from the one time he'd been.

"Up and running and all cleared out. Maybe not good as new, but . . . good."

"Cleared out . . . of infected?"

The old man nodded. "That's right. Go ahead and tell whoever you see. Word needs to spread across the border that our towns are ours again. Otherwise, nobody's moving back here. Capitol Hill's word ain't good enough. 'Least not after what they've done in the last two years. People need to hear it from their friends. From their old neighbors. That you can move back."

Gonzalo didn't reply. This was the first he'd heard of the CNC, but he wasn't surprised. What he had heard was that the government had said Coloradans could move back *at their own risk*. He couldn't imagine too many young families moving back anytime soon, but the extremists and the displaced were probably on their way in a slow trickle.

"Hey, all you troopers out there," the DJ said, *"a little celebration is in order, and a lot of appreciation is due to Team Freedom in the north of Russell County. They smoked out a den of fifty-three white-hairs this afternoon and laid every single one down."*

The old man gave the steering wheel a happy little pat.

"Good on ya, Team Freedom. Colorado's a little safer, thanks to you."

The old man's eyes drifted Gonzalo's way, waiting for a reaction. A happy hoot or a grin, if Gonzalo had to guess. He didn't play along. He kept his face blank.

"You on patrol?" Gonzalo asked. "That what you're doing out here?"

"That's right. You seen any infected?"

Gonzalo shook his head.

"Mind if I ask what you'd do if you did?" the old man said.

"Run like hell."

The old man smiled.

"You were infected, weren't you?"

Gonzalo tilted his head and looked the old man dead in the eyes. *Fuck this guy.*

"Nothing I could help," Gonzalo said.

"That's gonna get you killed out here."

Gonzalo's stomach tensed up.

"Are you gonna be the one to do it?" Gonzalo asked.

"Relax, son. I'm trying to give you some advice."

"Yeah, what's that?"

"Don't fool yourself," he said. "You're not one of them no more. You're a man. And there's things a man's gotta do to stay alive. Topmost on that list is putting those creatures out of their misery when they cross you."

Gonzalo wanted to fight this guy, to tell him how wrong he was. How could he treat Gonzalo like a human being now, but a year ago he would have shot him on sight?

"You know how many infected I've killed?" the man asked.

Gonzalo's skin itched.

"By yesterday's count," the old man said, "I'm at three hundred and twelve."

"You're full of shit," Gonzalo said, unable to keep his lips shut this time. He tried to stuff his emotions down. "What, did you burn down a building?"

"Individual kills," the old man said with pride. "I'm good with a rifle. I'm steady. Got hands like I was twenty-five. And I don't quit."

Gonzalo's mind was already wandering to Sasha, figuring

out numbers, working on odds.

"Anybody else hitting those kind of numbers?"

"Not alone. Not that I know of. Most folks work in teams. That's just not how I'm built. I grew up hunting. Been doing it since I was ten. It's a private thing for me."

"The people you're talking about, they're not animals."

"You're right. I guess there is a difference. To hunt an animal on its own turf and kill it, there's something primal about it that's satisfying. Spiritual. I don't get that feeling with these infected. They need to be eradicated for the sake of public safety, plain and simple."

Gonzalo looked out the window. Anything to not look at this old bastard.

"What are you doing out here, son?" the man said. A cheery, guitar-jangling song was playing on the radio now.

"I made a promise."

The old man grumbled softly. "Well, that's noble, but this ain't Camelot. Sooner or later, you're gonna need to kill one of them so you can live. Whether you were one of them or not won't matter to them."

Gonzalo couldn't help thinking about Janine and how she instinctively had hated him. And then the maniacs with the hubcaps on their chest killing that mother and father right in front of their son.

"You ever kill anyone when you were infected?" the old man said, his eyes sharp.

"No," Gonzalo said, swift and firm.

"You're lucky then. Consider it a blessing. You probably don't even realize how demented you were when you were infected. I've seen lots that were in a fog. Not human at all. *Creatures*, I call 'em. This virus is so evil, so deadly, that it cancels out these youngsters' humanity. None of what they are or could be can ever make up for the death they cause, for the people they've already killed. Every time I come across one, I think about all the lives I'm saving by putting them down. I think about the safer world I'm creating with every kill. And I sleep fine at night."

The old man nodded as if to say, *Amen*. Gonzalo was glad the man was done because he couldn't bear another second of listening to him. They spent the remainder of the ride to Greeley listening to more country songs and not speaking. Three hundred and twelve kills. The number weighed heavy on Gonzalo's brain. In an ordinary world, killing just *twelve* people made you a mass murderer. Gonzalo couldn't stop himself from wondering if any of them had been people he knew from McKinley, if one of them happened to have been Sasha. Gonzalo wanted to ask if this guy had been to Pale Ridge, but what if he hadn't? What if all Gonzalo ended up doing was tip him off that there were more infected to kill there?

When they reached Greeley, the old man wouldn't stop the truck. He continued to cruise the streets.

"Thanks for the ride," Gonzalo said.

"You got a plan?"

"I'll figure something out."

The old man brought the car to a stop in the middle of an intersection.

"You're a strong S.O.B., that's not lost on me. And I can tell you have some strong feelings caught up in this. I can respect that. I lost my wife and my . . ." The old man's throat closed with swelling emotion. "I still can't talk about it. But I know what it feels like to need to do something about it. We could use somebody tough like you in the CNC—"

Gonzalo opened the door and got out.

"Naw, man."

"Stay safe out th—"

Gonzalo shut the door before the man could finish. A moment later, the engine roared and the truck shot off down the road.

8

"WHAT THE HELL, GONZALO?" SASHA SAID.

"You came on all strong and you joined the Mice, and then you just backed off. I don't get it—you want to be *buddies* now?"

Gonzalo didn't know what to say. She'd nailed him. In the months since he'd joined the Mice, he had been avoiding her. Baxter's threat to kill him if he pursued Sasha had stuck in Gonzalo's head. The guy had made the threat while he held Gonzalo's life in his hands. Hell of a time to joke around. At first, he had tried to convince himself that Baxter's threat was empty, but the more time he spent around Baxter, the more he began to suspect there was something seriously wrong with the guy.

Baxter spoke endlessly about rules he wanted to institute— that they should all sleep in one room, that the Mice should all dress the same, that they should have the same haircut: a shaved head. Wiggles and Sasha were violently against that one, and Kent threatened murder if Baxter touched a single hair on Mona's head, but Baxter kept on making his proclamations as if he hadn't heard a single refusal. When they were all together, he spoke about the grand future he envisioned for the Mice, where they would steal so much of the school's goods that they could open a store and control the prices. They'd have the whole school by the balls, he said, charging twice the value just for people to buy back their own stuff. When Baxter and Gonzalo were alone, however, the big ideas fell away. He'd turn talk immediately to the subject of Sasha and repeat his threat—if Gonzalo made a play for Sasha, he would end up dead. When someone talks about ending your life, the safest bet is to believe them, and Baxter had such an unhinged look in his eyes, pupils shivering, eyelids twitching, that Gonzalo believed the threat was genuine. Baxter would never say anything else when it was just the two of them in a room, just that one threat, and then complete silence. Gonzalo had followed Baxter's one rule with devotion, even going so far as to avoid Sasha sometimes, but now she was calling him out.

"I'm serious, Gonzalo," she whispered. "I want an answer."

Gonzalo scanned the room in a panic, sure someone had just heard her whispered tirade. They'd snuck into Freak territory to do a little late-night thieving. Freaks were asleep all around the room, including a snuggled couple between Gonzalo and Sasha's feet. Sasha held a digital projector in her hands that they'd just lifted from a rolling AV cart in the corner. The walls were charred black with pentagrams, penises, and pregnant cows carved into the white drywall underneath. Two of the walls had eight-foot-wide holes busted through them that connected this room with rooms on either side, each containing more slumbering Freaks.

"Is this really the best time to talk about this?" Gonzalo whispered.

"Uh, yes, it is," she said. "I've been waiting longer than any girl should for you to do something, and I think I deserve an answer."

The look on her face stabbed him. Her eyebrows twisted upwards. Her eyes were insistent, and she looked hurt. She probably thought he didn't like her anymore, that he'd gotten turned off once he got to know her, or that he never liked her at all and just used her to get into a gang where he'd been enjoying steady food and safe shelter ever since. Gonzalo felt like a coward. He couldn't tell her it was all because he was scared of Baxter.

"Well?" she said.

"Let's go on a date," he said without thinking.

"A date?"

"Yeah."

She narrowed her eyes and pursed her lips.

"What's wrong?" Gonzalo whispered.

"I'm thinking."

The Freak below Gonzalo ripped out a wet snore that

sounded like a failed attempt to start a lawn mower.

"Sasha," Gonzalo said. He dropped to one knee by the sleeping Freak's head and looked up at her. "Will you please go on a date with me? I'm begging—oh my god, this guy's breath smells like rotten butter."

Sasha laughed without making a noise. She smiled and grew suddenly demure, only making eye contact for a few seconds at a time.

"Pick me up at The Hole at seven," she said with a chuckle.

"Eh, can't it be somewhere else?"

"Why?"

"Somewhere without . . ." He wanted to say *Baxter* but settled on, ". . . the others."

She frowned. "You . . . don't want them to know?" Her voice broke out of a whisper. "Why not? I'm not some side chick, you know."

"I know that. Easy."

"Then, why are you ashamed for the others to know?"

"I'm not," he said. "The Hole's fine."

"Great. I'll see you then," Sasha said and shoved the projector into his hands. She turned away with a huff and padded toward the vent with dirty, bare feet.

Gonzalo called out in the softest whisper he could manage, "Hey, where are you going? We're in the middle of a robbery."

She looked over her shoulder and smiled. "Gotta get ready for my big night."

Sasha crawled up to the vent and disappeared into the darkness beyond. Gonzalo wished he could smile—this was everything he'd wanted—but all he could think about was Baxter's reaction. His crawl back to The Hole was long, and Gonzalo's back was killing him. Actually, his back killed him all the time—so much so that he wished he could reach under his skin, grab the lumbar section of his spine, and wrench it all around like a joystick until all the tension cracked away. His legs hurt too, and his neck, and he knew why. He'd been growing.

At first he'd thought that he was getting the flu, or that spending so much time crawling on all fours was making the muscles on the front of his body too strong and the ones on the back too weak, but it was neither of those. He'd realized the truth when he'd noticed his clothes felt like they'd been shrunk in a dryer, which was impossible since he hadn't laid eyes on a dryer or a washing machine since the quarantine. The ducts had started to feel tighter, and last time he'd measured, he'd grown four inches in the three months since joining the Mice. Despite his growing pains, the thought of growing bigger thrilled him. It was possible he'd get a lot bigger, considering the average size of the men in his family. Soon he would be big enough that Baxter could never beat him in a fight. He wished he was already that big, but Sasha had her own timeline for things.

He arrived back at The Hole to find it spotted with

four-foot-high piles of random sneakers. Everyone was pitching in, matching the shoes into pairs and organizing them by gender and style. Baxter acted like he was overseeing it all, preaching about how this plan to steal the school's sneakers and sell them at high prices to a fence named Smudge was going to make them richer than Varsity. Wiggles was depressed. She sorted sneakers as if weights hung from her arms. She'd grown more and more morose over the Skater she loved from afar. She'd never ended up talking to him and was convinced that he could never love her. Baxter kept yelling at Kent because he kept brushing Mona's hair instead of sorting sneakers. Mona read a celebrity gossip magazine with old news about pre-virus pop culture that she'd found in a biology teacher's desk. As they pitched in to help, Sasha and Gonzalo shared secret smiles that only showed up in her eyes. But Baxter blabbed on, and the confidence Gonzalo had felt on the crawl back thinned as their date approached. There was a plastic circular clock on the wall, and he could see that the minute hand already leaned past twelve and the hour hand was on the seven.

He peered past the pile of shoes in front of him and saw Sasha stand up in the middle of the room, wearing a pastel-pink leather jacket and holding a pair of fresh white tennis shoes. Baxter had been walking around one of the piles counting out loud, but he'd stopped and was now staring at Sasha quizzically.

Gonzalo stepped out from behind his pile. He hadn't even thought about changing his clothes, he'd been so busy anticipating this moment. He didn't want see that unnerving twitch in Baxter's eyes, but he forced himself to. If he was going to do this, he had to do it all the way.

Gonzalo saw the moment when Baxter figured out what was happening. Gonzalo expected rage, but instead surprise rippled across Baxter's face like an aftershock. Gonzalo pounced on the moment.

"Ready for our date?" Gonzalo said loudly and clearly as he reached Sasha.

She smiled. He knew she liked him saying it in front of everyone that way. Her smile widened as Kent and Mona started whispering about it and Wiggles clapped. Mona was staring at Gonzalo with an interest he'd never seen from her before, and Kent seemed angry about it.

"You two are going on a *date*?" Baxter said to Sasha.

"Yes, and we're already late," Sasha said.

"How long has *this* been going on?" he said, and took hold of her arm.

She shook him loose. "Ew, Baxter, what do you think, you're my dad?"

"It's none of your business, man," Gonzalo said.

Baxter looked at Gonzalo. His mouth was a flat line, but his eyes were angry. Gonzalo had broken Baxter's one rule, and now was the time for Baxter to do something about it, to back up his big words with some sort of action. The silence between them stretched, and the whispering from Mona and Kent dwindled. Baxter blinked a few times.

"Enjoy yourselves," he said and went back to counting shoes.

And that was that. Gonzalo led the way into the ducts. Sasha followed him. No vicious words. No blood was shed. Baxter just looked like someone had stolen his teddy bear. He was like a lot of bullies: he crumbled when someone stood up to him. Gonzalo felt a warm flood of pride, knowing that he'd faced his fear and done as he pleased rather than listen to someone else's empty threats. Not only that, but he had Sasha now. He didn't know where he was taking her, what they were going to do when they got there, or what he'd say. He hadn't thought of anything, but he couldn't get himself to care.

He and Sasha were finally going on a date.

9

THE SMOKE FROM GONZALO'S LIT CIGARETTE
wafted up in a straight line. Even on the top of the four-story
brewery, there was no wind. He gripped the waist-high wall
that penned in the flat roof, the cigarette poking out between
his thick, clenched fingers like an apple stem. He wasn't finding this particular smoke very enjoyable. He scanned Greeley
with tired eyes.

Gonzalo had investigated every square foot of this old
industrial building and hadn't found a soul. In fact, he hadn't
found evidence that anyone had even been there for months.
Just the occasional food wrapper or crunched can, but nothing that indicated that this was some haven for the infected
community, like he'd hoped.

He'd been hearing about an infected underground network,
where all kinds of kids worked together to survive. He'd heard
about a blimp hangar full of a thousand kids. A cathedral

where hundreds lived in a big, hidden room behind the organ. Secret trails that linked places like that. But he'd checked most of them out and found nothing. After searching the brewery from basement to rooftop, he was starting to think all these hideouts were just legends.

He'd found a *Yellow Pages* in the manager's office and had plunked it down on the wall's ledge. The water-stiffened pages crackled when he turned them. He thought that maybe he could find something else in town that had "brewery" in its title, like a bar or a restaurant, and that maybe Dan had left out a key piece of information.

Dan. What a piece of shit that guy was. Gonzalo felt like an idiot for ever thinking Dan had good information. Of course he didn't. He was an adult. He was a predator. He was a liar. And in the eyes of Janine, Dan's victim, Gonzalo had been no different. To the infected, Gonzalo might as well have been forty. He was an adult to them, capable of as much evil as any other. He was on the outside now, and as long as he was, he'd always be chasing down outdated information, like "there are teens at the brewery in Greeley." Even if that had been true at some point, by the time that information got to adult circles and landed in Gonzalo's ear, it couldn't possibly be true anymore. Infected stayed alive by staying under the adult radar.

But that was going to get harder with groups like whatever those assholes called themselves in Lehman—the CNC—stepping up their game to "clean up" Colorado. They were organized, and eventually they'd have more numbers. If that old man had killed over three hundred kids single-handedly, how many had all the hunters killed, total? Whatever that number was, it was bound to double soon with more re-settlers, and then triple.

What are the chances Sasha would survive? If she hadn't been killed already.

Gonzalo tried not to think that way. With people moving back, he was running out of time. In the early days of his search, he thought he could find Sasha by thinking like she would have, fresh out of McKinley, probably with other Loners. He'd even tracked down her family home in Pale Ridge, then her extended family in other counties, but it had all led to nothing. And now, he had no idea what to do.

Gonzalo flicked his cigarette off the roof, and it spiraled down silently to the loading dock below. He rubbed his forehead. His brain felt empty. He would crash at his uncle's old apartment tonight, which wasn't too far. Some sleep in a familiar place and a little bit of food would do him some good.

He picked up his gas mask and noticed a little sliver of vibrant green out of the corner of his eye. He leaned out over the edge of the building to get a better look. Through an alley, two blocks down, he spotted his lime-green Honda Fit.

Gonzalo got to the street as fast as he could. He pulled on his gas mask and hoofed it through the dead streets, his heart thumping. If that was his old car, then Janine had to be close. Maybe that meant there were others.

He was gasping for breath by the time he reached the car. He needed air faster than his mask's filter could process it, so his mask sucked in toward his face with each inhale. He leaned on the car for support. It was still running. The keys were in the ignition. It was parked, half on the curb, half on the street, outside a fabric and yarn store called Sew Fun.

"I'm not giving it back."

Gonzalo spun around to see Janine coming out of a Goodwill on the other side of the street. She'd ditched the Colorado Rockies jersey for a pair of black jeans, a stained sweatshirt, and a woman's wool overcoat. But she still had Dan's broken pool cue. Evidently, it'd become her weapon of choice.

"Relax, Janine. I just wanna talk."

"Don't say my name. You don't know me."

Gonzalo put his hands up. "Take it easy."

"You won't be saying shit when I poke right through that mask."

She walked toward the car, the splintered cue thrust out at him.

"You really screwed me over back in Loveland," he said. "I had to ride a lawn mower to get here."

She didn't crack. "Good, then you don't need this car anymore."

"Well, I found it first."

"Well, I found it second, after your asshole friend locked me in a fucking fish tank and—"

"What are you doing in Greeley?" Gonzalo asked.

"Don't worry about it."

"Are there others here?"

"I'm not telling you anything. Now move!"

Janine was feisty, and she was strong, he could tell. He wondered if Sasha would have the guts to stand her ground like this.

Gonzalo softened his tone. "I just want to find my girlfriend. That's all. But I don't know where to look. If you don't want to tell me where kids are, maybe you could ask for me . . . Her name is Sasha."

Janine's face changed. She relaxed her grip on the spear and stopped moving forward.

"You know her?" Gonzalo said, excitement brimming within him. "Is she okay?"

Blood exploded from Janine's chest, then he heard the gunshot echo. She crumpled to the ground with a ragged crater under her left collarbone. Gonzalo staggered backwards. Blood gurgled from her wound. A pond of it spread out on the asphalt around her. It seeped fast into her coat. She wasn't moving. Gonzalo took cover against the side of the car and whipped his head around, looking for the shooter. He looked up, eyes snapping fast from ledge to rooftop to window. His breath heaved in his mask. Where? Where? And then he saw.

A familiar black pickup truck sat parked, peeking into an intersection a hundred yards away. The old man who'd given him a ride to Greeley leaned out the driver's-side window. He retracted a rifle with a scope from the open window, and when Gonzalo stood up in shock, the man raised his hand in the air, palm out, like he was saying hello. Before Gonzalo could think of how to respond, the man nodded and drove away.

Vomit flooded the inside of Gonzalo's mask. He couldn't stop it. He also couldn't breathe. His mouth and nostrils were submerged in stomach acid, gin, and peaches. Gonzalo had to run away from Janine's body. He needed to be a safe distance upwind of her before he could rip off his mask. He ran down the block and around the corner, vomit splashing up his cheeks and into one eye. Another thirty feet and he tore the mask from his face. He fell to his hands and knees and regurgitated again, is back in a hunch, like how a dog throws up. Less and less of the burning peach-gin stew was coming out each time, but his stomach kept clenching.

It was too much. That was what he kept thinking, over and over. Seeing Janine shot dead was more than his brain could handle, than his nerves could handle, clearly more than his stomach could. If Sasha were about to die out here, eliminated by some hunter, he'd just seen exactly what it might look like. Before, it was only an abstract possibility, but to witness the reality of it was so much worse.

He'd been looking Janine in the eyes. He'd felt her shock the moment the bullet blew through her. He'd seen her confusion. He'd seen her try to process what had just happened for a fraction of a second before she fell. He'd seen how terrified she was as her legs gave out and she crashed to the ground. She was alive, then *bang*, she wasn't. And whatever she'd been about to say, whatever secrets she had, whatever she knew, it'd all died with her.

He wasn't sure how long he stayed there in shock, but eventually he rose to his feet and did what had to be done. He found an old shovel in the garage of a single-family house nearby. Digging the hole wasn't hard. The ground was soft. The digging was just work. Sweat and strain and labored breathing. The longer he worked, the deeper he stood in the ground, until only his head cleared ground level. He'd left one side slanted so it wasn't hard to climb out.

What was hard was the walk back to Janine's body. Touching her body was even harder. Her skin that had been facing the sun was warm, but underneath, it was cold. Like the rest of her body. He tried to be delicate when he picked her up. It seemed somehow respectful. He carried her like a dead bride. He had to stare at the clouds because he couldn't watch her bent-back head wobble and swing to the rhythm of his walk. Or look at that wound. It was a sinkhole of ripped flesh that tunneled through the meat of her heart and out her back.

Gonzalo did his best not to make contact with any of her blood. Some people said that infected blood had more concentrated toxicity, but it was hard to know for sure. What he did know was that the poison that killed adults seemed to just emanate from infected, like a scent or a pheromone. Maybe there was a layer of the virus on all infected skin. Or maybe their lungs produced the poison and it was their breath that was toxic. He'd heard lots of theories, and every one sounded like the person was talking out his ass. All Gonzalo knew for sure was that he'd wash himself thoroughly afterwards and probably burn his clothes.

Gonzalo walked into Janine's grave. He laid her down in the dirt as gently as he could. He was glad to walk away from her and climb out. He wasn't proud, but he shoveled the dirt onto her face first. He thought it would make the rest of the burying easier, but he kept feeling flashes of deep sadness when he thought about how hard life had been on this poor girl. She had been maybe seventeen, maybe not that far from phasing out of infection. She'd just escaped Dan, after some awful shit had gone down, and who knew what she'd been through before him. And now here she was, about to be planted in the ground to rot into nothing. She hadn't made it. No matter what she'd hoped and how hard she'd fought along the way, there was no happy ending for Janine.

Filling her grave was strenuous and repetitive. The more Gonzalo shoveled, the more he kept his thoughts at bay as they took a new, even colder direction. A nagging idea had inserted itself into his brain at the moment of Janine's death.

He wanted to quit.

10

behind him. Her voice buzzed off the walls of the dark metal duct.

"Wet Street."

"Oh."

Gonzalo waited for more but got nothing, and there wasn't enough room for him to look back and read her face. "Just oh?" he said.

"I don't know what you expect. You give a girl all that time to cool off, then expect her to get boiling hot again?"

Gonzalo stopped. "Wait, you were boiling hot before?"

"I was a cup of tea that had been left out for an hour."

"That still sounds warm."

"Barely."

"What about now?"

"I guess that depends on Wet Street," she said.

He prayed Wet Street was as cool as he'd heard, because if it wasn't, he had nothing. Supposedly, it was a hallway near the ruins of the East Wing, where a pipe had burst along the ceiling, raining down water in a continuous spray. He'd heard people say they played in the spray like it was an open fire hydrant in the summer, and that the floor was deeply bowed so the water collected into a kind of pond where you could sit and soak. He hoped she liked it, because it was bothering him way more than he wanted to admit that Sasha didn't seem all that excited to be here with him. He was dying to get right back to how electric things had felt when he'd first joined the Mice, but it was possible that he'd waited too long.

Gonzalo pressed the home button on the broken iPhone Wiggles had given him. The screen lit up a flat gray behind the shattered glass. Lighting up for thirty seconds at a time was the only thing the phone could still do, but it provided enough light for Gonzalo to check for directional markers, which were drawn in Sharpie at every duct intersection:

They stood for North, South, East, and West, in that order. He led Sasha east and eventually came to where the ducts bent at wild angles, warped from the explosion that'd happened in the east end of the school just before the quarantine. They came to what he thought was the right vent. He popped the cover off. It swung down and was stopped short of slapping the wall and making noise by a taut white string. There didn't seem to be a vent cover in the whole school that the Mice hadn't rigged. Gonzalo dropped out of the vent and landed on the slick, wet floor of the hallway. Sasha followed him out and nearly slipped when she landed, but he grabbed her hand and helped hold her upright. She let go as soon as she was steady.

"I would have been fine," she said.

He wasn't going to argue. As long as his navigation was correct, they had to be right around the corner from Wet Street, and playing in the water would hopefully lift her spirits. Wet Street did prove to be around the corner, but it was not as advertised. There was a broken water pipe by the ceiling, just like he'd heard, and water did spray down continuously, but it sprayed down into a twenty-foot-long gray puddle with a film of swirling oil on the surface. It stunk of mold and old eggs. The ceiling above sagged as much as the floor that formed the "pond." The floor was slick with a sludge of wet dust. The soaked walls on either side bulged like bellies, dripping with sweat.

"What do you think? Is that puddle half piss, or more than half?" she said.

Gonzalo laughed, but Sasha didn't. She wasn't even smiling either. She was looking around like she was . . . disappointed.

"This is not what I expected," Gonzalo said.

"A lot of things haven't been what I expected lately."

He looked at her, but she was avoiding his eyes, like she'd been since they'd dropped out of the vent. He wanted to explain himself, but he didn't want to tell her that he'd been scared of Baxter. His Uncle George had been popular with ladies, and so had his cousins, and Gonzalo couldn't imagine any of them telling a girl they were scared, not under any circumstances.

"Let's walk somewhere else. Get away from this smell," Gonzalo said.

"Where?"

"I don't know."

She didn't like that and started walking back to the vent. He didn't want to go back to the ducts. Once they were in there she might just say, "Let's go back to The Hole." He needed to move things forward, not take a step back. He caught up with her under the vent and touched her shoulder. He hadn't come up with anything to say, but he didn't think he was going to win her over with words—he had to show her.

"I got something for you," he said.

Gonzalo reached into his pocket and pulled out a ziplock bag containing three sugar cubes. Her eyes narrowed.

"Where'd you get those?" she said.

"Found 'em stashed just behind a vent cover by the library. Someone wanted to hide this bag from the rest of their gang."

"So, these are all for me?" she said.

"Well, I get one," he said, fishing one out as he passed her the bag with the other two.

She smirked. "You sure you understand how gifts work?"

Sasha plucked out one sugar cube for herself, leaving the third behind. They popped the cubes in their mouths at the same time, staring into each other's eyes. Sasha writhed and shimmied like she was tasting the sugar with her whole body.

"Mmmmmmhhmmhmmhmm," she said as she swallowed, and her mouth opened with a pop. "That was amazing."

Gonzalo was still savoring his. The *zing* of the sugar on his tongue made him smile.

"What are you smiling about?"

"When I found that bag, there were twenty sugar cubes in it."

Her eyes went as big as gum balls. She punched him in the arm. "You greedy a-hole!"

Sasha fished out the last sugar cube. She popped it and started swishing it around, way too fast.

"Hey, slow down, rookie," he said. "It's the last one. You have to savor it."

She stared at him, maybe more *glared* at him, but she stopped attacking the sugar with her tongue.

"If you want to get the most out of it, you have to close your eyes," Gonzalo said.

She cocked her head skeptically, but then slowly, very slowly, she let her eyelids fall.

Gonzalo's heart clapped against his ribs. She stood in front of him with her eyes closed, tongue rolling in sweetness. This was the moment. He imagined his Uncle George was there watching, telling him—and it gave him the push to go for it. With the sugar still melting in his mouth, he closed the distance between them, cradled her head in his hands, and kissed her. Sasha's lips went firm but then softened and moved with his.

Then Sasha pulled away. They stared at each other. Gonzalo could only handle it for about three seconds before he kissed her again. Sasha kissed him back. It heated up fast, their hands in each other's hair, their candied tongues in each other's mouths, their breath in each other's lungs. It wouldn't have stopped if he hadn't felt her try to steal the remains of his cube with her tongue.

"Hey!" he said.

She laughed, and swished the stolen lump of sugar around in her mouth.

"So sweet of you to give me all three," she said.

His body was rushing with feeling.

"I'm a nice guy."

Her face went earnest.

"You *are* a nice guy," she said. "You know I watched you from the vents for a long time?"

"You did?"

She nodded.

"Why me?"

"Well, it wasn't just you. If you look out from the vents, you see a lot of people."

"Yeah, but you said you watched *me*."

"You popped up from time to time."

"And? I was your favorite character?"

She grinned and nodded. "Something like that. I saw you help people. Protect people. And I saw that you never gave up."

"Is that why you saved me?"

"I saved you to save you."

"Not because you liked me?"

"A girl can't care about another human being's life?"

"But you have to have seen hundreds of fights through the vents before. Did you save any of them?"

"Nuh-uh, Gonzalo. That's not how it works. You have to say something nice about *me* now."

Gonzalo rifled through all the feelings he could share with her. That he wanted to have sex with her. That he *really* wanted to have sex with her. He could tell her how many times he'd already had sex with her in his own head, even though the only real sex he'd ever had was a semi-painful hand-job he'd received from a neighbor girl in her tree house the day before she and her family moved across the country. His gut told him not to tell her how horny he was. He needed something deeper. Something like what she'd said. He felt ambushed, like she'd recited a perfect speech she'd written and now expected him to improvise his own.

"I don't trust anyone. And I trust you," he said.

"Why?"

Rats. She'd stumped him again. Couldn't she just take a compliment?

"Because . . . you saved me. And you didn't have anything to gain from it."

She smiled.

"I've trusted you ever since," he said.

"Is that it?"

"And because . . . you're hot. I know that's a bad reason, but—"

"No, that's a good reason."

"I did good?"

"You did all right. But I'm going to need to hear more. Much more."

Gonzalo didn't get the chance to tell her more because Sasha smothered his lips with hers. When they came up for air, he felt a thousand times closer to her.

"Do you like it in the Mice?" Gonzalo asked.

She frowned and didn't answer right away.

"I think about leaving the Mice sometimes," she said.

"You do?"

"I see other gangs from a distance, and on their own turf they get to be who they want to be. I've never felt that way in the Mice. We have to be quiet so much, we have to stay secret, and, Gonzalo, I don't want to be quiet. I want to be LOUD, you know? And there's just so few of us, and it gets so tense all the time. I mean, when I was little I remember being excited about being a teenager, about going to high school, and look at me—my social life is on its deathbed."

"I've been thinking about leaving a lot too lately."

"'Cause the others have been riding you so hard? It's just because you're new—"

"I'm growing. Soon, I'll be too big to fit in the vents and I'll have to live in the halls again. But maybe I'd be big enough that I could really fight on the quad. Get a whole lotta food. And I guess I just wanted to know . . ."

He felt out of control. He shouldn't be asking her what he was about to ask her. It was too soon. She was gonna get freaked out. She'd think he was desperate. But he said it anyway.

"If I left the Mice, would you want to come with me?"

She stared off away from him, and then a grin spread across her face.

"I'd go."

"You would?"

"Yeah, but I'd pull my own weight."

He wasn't going to argue. He liked that she wanted to be a team. They talked longer, about dumb stuff, about funny things they'd seen happening in the halls, about the meals they craved from before the quarantine, about anything and everything, until Sasha got tired.

"I'm gonna go to bed," she said though a yawn.

"Can I come?"

She laughed. "You may not."

They kissed again before she crawled into the vent and left. He still didn't know where she slept, and she wasn't about to tell him. He waited for a minute like she'd made him promise so that he wouldn't see which way she went. It was Mice rules.

Gonzalo had soda pop in his veins. He'd never felt this way before. Warm all over, tingly, and full of enough energy to sprint a mile. He'd wanted Sasha so badly, and waited so long, and everything had actually worked out. It was kind of mind-blowing. The quarantine didn't seem quite so oppressive anymore. The universe didn't seem out to get him. He was feeling something that he'd forgotten you could feel in McKinley: hope.

That was probably why he didn't hear the person behind him until the last second, when they were able to crack their baseball bat into the back of his head. The world went blank.

When Gonzalo awoke, he was in a small bathroom he didn't recognize. His vision was a haze, and it was dark. Two candles were lit, sitting on the seat of a wooden chair by an open door. The candlelight drew a rim of light around the silhouette of a short, little boy with a handsome face.

"Cute date," Baxter said.

Gonzalo got his feet underneath him and stood, but it felt like his head was spinning in two different directions. He looked down and realized his ankle was tied to a water pipe that ran from the ceiling to the floor. Gonzalo picked at the knotted nylon cord and pulled the first knot apart, but there had to be fifty knots to go.

"What are you doing?" Gonzalo said.

"You should take a look at your surroundings and get comfortable. You're going to be here awhile."

"This isn't funny, Baxter." Gonzalo glanced around the room as he tore at the next knot. There were crates of bottled water and piles of canned food stacked up against the wall. A ridiculous amount.

"You're a problem, Gonzo. The others are starting to like you. Sasha seems to like you. I can't have that. The Mice is my gang. There's not room for two leaders."

"I'm not trying to be the leader. This is about Sasha, and you know it."

"I've left you enough food for three months. That should be long enough."

"Long enough for what?"

"For you to get too big to ever come back," Baxter said.

Gonzalo stared at Baxter in disbelief.

"Don't be so shocked that I know your secret," he said. "I see everything."

"Don't do this, Baxter," Gonzalo said. He yanked at the knots, trying to untie them with as much speed as possible, but Baxter was already backing out the door and pulling it shut.

"Baxter!"

Gonzalo heard the lock engage with a click.

11

THE SKY WAS A DEAD WHITE. IT LEECHED THE
color out of everything. Gonzalo was ripping down the road in
his Honda. On the seat next to him were some things Janine
had found between Dan's house and dying. An old hairbrush.
Two cans of pepper spray. A wire-bound notebook. She'd only
written one thing on the first page of the notebook, and the
rest of the pages were blank. In plump, looping letters, she'd
written two words:

"All dead."

Gonzalo tapped the brakes. A black minivan was parked on
the side of the road ahead. A pair of legs extended into the
road. The rest of whoever they belonged to was under the van.
Gonzalo slowed to a crawl as he approached. The van looked
like it had been washed within the week. Its rear doors were
wide open, revealing a bed and some built-in shelving. A rusty
car jack lay in the dirt nearby. Two tires, a spare tire and a

full-sized one, were on the ground.

Gonzalo pulled up beside the van and stopped. The van was parked on a slope, and something about the angle of the jack had made it break or slip. Now the stripped metal rotor of the wheel was sunk into the abdomen of the body pinned under the van. A blanket of burgundy blood spread out around the legs. It was a miserable way to go, and Gonzalo pitied the poor bastard.

The left leg shuddered.

"Goddamn it," Gonzalo muttered inside his mask.

He turned off the ignition, pocketed the keys, and got out. Gonzalo hurried toward the outstretched legs and crouched down. When he looked under the van, he saw a man looking back at him. No gas mask. He was in his fifties. Brown and gray beard. Meaty face that had gone pale blue. A web of branching capillaries spread out across his nose and cheek bones like sprinkled saffron.

"You're gonna be all right. I'll just . . ." Gonzalo said, but then he looked again at the rotor buried in the man's gut. It looked like it'd sunk straight through him and was making contact with the ground. Blood still oozed up from his stomach like jelly from a bitten donut, fresh and red.

"S'too late," the man said. His voice was thin. He gurgled when he drew breath.

Gonzalo didn't argue. The man was right. This was tragic, but what Gonzalo hadn't expected was how awkward it was. What do you say to a dying man you just met?

"What's your name?"

"Buddy."

"I'm Gonzalo."

"No . . . ," he rasped, "my son. Buddy is my son."

Speaking was incredibly hard for him. He heaved and spit.

"You have to find him," the man said.

"Listen, man, I—"

"Please," the man said, louder than Gonzalo would've thought he could.

"Is Buddy infected?"

The man fixed Gonzalo with a suspicious stare, and his eyes seemed to clear for a moment.

"Take off your mask," the man said.

Gonzalo hesitated for a moment, but didn't see any reason not to comply. Whatever the man was hoping to see in Gonzalo's face, he saw it. His expression relaxed back into agony, and he closed his eyes.

"Yes. He's infected."

Gonzalo winced.

"You have to tell him I love him."

The man reached out for Gonzalo's hand, and Gonzalo took it. The man's grip was fearsome.

"Tell him to be a good man," he said and coughed. "Tell him that when he transitions out, it's his job to take care of his mother and his sister. There's a little money hidden in the basement of our old house. Not a lot, but enough for a few months.

You have to tell him that I never stopped looking, okay?"

Gonzalo nodded.

"You'll tell him that?"

"I will," Gonzalo said. He was just comforting the guy at this point. The man's grip lost strength, and his hand dropped down to the dirt. His eyelids drooped. This was it. Death was taking him.

The man took a sharp breath in, and his eyes widened.

"I know where Buddy is," the man said.

There was a fire in the dying man's eyes that made those words worth believing. Gonzalo moved closer.

"Tell me," Gonzalo said.

"They hide," the man said. "The locations change—they move around—but they're out there. A whole infected underground. So many that you wouldn't believe it."

Gonzalo's heartbeat quickened. "You've seen this?"

"Head to the sewers in Longmont." Air hissed and popped from his wet throat. His eyes drifted shut. "In the Slough."

The man's face and the tendons of his neck went slack. He let out his final breath.

It was an eerie feeling seeing a man die while hope was catching fire inside him. Despite what had just happened to this man, the blue sky seemed richer to Gonzalo now, the air more fragrant. He heard the low hoot of an owl. A woodpecker somewhere nearby did a drumroll against a tree. He couldn't give up now.

12

FOR HIS FIRST FEW WEEKS OF IMPRISONMENT,
Gonzalo had been full of furious energy. He'd fly into fits of
rage. He'd curse Baxter's name at the top of his lungs. He'd
batter the door and throw his weight into it repeatedly, but
the wood never gave. There was something large and heavy
barricading the other side of the door. Eventually, he gave up
trying. There were no vents in the wall of this stripped-down
bathroom, and he'd torn out the ceiling panels to inspect
above him. He'd hit concrete in every direction. There was no
way out of the room.

He counted off the days by marking the wall with a ballpoint
pen he'd found under a radiator. The school's lights were on
a timer. They came on in the morning and went off at night.
It was the only way he could tell that a day had passed, and
thirty days passed like a year. The pitch-black nights were
endless. With no book or anything to look at, he was forced to

occupy his mind with memories. Good ones just made him feel bad, and bad ones filled him with regret, so most of the time he focused on what he would do to Baxter when he got a hold of him. Gonzalo didn't even have a toilet—only a hole in the floor where a toilet had been ripped out. If he rationed water, he could use some of it to flush the pipe clean. Well, clean*ish*. There was no getting rid of the smell.

The second month was harder, mainly because he hadn't really believed Baxter would leave him in there longer than a month, and so he hadn't rationed his food properly. It had been hard to restrain himself with nothing to do, and with a growing body that craved so much sustenance. He tried to see how long he could stretch little bits of food. His aches and pains got worse, interrupting his sleep every night. He'd fall asleep telling his body to stop growing, but it never worked.

At sixty marks on the wall, Gonzalo's clothes began to rip at the seams. The button had popped off of his jeans from strain. He was getting big. Really big. Every minute felt like his body was being drawn and quartered. The pain was so massive that he wondered if he might actually be able to see his limbs getting longer if he only watched closely enough.

He started doing pushups. He learned to do handstands. One-handed handstand pushups. They weren't perfect or anything, but eventually, with a little help from the walls, he could lower himself down at a controlled pace and grind his way back up. He challenged his body to do impossible things because there was nothing else to do. And when he slept, he dreamed of the day Baxter would let him out and how Gonzalo would pummel him into the ground.

On his ninetieth day in captivity, Gonzalo ate his last piece of jerky, drank his last bottle of water, and waited for the door to be unlocked. Baxter had said he'd let Gonzalo out after three months, but nothing happened. The door stayed locked all day. The next day he stood in front of the door and waited again, until he fell asleep. For four days, it went that way, with Gonzalo surviving only the sludgy, rust-colored water from room's broken sink, until a horrendous possibility began to terrorize him.

Baxter wasn't ever coming to let him out. He wanted Gonzalo to die in here. Or maybe, something had happened to Baxter. What if someone had killed Baxter? Or he'd gotten a wound and it'd gotten infected, and fever had struck him, and Baxter had died without telling anyone that Gonzalo was in here? What if the quarantine had ended, the whole school had been let out, and no one would ever know that somewhere back in McKinley High, there was a boy locked in a bathroom?

On the morning of the ninety-sixth day, Gonzalo tried the doorknob, like he had done every other morning, and for the first time, it turned freely. He pushed on the door. It swung open. Beyond the door was a short hallway that dead-ended with a door on the right wall. That door was ajar. Gonzalo's heart started to thud with nervous excitement.

He couldn't believe it. He was free.

Gonzalo burst out of his room. He had to duck his head down so he wouldn't knock it into the door frame. Three desperate months fueled his pace as he scrambled down the hall. He felt like he was going to fall down—he wasn't used to the awkwardness of his newly stretched frame.

He realized he was in the ruins, near where he'd kissed Sasha when he'd first come to Wet Street. He stomped through the water until he reached dry floor. He knew exactly what he wanted to do first. He found an empty classroom, waited until he was sure there was no one coming, and then pulled the vent cover off of the wall. This was the moment he'd dreamt of. Revenge waited for him. And more: Sasha.

The hole in front of him looked small. Smaller than he remembered. No, he was probably just psyching himself out. He stuck both hands into the duct, and then his head. The problem came with his shoulders. They were wider than the duct. He could sort of jam them in if he got one in first and then the other, but only partway. He tried feet first too, even though he knew it didn't make any sense, and he failed again.

It was all sinking in now. Baxter's plan had succeeded. Gonzalo was too big to ever return to the ducts.

Gonzalo walked the halls in a stupor. His frizzy hair had grown longer during his imprisonment. It hung in front of his eyes. He wandered to more populated areas of the school. People stared at him. Usually kids in gangs tended to ignore Scraps like him, but they were looking at him now—looking up at him. He started staring back. They moved out of his way, even if they were in groups. No one spoke to him, and he was glad. He didn't want to talk. He didn't trust anyone. Not after what Baxter had done to him. Baxter had been someone he'd known—who knew what a *stranger* might be capable of?

He picked up his pace to a jog. In the last three months, he hadn't been able to walk more than three steps without having to turn around, so this felt good. It felt good to push the world behind him with each step. His legs felt strong. His stride was longer than before. His muscles pushed harder. He hadn't grown muscular and bulky. Rather, he was lean, and his muscles were ropy and hard. He'd come out much stronger than he'd gone in.

And angrier.

He thought of Baxter's pretty-boy face, and he threw his fist into a locker. The metal dented. Gonzalo stopped and gazed at the depression he'd left. It felt good to damage something. He wanted to do the same thing to Baxter, put a dent in his head. Baxter'd stolen three months of his life. He unloaded on the locker again. The locker door bent inward. Baxter's face bent inward in his mind.

A familiar noise distracted Gonzalo. In the distance, he heard the low rhythmic thupping of a helicopter. The food drop, he thought. Gonzalo's mouth flooded with saliva. Hunger attacked his gut. It felt like there was a rat in his belly, trying to gnaw its way out.

He broke into a run. He wasn't far from the quad. There was food out there, and people to hit. He wanted to keep hitting something, and people were much softer than lockers. The chopper's beat grew louder the closer he got. He burst onto the quad, and the pounding of the helicopter blades thumped at his eardrums.

The gray canopy convulsed overhead. Quivering waves radiated from the center out to the four sides of the quad. The slit in the center of the canopy was agape, revealing a tangerine sky beyond, drenched in the light of the rising sun. The clouds were rimmed with gold. The block of food and supplies had already breached the opening and hung underneath it, swinging.

The gangs were screaming. Shaking their weapons. Their numbers were greater than Gonzalo remembered. Their dye-jobs looked better than he'd ever seen, more vibrant. He ran his hands through his white hair. The last time he'd been here, he'd gotten stomped, robbed, and knocked out. He hadn't thought he would ever come back. He'd been terrified, but he couldn't find that fear today.

He felt only impatience.

The blue-haired Freaks were to his right. Five of them were watching Gonzalo cross. To his left, he saw Varsity. Fucking banana-heads. He wasn't as big as their biggest guys, but he was getting there. They didn't like him. They mad-dogged him, like he'd just felt up all of their sisters.

Gonzalo was the only white-haired kid standing at the front lines with the rest of the gangs. The rest of the Scraps hung by the walls, or in the halls, and would wait a few moments after the gangs ran for the food pile before entering the fray, as they always did. Gonzalo knew that rule, even though no one had ever spoken it out loud, and he knew he was violating it. He knew that the glares he was getting from the Freaks and the Varsity guys were meant to warn him that he'd better not think about running at the same time they did.

They could go fuck porcupines—he'd be running the second that block dropped. No one was ever going to control him again. He wouldn't allow it. Not after what Baxter had done to him. He didn't want to feel that helpless, that utterly controlled and contained ever again.

There was a plink as the cable detached from the block, followed by a breathless silence and a resounding crash. Gonzalo sprinted forward while the silver packets of powdered soup were still flying through the air. All the gangs launched forward a second after him.

The broken plastic wrap and securing straps that had held the block together lay in a tangled mess with the food and water and medical supplies, the blankets, the socks, the toothpaste and tampons, soap, deodorant, condoms, Bibles, and everything else. It might as well have been a pile of cash. Gonzalo got his paws on a box of powdered milk and clutched it to his chest. The rest of the gangs ripped into the perimeter of the pile.

Gonzalo whipped around to leave and found himself faced

with a pack of Varsity. One of the Varsity guys who had been glaring at him earlier lunged for the box of milk. Gonzalo scrambled back up onto the pile of supplies. The Varsity and his buddies crawled after him. Gonzalo scurried on his back over water jugs, bags of white shirts, twenty-four-can packs of chicken soup. All around him the battle crashed against the edges of the pile like a stormy ocean against the rocky shore. The slap of body against body, the chorus of grunts, wails, cuss words, and shouted commands filled his ears. The other Varsity started to lose interest, but the one who had made a grab for his powdered milk gained on him. Gonzalo couldn't scramble backwards as fast as this guy was coming at him. He should have rolled right and then slid down the pile to try to outrun him, but he didn't. He stopped. Because he hated this guy's face. Because he wanted to hurt it. Because he wanted to hurt Baxter. Gonzalo rushed the Varsity and slugged him straight in the chin. The guy went to sleep in a heartbeat, and toppled to the ground. He had an empty duffel bag slung over his shoulder. Gonzalo took it.

While the other gangs snatched up everything around the edges of the pile, Gonzalo focused on the middle, right where he stood, on top of it all, filling his duffel with what he'd need to survive for two weeks, until the next food drop. He got nearly a dozen cans of chili, a twenty-eight-ounce bottle of orange Gatorade, a twelve-pack of toilet paper, a plastic jar of Bazooka Joe bubble gum. Chili for every meal, a bottle to drink out of, and gum for dessert. He saw a plastic-wrapped stack of three bars of Zest soap. He grabbed it, and someone kneed him in the temple.

Gonzalo fell to his side. His hand went to the flaring pain in his head. He saw a fat Freak above him swing his leg back like a pendulum before delivering a kick to Gonzalo's stomach. Gonzalo squinted up through the pain at something he couldn't understand. The Freak's chemical-blue hair was parted in the middle, and his face was upside down. It took a moment to realize that the Freak had painted a realistic smiling face upside down on top of his actual face.

Gonzalo did his best to spring to his feet, but not before the upside-down-faced Freak had snagged the duffel and taken off. Gonzalo staggered out of the pile. He ran between fights, between Sluts and Skaters, before he spotted the Freak with the bag again.

Gonzalo weaved faster through the chaotic battlefield. Past Nerds shoving a little Geek around. Past a Scrap who'd been pants'd and was running bare-assed for the hallway, trying to cover himself. Past a tall Geek trying to run a box of bottled water back to the guarded Geek loot pile on the other side of the quad. She couldn't stop people from stealing individual bottles from her. She could kick at them, but she needed both arms to carry the box, so she became a pissed-off water girl handing out refreshments. Gonzalo navigated past all of these little scenes as he closed in on the punk who'd stolen his bag.

He caught up with the Freak near the Skater loot pile, grabbed the dude's head, and whipped it toward the ground. The Freak hit the dirt face-first. Gonzalo tore the bag from the Freak's grip. The paint on the kid's face was half scraped off, and his skin was scoured with abrasions and streaked with dirt. The Freak popped up and tried to swing at Gonzalo, but Gonzalo kicked him hard in the chest. The kid fell onto his back, wheezing and choking for air.

The Skaters gathered at the loot pile all winced, their faces scrunched up like they could imagine the Freak's pain. Gonzalo pointed his finger at all of them and then slapped his chest. A few of the Skaters flinched.

It didn't seem like any of them were going to make a move for his bag. It almost seemed like he'd won their respect. Gonzalo looked to the pile, which was nearly gone now. He saw the desperate struggles across the quad. So much violence to deal with out there, and not that much stuff left to fight over. He decided to call it a day. He'd gotten what he'd come there for. He snuck off the quad before any of the gangs had finished gathering their stuff together. He didn't want anybody else to get ballsy with him simply because he was alone.

Gonzalo ran to the nearest hallway, past the Pretty Ones who looked at him like he was an animal, and past a wide-eyed Scrap who gazed at him in wonder. He made it to the halls without incident and wandered into the school, bag in hand, in search of someplace safe.

13

AS FAR AS LIFE IN THE INFECTED ZONE WENT,
Gonzalo was rich. The van he'd inherited was decked out for living in, complete with a mattress, a mini-kitchen with a hot plate and camping cooking equipment, and a filtered-water pump. The whole thing was sealed airtight so that he never had to wear a gas mask, even though he kept one handy on the passenger seat. He now owned crates of dehydrated meals, cans of instant coffee, and a bottle of Scotch. He had the dead man's backup toothbrush, still unopened in the box, toothpaste, soap, and shampoo. He even had camping deodorant that was supposed to stop you from sweating for two weeks. Gonzalo had been smelling like roadkill lately, so he'd had to try it. Even though he'd felt like he was giving himself armpit cancer when he'd smeared it on, he now smelled like a pine forest. He had a big first-aid kit which he'd cracked open to dress his bite wounds, a shelf of mystery novels, a survival

knife, a hunting rifle with a scope, an aluminum baseball bat, a brand-new gas mask with a full, clear face shield, and twenty-two replacement filters.

With that much luxury, it was hard to leave the van, but if he wanted to make any progress, he had to. Instead of kicking back with a Scotch, a smoke, and a paperback, Gonzalo was now standing over a vat of stewing sewage at the Longmont Water Treatment Facility. He was glad he had a gas mask on so that he couldn't smell the unholy aromas that had to be wafting up from the mudwater. Machinery suspended over the vat had once dragged a metal comb with hundreds of long teeth through the brown liquid, probably to break up the solid matter. Gonzalo looked away and gagged a little.

But it didn't matter how gross it was. What mattered was that the dying man had tracked down his son, Buddy, and had been headed here to finally catch up with him. Everything in the man's notebook concluded that there was an infected community here. The man theorized that teens were able to move through Longmont using the larger sewer tunnels, entering or exiting through manholes when they needed to. All those sewer tunnels led to one place—this facility—and that meant that Sasha could be here, maybe just a hundred feet away.

Huge, odd-shaped machinery filled the grounds. There were eight single-story buildings along the edge of a wide creek, and a two-story structure with a silver, domed roof that looked like a half-cooked Jiffy Pop pan.

Gonzalo felt close to a real breakthrough, and he'd never been better prepared than he was now to interact with infected. Not just with the rifle he held in his hands, but thanks to the message he'd promised to give Buddy from his father, he had a way to win favor with these infected in particular. He came to a section with four concrete canals of brown sewage. They were as long as football fields, but only about twenty yards wide, separated by slim concrete and steel walls. A tan-colored scum coagulated on the water's surface.

He pushed on toward the building with the reflective domed roof. Inside, he found a two-story vat, like a giant above-ground swimming pool, with a staircase that wrapped around it. The domed roof was actually translucent, and dimmed sunlight passed through. Gonzalo walked up the stairs, every step echoing off the high ceiling and making him edgy. At the top of the stairs was a metal platform that wrapped around the upper rim of the vat. Inside was a supply of clear, clean-looking water. Sunlight sparkled across the water's surface.

As he turned back toward the stairs, something scraped under his shoe. He lifted his foot and spotted a black metal bobby pin on the floor. Girl droppings. A good sign. His heart beat a little faster as he descended the staircase. He scanned the first floor again for more signs of human life, and stopped when he saw a slight glint in the dust. A long, white hair, disappearing into a crack between the concrete slabs of the floor.

He reached down into the widest part of the crack and felt that the slab was loose. His breathing was short and excited now. He tried to lift the slab up. It was heavy, but it moved freely. Once he had it on its end, he was able to lean it against the wall. Underneath was a ladder leading down into a dark tunnel. He muttered his disbelief. It was happening. This lead was actually paying off.

Gonzalo stepped onto the ladder and descended into the darkness. At the bottom, he clicked on a small LED flashlight, another perk from the van. He was in a narrow passage. A tangle of pipes ran on both sides of him, making the passage tight. He came to a latched metal door and opened it.

A rush of voices filled the passage.

Gonzalo pulled the door wide to see a shallow underground river of clean water in a catacomb-like tunnel. On either side were concrete-slab embankments, where a hundred kids were camped out in tents or gathered in circles with lawn chairs and sleeping bags. Two guys in swim trunks were throwing a Frisbee to each other across the river. The infected underground was real.

Gonzalo slipped in quietly for a better look. He stayed as hidden as he could and moved slowly until he was just behind a transformer box. He marveled at the fun going on in this secret oasis until a piercing pain on one side of his head made him yelp involuntarily. He flailed and fell away from his hiding spot as he reached up to his head. He plucked a throwing dart out of his scalp, and before he could figure out how it had gotten there, someone snatched his rifle out of his right hand. He felt half a dozen hands shove him from behind, and he was launched onto his stomach, out into plain sight, where all of the infected in the tunnel could see him. Gonzalo looked back to see five white-haired teens standing behind him in an alcove he hadn't noticed before. A dart board hung on the concrete wall behind them. Two girls and three guys stared him down, all angry and all in beachwear. One had a handful of darts, one had a scorecard, and one pointed Gonzalo's rifle at his head.

"Don't move!" the kid with his rifle shouted. He was missing one of his two front teeth, and looked about seventeen.

Gonzalo got himself stable on one knee. He put up both hands.

"I'm looking for someone," Gonzalo shouted through his mask.

"Someone to shoot."

"No, not to shoot."

"Then why'd you bring the rifle?"

"For protection. That's all. Look, I've got a message for Buddy."

"I don't know a Buddy," the kid said. "Does anyone know a Buddy?"

Heads shook all down the concrete embankment on the other side of the canal. Now that he was among them, the beach-blanket fantasy didn't seem as charming. They were malnourished, with blotchy, pale skin and hollow eyes. A few sucked on soda and smacked bubble gum, but all of them pointed something dangerous at Gonzalo. They gripped pocket knives, wooden spears, and a few antique guns. As scared as Gonzalo was, he still scanned the bony crowd for the shortest girl.

"Kill him," someone said.

"No!" Gonzalo shouted, and the kid paused. "Don't do that. Please. Listen, I'm not here to hurt anybody."

"Yeah, sure. We've seen your kind before," Missing Tooth said. "The ones who bring guns always end up firing them."

"That's not me. I'm not a hunter. I'm just looking for someone. A girl named Sasha. She's all I care about—she's all I'm looking for."

"You guys know a Sasha?" Missing Tooth said to the crowd.

More head-shakes, *nahs*, and *nos*.

"Too bad for you, guy," Missing Tooth said. He raised the rifle up to his eye and peered down the barrel into Gonzalo's eyes. Gonzalo tensed up.

"Wait. I know this guy," someone said.

Everyone turned to see who'd spoken. His voice seemed to command some level of respect from the others, because Missing Tooth lowered the rifle. The crowd parted, and when Gonzalo saw who it was, he wished Missing Tooth had pulled the trigger. Aside from the limp in his step and the Hawaiian shirt he was wearing, he hadn't changed a bit. Same tiny body. Same handsome face.

Same old Baxter.

"Shit," Gonzalo muttered.

"How do you know him?" Missing Tooth said.

"From McKinley," Baxter said, and that prompted some chatter in the crowd. "His name's Gonzo."

"Gonzalo," Gonzalo grumbled.

"He used to be infected," Baxter said. "That girl he's talking about, she's real. I knew her."

"So, you're saying he's telling the truth?"

"That's what I'm saying."

"He can't be here," the big kid said.

"Don't tell us about it, Ronnie. You're the one that was on guard duty," Baxter scolded. "You let him walk right in."

"I—"

"Save it. He's in here now. He knows about us. Let me have that."

Baxter took the rifle from Missing Tooth, who seemed relieved to hand it over.

"I'll take him outside and do this."

Missing Tooth stared at Baxter, mystified. "I thought you just said you knew the guy."

"Never said I liked him," Baxter said and grinned. "On your feet, Gonzo."

Gonzalo grimaced and lifted himself up to full height. At the sight of his stature, everyone took a full step back. Baxter laughed.

"Don't worry. He's as dumb as he is big. Like a big old moose."

Gonzalo gritted his teeth in anger. Old emotions were crashing around inside his skull. Baxter jabbed the rifle at him.

"Get going, moose."

Gonzalo did as he was told and walked to the door out of the sewer. As he walked through the crowd, he scanned all the female faces for Sasha. Baxter jabbed him in the ribs for being slow. He pushed him out the door and into the dark passage. Baxter threatened to shoot Gonzalo five separate times as they climbed the ladder. Gonzalo never said a word. He just stewed, waiting for Baxter to slip up. But the kid kept his distance until they were above ground and near the facility's front gate.

"You're the best thing to happen to me all week, you know that?" Baxter said. Gonzalo guessed he was about five paces behind him. "Whoo, I was getting sick of that place. Bunch of beach bums. They say they don't piss in that river but I don't believe them. I saw a lot of rashes."

"If you're gonna shoot me," Gonzalo said, "spare me the bullshit."

"The taunting's the best part."

Gonzalo reached the front gate in the chain-link fence. He

could see his van parked just outside. Dying by Baxter's hand was going to make him one pissed-off ghost. He couldn't let it happen.

"Listen, man—" he started, still facing away from Baxter.

"Ooo," Baxter interrupted. "Is this the part where you beg for your life?"

"It could be."

Baxter didn't say anything, which Gonzalo took as his prompt to start pleading. Even with death hanging over him, begging Baxter to spare him felt impossible. He gritted his teeth and dug deep.

"I know we've had our diff—"

KRACKOW! The rifle exploded behind Gonzalo. His whole back jerked, but he felt no pain. He whipped his head around to see Baxter, with the rifle pointed up in the air, a tongue of smoke lolling out of the barrel. He was smiling up at Gonzalo.

"What—?" Gonzalo sputtered. "What the hell, man?!"

"Any longer and they don't hear a gunshot down there, they're gonna come up wondering why."

"I don't . . . I don't get it."

"Those are your wheels, I assume?" Baxter said, flicking his head toward the van.

Gonzalo turned his whole body to face him. Baxter had leveled the rifle at Gonzalo again, with a proper grip, like he was ready to shoot.

"Yeah," Gonzalo said.

Baxter made eye contact and smiled. His smile grew into a chuckle. He approached Gonzalo, and Gonzalo braced himself.

"Great," Baxter said and handed Gonzalo the rifle. "Then let's get going."

Gonzalo stared at the rifle in his hands, confused, and then looked to Baxter as he breezed past. "Did you become a Christian or something?"

"No, I think we should partner up."

Gonzalo started after Baxter, still trying to pick up the pieces.

"Uh . . . why would I want to do that?"

"Because we want the same thing."

"I'm waiting."

"Well . . . Sasha, of course."

"What do you mean, you want Sasha?"

"You're not the only one who cares about her, you know that."

"But why would I want to help *you* to find her?"

"Because I know all the secret places like this one. And I can vouch for you. I mean, look at what just happened. You got in, and you were a total embarrassment. You want that to happen again? Seriously, Gonzo, you thought you could walk in and convince them you're a nice guy? I knew you were dumb but . . ."

"I haven't forgotten what you did," Gonzalo said.

"That's in the past. I'm talking about right now. I know places that people have seen her. I'm on her trail. Are you?"

Baxter pushed open the gate. For the first time, Gonzalo started to take him seriously.

"You've seen her?"

"I've talked to people who've seen her. What do you got?"

Gonzalo didn't answer. A grin spread across Baxter's tiny face like smeared butter on toast.

"That's what I thought," he said.

"So, you want to join forces out of the kindness of your heart?"

"I need your help too."

"Is there a high shelf somewhere you need me to reach?"

Baxter didn't laugh. "I need a ride."

"You want me to drive you?"

Baxter rolled his eyes. "Have you been seeing a lot of infected out in the open? We travel in secret, and it's slow as hell. You have a lot of space in that van. I can't get to the places without you, and you don't know where to go without me. We need each other, buddy."

Gonzalo looked at the van beyond the gate. There were no leads left to explore from the dead man's notebook. The sewer had been it. If he said no, he'd be back at square one, wandering blind again in the hope that he'd just get lucky. What Baxter was saying made sense, if he could trust him. He definitely *couldn't* trust him, but there was one thing he felt he could depend on, even though he hated to admit it. He could see the passion in Baxter's eyes when he spoke about Sasha. It was the same way Baxter used to look at her in the Mice. Like a prized possession.

They did want the same thing.

"So, what do you say?" Baxter swung his arms out and let them flop down to his sides.

Gonzalo's palms began to sweat, which was something that happened to him sometimes when he feared that he was about to make a mistake. But he ignored it because if he walked away, he'd never know if this could have been the thing that would have led to him finding Sasha.

"If your lead doesn't pan out, it's over," Gonzalo said.

"Great." Baxter limped his way to the passenger side of the car. Gonzalo got into the driver's seat and shut the door. Baxter waited outside for Gonzalo to unlock his door. Gonzalo massaged the back of his neck. He wouldn't be able to take his mask off inside the van anymore with Baxter in it.

Baxter knocked repeatedly on the window. "Hey, do you have any snacks? What's the music situation? Are you gonna open up or what?"

Gonzalo sighed and pushed the power-lock button, and Baxter opened the door. He threw off his Hawaiian shirt and left it on the ground. Underneath he wore a black T-shirt with white letters that said: I don't think so.

"I have a small bladder, so I will have to pee soon," he said as he climbed into the van. His little sneakers were covered in brown muck.

"No. Those sneakers are not coming in here like that. Yo, man, find a hose."

Baxter continued to pull himself up onto the seat.

"At least wipe them—aw, goddamn it."

Baxter shut the door. His feet were all over the floor mat.

"It's just mud," Baxter said.

"It better just be."

14

GONZALO WANTED THEM TO THINK HE WAS A
monster. He growled at people as he passed them in the halls.
He ate his food with his hands. He never spoke. He did whatever he could think of to make people think he was a beast, a
wild animal, something that you didn't want any trouble with.
He walked around barefoot. He never washed his clothes. He
shat in the halls while staring people in the face.

All of this behavior freaked people out. That was good. That
was what he wanted. People hugged close to the lockers now
when he came walking by. They quit trying to mess with him
so much. Fighting for the food at the drop was only the first
step. The fighting always continued over the next two weeks,
straight until the next food drop. In his first weeks of freedom, he'd fought off daily attacks from gang kids who wanted
his food, who thought they could take from him. Sometimes
they did. He started splitting his food up and hiding it in

different locations so that if he did get jumped by a group of people, he wouldn't lose his entire two-week supply.

But that wasn't the worst of it. He couldn't stop thinking about Sasha. Gonzalo searched for Sasha's face in every air vent he passed. He'd go back to specific vents they used to frequent in the Mice. She was never ever there. If he heard the pop of warping metal from up above, the hairs would stand up on the back of his neck. He'd call out for her, but she never answered. He wondered if she'd heard him but didn't want anything to do with him. But then he would wonder if it was actually Baxter, watching Gonzalo and snickering.

It made him furious that his new body was so capable of crushing Baxter in an instant, but now he had no way of laying his hands on the bastard. He was growing bigger by the week. His body was in constant pain because of it. His hands were growing large and thick. He was becoming a more imposing figure the longer he stayed alive, but it still wasn't enough. He needed more. He had the reputation of a crazy person and a fighter, but when he had anything valuable on him, there was always someone who still wanted to have a go, no matter how much he yelled or acted deranged.

He needed something that would scare the shit out of them, and when the idea finally hit him, he felt like he might legitimately be a genius. He was always searching for a new place to call home because he was always getting robbed. Robbers would come back once they knew where he stayed. But there was one place he could live where no one would ever want to go. Someplace where even Baxter couldn't spy on him. A place that had been boarded up since the early days of the quarantine because what was on the other side needed to be forgotten.

The senior lounge.

Before the military had instituted "graduations," waves of seniors had died when they transitioned out of the virus, poisoned by all the fatal fumes of the underclassmen. So the last remaining seniors holed themselves up in the senior lounge and boarded the doors shut from the inside when their noses began to bleed. They thought that if they sealed the lounge shut, they could keep the virus out. They didn't do a good enough job. The virus got through anyway, and they all died. No one had ever pried the doors open again because they knew what was in there.

Gonzalo made quick time to the third-floor senior lounge. Now, standing in front of the double doors, his stomach was fluttering. The lounge was a crypt. A resting place for tortured souls and their rotten flesh. Gonzalo took a deep breath.

He jammed the broken shaft of a lacrosse stick between the two doors and leaned into it. Gonzalo worked the stick deeper and pushed with all his weight. He could hear the nails popping out of boards on the other side.

With a dry crack, the doors popped apart. Dust rained from their inner edges. The left door swung in slowly, wobbling on its hinges. Gonzalo pinched his nose in preparation for the smell. No one had been in this room since it'd all happened.

It was dark inside. He stayed still. He felt a visceral resistance to entering the room. He made himself calm down. Everything he was feeling was only proof that this plan would work—no one would ever follow him in here. They'd want to turn around, just like he did. Gonzalo forced himself to walk through the doors.

It was hard for him to see anything at first. He reached for the wall with his free hand. With each step he scraped his bare foot along the gritty floor like a blind man's cane, feeling for obstacles, paranoid about what horrible thing he'd land on if he tripped and fell. He was still pinching his nose and was afraid to stop. The air had to be polluted with the stench of mass death. He felt around the wall for a light switch and hoped the lights still worked. He slid his palm up and down the glossy painted wall. His fingers skimmed the toggle of a light switch. He flipped it.

The lights worked too well. Their cold, fluorescent light revealed a triangular room with a landscape of corpses strewn over padded furniture and piled over each other. The floor and walls were a collage of brown blood splatters, including the dried and crusted-over lake of umber at Gonzalo's feet.

Gonzalo's legs went soft and he almost fell. He caught himself on a dusty love seat and sat on it. He made himself slow his breathing. This was too much, even for him. He didn't know what he'd been expecting. He knew there would be dead bodies here, but knowing something was true and seeing it were two very different things.

The bodies didn't look like people anymore. The bones hadn't changed, the limbs were still in place, but the flesh was different. Shrunken and dried. Thigh muscles reduced to sheets of beef jerky stretched from hip to knee. Some of the corpses were naked, some were bottomless, some topless. Lord knew what kind of things had happened in here once they were locked inside and the first person puked up their lungs and died. Maybe some of them held out hope that the military was going to swoop in and pull them out before the end, but just as many probably knew that these were their final days and they'd better make the most of them.

All the exposed flesh Gonzalo saw was cracked and brown, like an unwrapped Egyptian mummy. The stomachs were caved in as if a vacuum cleaner had sucked everything out of them. Every face had been sucked tight by the drying process, their eye sockets emptied. Skulls with leathery, shrink-wrapped skin. Full heads of white hair still attached to the scalps as if the corpses were wearing wigs. Each corpse sat atop a dry puddle of brown and black that ruined the cloth cushions of the furniture underneath.

Three of the less-clothed seniors were piled on top of each other, and it made Gonzalo gag to see the way their shrunken bodies had melted into one another. They were just one mass of twelve limbs and multiple rib cages and pelvises rising up out of the pile of bone and dried skin.

Gonzalo struggled to his feet. He'd let go of his nose when he sat down, and now he realized he was smelling the room. To his shock, it wasn't so horrifying. It smelled like garbage, like a particularly sour Dumpster, but it wasn't the kind of putrid that he'd expected. At one time, though, when these bodies had all been rotting at once, expanding and filling with gas until they became so bloated that they evacuated their liquefied organs everywhere, the stench must have been overpowering. Now everything was dry as a bone. The bacteria and maggots were long gone.

He wandered through the room, navigating the maze of twisted corpses on the floor and couches. His eyes panned across dead boys and girls and more dead boys and more dead girls, still twisted in the same position as when they'd coughed out their lungs and died. Gonzalo guessed there were about fifty or sixty bodies in all. Fifteen of them were stacked like bricks against the back wall of the room.

Beside the stack of dried bodies was a half-open door.

He made his way to it and pushed the door all the way open. He flipped on the lights and saw a hallway, no more than ten feet long, with two doors at the end. There were no corpses in the hallway, and although the floor was dirty from foot traffic, it wasn't stained with old blood like the lounge. He sighed in relief, but his heart hadn't slowed down any.

Gonzalo stepped into the hall and closed the door behind him. Behind the door was a red box with a glass front and a blazing red fire ax inside. The glass said "Break in Case of Fire." He took off his shirt, wrapped it around his fist, and shattered the glass with a jab.

The ax's wooden handle felt good in his hands. He stared at the heavy wedge of metal at the end, and its perfect, sharp blade. He realized he was grinning. He couldn't believe his luck. He'd never seen anyone in the whole school who had a weapon this lethal. If it hadn't been locked up in the lounge, someone would have claimed it long ago. But it was his. No one would take potshots at him now. Not even in big numbers. No, they would run the other way when they saw him coming with this.

It felt like a sign. He walked forward, excitement building. The doors at the end of the hall led to bathrooms. Someone had written "CLEAN" in Sharpie over the girls' room. The boys' door had "DIRTY" written across it. He checked out the two bathrooms and found that the DIRTY room had apparently been used as a bathroom. There was one corpse in there. A tall boy on the floor.

Gonzalo backed out. When he investigated the CLEAN room, he was relieved to find no dead bodies. It seemed that the CLEAN room was where people had slept. There were couches in there, and clothes and the remnants of a food supply. Gonzalo might have been losing his mind, but he could see being comfortable back here. The cleanliness of the room, the hallway separating him from the dead people—if he dragged the body from the DIRTY room back to the lounge, it wouldn't be that bad. His own place, with a separate bathroom. Not many Scraps could claim that.

He almost felt safer here than he had in the ducts. It was just the death room he had to get used to. As long as he didn't lose his mind, he'd be fine. Staring into empty eye sockets day in and day out had to do some kind of damage eventually, didn't it? But if he walked through the lounge quickly each time, and maybe learned to do it with the lights off, and if he spent all of his time either back here or out in the school, he could probably deal with it. Other people wouldn't be able to, though. No one was that desperate. The lounge would be like a moat, protecting his castle. He felt safe with an ax in his hand, separated from the school by a room full of fifty corpses.

Gonzalo sighed and lay down on one of the couches. It was soft. Softer than the vents, that was for sure. Softer than the floors he'd been sleeping on for months. Not bad. Not bad at all. Gonzalo put his hands behind his head and chuckled. This was a batshit crazy idea of a place to live, but he'd already made up his mind the moment he'd lain down. He was home.

15

"YOU MEAN TO TELL ME THAT YOU'VE BEEN out here for six months and the water plant was the first infected hideout you found?"

Baxter laughed so hard that droplets of spittle sprayed from his mouth.

Gonzalo kept both hands on the wheel and his eyes focused on the road ahead. Baxter had been trying to bait him into flying off the handle since they got in the van. The road was dark, but the van's xenon headlights were strong. Gonzalo had insisted on having the interior dome light on so he could keep an eye on Baxter.

"Gonzo," Baxter said, "there's a whole world of infected out here. Tons of hideouts. We're everywhere. How could you have missed us? Were you in a coma for part of the time?"

Baxter's laughter overtook him again. The piercing pitch made Gonzalo cringe. Gonzalo shot his passenger a look.

Baxter kicked his little feet with amusement. When he let them hang, his feet didn't reach the floor. His head barely made it to the headrest. He had a road map laid out in his lap like an activity book. Gonzalo was riding with a ten-year-old. The guy hadn't grown a bit since Gonzalo had seen him in school. He could knock him out with one finger.

Baxter caught Gonzalo eyeballing him, and his smile deflated. The van rumbled along the cracked road. Baxter's stare sharpened. He wasn't laughing anymore. His nose and brow began to twitch. Maybe he knew what Gonzalo was thinking. Gonzalo grinned softly and put his eyes back on the road.

A fallen traffic light blocked most of the intersection ahead, and Gonzalo had to swerve to avoid it.

Baxter groaned. "You missed the turn."

"Whose fault is that?"

"Yours. I told you to turn on Broadmoor. That was Broadmoor."

"You've got one job—to tell me where to go," Gonzalo said. "I'm just the driver." Gonzalo slowed the van and made a U-turn.

"When you try to do two things at once, your brain hurts, huh?"

"You're a punk—"

"Turn here, stupid."

Gonzalo turned onto Broadmoor. He had to drive onto the sidewalk to avoid the traffic light.

"So, when are you going to tell me what this place is?"

Baxter peered out his window. The van hit a pothole with a loud clunk, and the impact made them both slam down into their seats.

"I don't know," Baxter said.

"What do you mean, you don't know? You told me you had a lead."

"Calm down. All I mean is, where we're going isn't like the water-treatment place. It's not a hideout exactly. It's, like, a thing. At a toy factory."

"A thing?"

"Something's happening tonight at ten p.m. That's all I know."

Gonzalo checked the digital clock on the car stereo. It was 9:45.

"How do you know Sasha will be there?"

"I'm getting the feeling you don't trust me."

"Like I have a reason to."

"Look," Baxter said. "I know what I know. You're either with me or you're not. If the toy factory doesn't pan out, then ask away. Until then, watch and learn."

The idea that he was driving to a place where Sasha might be, in the flesh, right in front of him, sent a thrill rushing through Gonzalo. He tried to picture Sasha's face, and how she would look at him like she was seeing a mirage when he walked up to her.

"What are you smiling about?" Baxter asked, like it was an accusation.

"Nothing."

"I bet. You probably think about nothing all day. Just *duurrrrrr...*"

Baxter stared off into space, cross-eyed, with his tongue hanging out of his mouth like he was brain-dead, and kept on making that dumb noise.

"*Duurrrrrrrrr.* Food me want. *Durrrrrrr.* Where are infected. I no see them. *Duurrrr.*"

Baxter erupted with more laughter, but it sounded like he wanted to shout at Gonzalo and was doing it with laughter instead. Gonzalo let it slide. If they were close to Sasha, then spending time with the slithery sub-human midget in his passenger seat would be a distant memory soon.

Broadmoor Avenue was a dark stretch of road with a lot of overhanging trees. Driving it felt like Gonzalo was carving his path into a featureless void, where nothing existed past the reach of his high beams. Eventually, the trees thinned out and whole blocks began to be swallowed up by warehouses and factories.

"There," Baxter said and pointed to a dead neon sign. "Bumblebee Toys, that's it. Kill the lights."

Gonzalo parked the van right in front of the toy factory. It was a spooky-looking four-story building with painted-over windows and brick walls. The kind of place where people were probably dangling from meat hooks inside. A cartoon bee smiled down at them from the dirty, broken sign.

"Keep the keys in the ignition. In case we need to leave in a hurry. I'll be as fast as I can," Baxter said and opened his door.

"Wait, what? No way. You said you'd get me into places I couldn't get into."

Baxter gave Gonzalo a flat, slightly perturbed look.

"Yeah, in a place I know I can vouch for you, but not here. I don't know who or what is in this place. I might not be able to convince them you're all right."

"This is some bullshit."

"Gonzo. Let me do my thing. I'm good with people. If I don't get results, *then* you can bitch."

Gonzalo shook his head. Things were already getting shifty. "You're not holding up your end of the deal."

Baxter started backing up toward the factory entrance.

"Pal, if Sasha's in there, are you really gonna blow our chances, just 'cause you had to hold my hand? I could come walking back out here with her in a few minutes. Keep your pants on."

"Baxter!" Gonzalo said, but it was too late. He'd already slipped through the doors. He'd left the van door open. The wind moaned. "Goddamn it."

He couldn't trust Baxter. He knew this. What if the little creep did find Sasha, and instead of bringing her here, he walked her right out the back and never told her about Gonzalo? He might even tell her that Gonzalo was dead.

He had to go inside. He had to see what this was with his

own eyes. It was the only way. He grabbed a sweatshirt from the back of the van and pulled it on, putting the hoodie up over his head to hide his gas mask. For a second, he considered bringing a gun, but that had nearly gotten him killed before. He took the keys from the ignition, slipped out of the van, and locked the doors. The front doors seemed like a bad option. Even with the hoodie, he wanted to avoid as many interactions as he could. Straight on, it would take somebody less than a second to see he had a gas mask, which tended to evoke a response of "Adult!" or "Run!" or "Kill!"

He searched for another way in and found it where the windows were broken on the east side of the building. He climbed through and pulled himself into a wide-open room with a two-story-high ceiling. Moonlight lit up the space through high windows. He saw the silhouettes of big machinery and an assembly line conveyor belt that weaved its way through the room like a huge train set.

Gonzalo moved cautiously. There was no one around. As he walked deeper into the factory, he noticed piles of plastic water guns in the shape of Glock pistols. He picked one up and held it up to the moonlight. The translucent plastic of this one was emerald green, but others were royal blue, lemon yellow, and pink. Each one had the same smiling bee imprinted on the handle.

Gonzalo heard a steady, soft thump in the distance that he hadn't noticed over his own footsteps before. He made his way to the nearest door, and when he opened it, the thump got louder. It sounded like someone was running the kind of machinery he'd seen in the room he'd just walked through. Gonzalo stood in an echoey stairwell that led both up and down. The thump was coming from below. He took the stairs down slowly into the dark.

The stairwell ended with a thick wooden door below, lit by a single blue bulb. A moth kept swirling around it and crashing headlong into it. The thump was loud now, and it changed. It started to thump faster, and then Gonzalo began to understand—this wasn't just noise, it was music. And it was loud. The thump of bass buzzed the hinges of the old door. Gonzalo reached for the knob and pulled it open a crack. The music surged, and what he saw made him pull the door open wide without thinking of the risk. His grasp of what life was like for infected kids in hiding collapsed before his eyes.

It was a dance party. The dance music blared in the low-ceilinged concrete basement. There had to be two hundred, maybe three hundred infected teenagers in Halloween costumes, dancing their asses off to a relentless drumbeat. The bass walloped the room. He saw kids dancing with their eyes closed, lost in the music. Gonzalo stepped in and let the door close behind him. The area by the door to the stairs was dark, so he wasn't drawing any attention yet. With all the swirling and flashing DJ lights set up around the rest of the room, it looked like a nightclub on New Year's Eve. Blinding beams of purple and green and blue light cut through the room. He figured he had a decent chance of not being noticed.

Pushing into a mob of infected this large was insanity. He should have been crippled with fear, but his nerves were pulsing with anticipation. Baxter had been right. Knowing Sasha, it wasn't a stretch to think that if she had been somewhere in the area, she would have made her way here just to dance. Gonzalo scanned the crowd as he worked his way around the periphery, careful to stay in the darkness as much as he could. It was almost unbearable. Any face could have been Sasha's.

He watched kids pass each other pills and swallow. He saw lit joints. Lighter flames in glass pipes. He saw beer cans clutched in hands. Liquor bottles too. Kids in red jumpsuits walked through the crowd, dragging rolling coolers full of soda. Nearly every kid, dancing or talking, clutched a bottle of something or other.

He stayed pressed against the wall but crept closer to the front of the dance floor. There was a field of car batteries near the DJ, a hundred of them all lined up and wired to the lights, the fans, and the DJ equipment. The DJ was set up behind an office desk, on a series of wooden crates that raised him above the level of the crowd. He had long white hair done up in a floppy bun on the top of his head, and he wore a shredded tank top and tuxedo pants. He DJ'd off a laptop and danced behind the desk like he was auditioning for a Ritalin prescription.

Not everyone in the crowd was the best dancer. In fact, most were sort of clumsy, but they were doing it with all their heart. Like they needed the release. The thundering beat of the song grew louder and sped up until it was faster than a hummingbird's wings. The kids in the crowd were shaking. Scrunching up their faces. He couldn't tell if they were sweating or crying. Just when the pitch and speed of the beat was at its crescendo, an air-horn noise blasted out at the same time as a lion roar and the bass dropped in heavy. The dancers lost their minds. The new beat emerged as a fractured, distorted groove with stuttered bass and shrill, squeaky highs. The crowd bopped and humped around in sync.

Gonzalo pushed on. He kept his hood up high and his head tilted down so the flashing club lights wouldn't glare off his face shield. From under his brow, he examined the face of every short person he saw, hoping the next one would be Sasha's but never expecting what he saw next: Baxter, dancing his heart out. Sweating through his T-shirt. His eyes were closed and his brow was tight as he hopped up and down and threw his little body into each movement.

"Hold up, what?" Gonzalo said, although he couldn't hear himself over the music.

Baxter was taking a dance break? While Gonzalo was supposed to be waiting in the car? He wanted to walk right up to him and choke him, but he couldn't risk the attention. That little weasel. Gonzalo's instinct had been right—finding Sasha was entirely on his shoulders. Which was just fine by him, but to do it right, he needed to get closer to these kids, get right up in all of their faces, so that he really could be sure he hadn't missed Sasha. It was dangerous. Baxter should really be the one to do it. Gonzalo pushed into the crowd, aggravated. He saw the flash of a face in the crowd up ahead that made him hold his breath.

It was Sasha. He was almost sure of it, even though he'd seen her for only a second when the crowd thinned.

Gonzalo charged forward. He pushed people out of his way. He couldn't see her anymore among the taller kids. He plowed over to where she'd been, knocking people to the ground, and found her with her back to him. Gonzalo grabbed her shoulders and whipped her around—

It wasn't her.

The girl was Sasha's size and had a similar look, but he was staring into the eyes of a total stranger. And she was staring into his. Gonzalo looked around and saw that all the infected near them had stopped dancing and were gawking at him.

A snare-drum beat cut through the blaring music, but its rhythm was completely off from the music. The dancers screamed. The girl who looked like Sasha peered off to the right, and her face stretched in terror. Gonzalo followed her gaze and saw what had frightened her.

Hunters were storming into the room behind clear polycarbonate riot shields. They fired guns into the party. Clouds of fire burst from their barrels. Blood leapt into the air. Waves of infected fell dead, and the living ran, knocking each other over to get to the exits. Gonzalo thought for a split second of pulling down his hood and screaming at them that he wasn't infected, but he was too afraid of being shot. He ran with the horde. The snare-drum gunfire drowned out the music, its beat arrhythmic and rushed, and accented with screams.

He followed the flow of the crowd, pushing to the edge of the room. He was sure each pop of the snare would blast a bullet through his back, but he was able to make it through a pair of double doors to a stairwell. He climbed the stairs, glad to stand a foot over the crowd. The quieter the music and the gunshots became, the more he could hear the fear of the kids around him, the whimpers, the gasps, the unintelligible noises, angry shouts at the crowd ahead. Shoes slapped against the steps like applause. Gonzalo fought his way to the top of the stairs and through the doorway into a hallway. All down the hallway were windows to the outside, and the ones that weren't broken were getting kicked out by panicked kids. Streams of infected dove out the windows. Gonzalo did the same. The drop to the ground was over ten feet, but he was able to stick the landing with only a brief knife of pain in his ankle. All down the building, kids were pouring out of the windows like rats out of a flooding sewer. They ran full-blast in every direction away from the building—at least a hundred of them, scrambling.

Infected were knocking into Gonzalo as they ran past.

"Sasha!" Gonzalo yelled at the top of his lungs. His mask buzzed from the volume. He yearned for one of the fleeing infected to turn around at his shout. She still could be here. Even though there were hunters trying to slaughter everyone, she still could be here, running for her life. He shouted her name again, but no heads turned.

Another kid ran straight into Gonzalo. He looked down and saw it was Baxter. Before he could say anything, Baxter took off toward the front of the building in a wobbly run that favored his good leg. Moonlight glinted off something that swung from Baxter's hand. Gonzalo slapped his pocket and felt no keys.

"You pickpocket piece of shit."

Gonzalo sprinted to the van. Baxter was already backing up by the time he got his hand on the passenger-side door handle. He whipped open the door as desperate infected bolted past.

"Wait!" Gonzalo said.

Baxter threw it in drive and gunned it. Gonzalo dove in, one leg still hanging out the open door as Baxter peeled out. He pulled his leg in and shut the door, then tried to unfold himself into a sitting position.

"You stole my keys," Gonzalo shouted.

"Is this really the time?"

"You were going to leave without me!"

"You were supposed to wait!" Baxter's voice cracked. He kept his eyes flicking between the rearview and the road ahead. He sat on the edge of the seat with a straight back and crushed down on the steering wheel. Gonzalo had never seen him look so genuinely rattled.

Gonzalo twisted around in his seat and saw infected escaping into other buildings, crawling down storm drains. The van tilted as Baxter whipped it around the next corner, and then wobbled as he straightened out. Baxter relaxed his grip on the steering wheel as they sped away from danger.

"Well, that went pretty well, wouldn't you say?" Baxter said.

Gonzalo's gaze returned to his travel companion, and his mouth sank into a deep frown. The van zoomed forward.

16

SCARECROWS, CONSTRUCTED FROM THE BONES
of broken-down furniture and dressed in the clothes of corpses,
stood in a rick-rack line down the hall outside the senior lounge.
They were a warning. He'd built them and planted them there
when more and more people had started to frequent the hallway. He'd thought the senior lounge's reputation would have
been enough to keep them all at bay, but things had changed.

Gonzalo was the only Scrap in McKinley to consistently take
what he wanted from the quad, and to the other Scraps, who
had no gang, who lived in the dirtiest, darkest corners of the
school and starved alone, that was heroic. At least, accord-
ing to the whispered conversations he'd heard in the halls,
like the one two boys were having now as they each dared the
other to go first into the thicket of scarecrows.

"I'll go first and knock on the door if you do the talking,"
a white-haired kid said. He had the worst kind of buck teeth

imaginable. His four top front teeth, big beetle shells, stuck out over his lower lip, making it impossible for him to fully seal his lips.

"Deal," the other Scrap said. He was smaller. The light from his phone reflected off his high, gleaming forehead—he was going prematurely bald. He shoved the bucktooth kid forward. The kid crept past the first scarecrow, which wore a letter jacket around its jagged frame and had a rotten ham for a head. Gonzalo had scored an entire canned ham at a drop, but it was past the expiration date. He'd skewered it onto the top of the scarecrow, pinned condoms on as the eyes, and shoved a broken length of plumbing pipe straight through the side of it, like its head had been impaled. Now the ham was dried and shrunken and bent to the side from the weight of the pipe, and it tended to make people want to turn around. The Scraps walked past it.

If they weaved past five more, they'd be at the door of the lounge. Gonzalo watched them from behind the door, with it open a crack. He hoped they'd lose their nerve before they got close enough to knock. The bucktooth boy stopped just before the second scarecrow, which was dressed in a soiled dress Gonzalo had found balled up in a bathroom. He'd used a bag of trash for her head, with long, white hair hanging down, and where her face should have been was a shag carpet of bloated, dried tampons, taped to the bag by their strings. He'd originally meant to save the tampons as a gift for Sasha, if he ever saw her again. A box of tampons was like a dozen roses to a girl in McKinley. There were never enough to go around, and girls tended to hoard them. This scarecrow tended to scare guys off more than girls because Gonzalo had made a mud out of red Kool-Aid powder and a splash of water, then rolled all the tampons in them. These two Scraps shuddered at the sight of her, but they still weren't spooked.

"So . . ." the bucktooth boy whispered, "what are you gonna say?"

"Something like, 'We've seen you at every drop and, ya know, you're one badass motherfucker, and you probably don't need two other dudes hanging around, but we can pull our weight and we can do whatever you need us to—"

"I don't think we should start by saying, 'You probably don't need us.'"

"Shit, you're right . . ." the balding kid said. "So, why does he need us again?"

The bucktooth stayed quiet for a while, then said, "I don't know."

Gonzalo nodded in the dark behind the door. At least they were honest. He needed them to move on because the drop would be starting soon, and he wanted to get a good spot on the quad. But he actually didn't mind listening to them talk. Outside of little snippets caught here and there, he hadn't heard a friendly conversation in a while. He missed it.

"You're hilarious," the balding kid said.

"Huh?"

"I mean, you crack me up all the time. And . . . me, I got all kinds a' crazy stories. You always say that, right? So, how fun can it be living alone? We can entertain him."

"So, you're gonna say, 'Wanna be buddies'?" the bucktooth kid asked.

"Kinda."

"The guy lives with dead people. I don't think a dude like that wants buddies."

Gonzalo felt an odd pang of emotion that hadn't stirred since he'd started living at the lounge. It was a touch of sadness about giving up. Deep down, he'd known that by choosing to live with the seniors, he was sealing himself off from all human contact until it was his time to graduate.

The bucktooth kid kept whispering, "I say we just stick with the 'We'll do whatever you need us to do' angle. 'Cause it's true. If we're in good with Gonzalo, we won't have to worry about food ever again. I'm outta ideas, man. I seriously will do whatever he needs us to do."

"Me too," the balding kid said.

Gonzalo shook his head, starting to get frustrated. He didn't need anything from them. The bucktooth kid blew out a worried breath, and it whistled through his teeth. He stepped past the second scarecrow, then the third. Gonzalo clenched his jaw.

He raised up his ax and opened the door. The bucktooth

Scrap screamed at the sight of him, turned, and ran past his balding friend. The Scrap disappeared down the hall, leaving his smaller friend behind to reckon with Gonzalo alone. Gonzalo took one giant step forward, and the balding kid shook in place.

"We, uh—we, uh—ah, fuck it," he said and ran away.

When the Scrap was completely out of sight, Gonzalo lowered his ax with a sigh. He should have felt good. Two more Scraps out there to spread the word that Gonzalo was a madman and that even looking his way meant risking death. But the loneliness hurt, and even though he'd told himself otherwise, he was starting to think he couldn't make it to graduation if he kept going it alone. Maybe other people were as essential as food.

Gonzalo pushed past his scarecrows into the school. He could feel his bitterness festering. He thought about everything that had gotten him to right here, right now—the virus, Baxter, the stubborn growth of his bones—it seemed he was destined for pain. The gangs were filtering in from their territories as he reached the front foyer. Everyone was getting in the zone for the food drop, cracking backs, stretching, swinging weapons as they marched. All of the Varsity guys watched Gonzalo walk toward them. He could see the indecision play out on their faces.

Good, he thought, *let 'em bring something*. He let his acidic emotions twist and pull at the muscles of his face.

The group of Varsity stayed put, menacing him from a distance. As Gonzalo got close, he switched to holding the ax out in front of him with both hands instead of carrying it over his shoulder. Their nerves held for a few more steps, but once Gonzalo was within ax-swinging distance and still wasn't slowing down, they got out of his way. He saw the fear in their eyes. They believed he was a monster. His reputation was the best armor he could have. The group of Varsity split in two, parting for him to walk through. He heard them muttering after he passed. He eyed a Scrap in the shadows who'd been watching the scene, smile beaming.

The sound from the quad was rumbling. The crowd was all whipped up about something. He picked up the pace when he realized that the two Scraps he'd scared off at the lounge were standing by the entrance to the quad.

Gonzalo slowed to a stop just beside them. He expected them to jump again at the sight of him, but they didn't even glance over. They were too transfixed by what was going on in the quad.

Gonzalo followed their gaze outside and saw a group of Scraps lined up along the wall, assembled for the drop like the other gangs. They wore black war paint and linoleum-tile armor. He liked them right away. There were only nine of them, but they stood there ready to fight for their food like everyone else. It was bold, and his heart went out to them. They were definitely going to get their asses kicked, just on principle, but they were standing together, like a gang of Scraps. He'd never seen that before.

"What's the story with them?" Gonzalo said without thinking. His voice sounded odd. He'd barely heard it in months.

The smaller Scrap looked up and saw Gonzalo. He jerked away and grabbed his friend by the arm.

"Did you just talk?" the balding one said.

"To us?" the other said.

"What's the deal with those kids out there?"

The two of them stared at Gonzalo in silence until the bucktooth kid punched the balding one to get him to talk.

"Uh . . . you don't know? It's all anybody's been talking about for weeks. That's David. He killed a Varsity."

Gonzalo never heard gossip. He didn't go to the Market. He went to the quad, then home. That was all. Except maybe the occasional walk down one of the routes he knew Sasha crawled, listening for her.

"Which one is he?" Gonzalo said, looking out to the quad.

"The one in the front. The word is, David was defending a Scrap girl, but Sam's made it out like it was murder. He already tried to hang him in the Market, but David got away."

Gonzalo growled. He despised Sam. He'd seen the Varsity food pile with his own eyes. They thought they could get away with anything. He hated that they always did.

"They say he wants to start a Scrap gang," the bucktooth kid said.

The balding kid shook his head. "Varsity's gonna kill him today, and the Scraps who saved him in the Market. Sam wants everybody to see what happens when you kill a Varsity."

"He said that?" Gonzalo said.

"That's what I heard," the bucktooth one said.

"Fuck that shit," Gonzalo said.

"You gonna do something about it?"

Gonzalo looked down at the little Scrap, annoyed. It sounded like a dare, like a challenge to back up his words, and where did this scrawny kid get the balls to talk to him like that? But when he saw that the kid wasn't smirking, Gonzalo understood. He was asking out of hope. He wanted Gonzalo to do something about it, because he couldn't. Varsity would stomp him, along with the other nine Scraps. Gonzalo had the size, the power, and a deadly weapon. He could make a difference out there on the quad.

Thup-thup-thup, the helicopter thundered above.

"Look at the fat one!" said a voice from the Varsity crowd.

He heard laughs. Gonzalo looked at the nine Scraps standing by the wall, and saw that one of the girls was pretty big. She looked mortified, and Gonzalo got angrier.

"No fair! Elephants aren't allowed to fight at the drop!" someone shouted.

Varsity laughed louder. It pissed Gonzalo off. People in the other gangs covered their mouths, embarrassed for the Scraps but still laughing.

Sam's voice cut through the crowd: "I heard there was a new gang!"

Sam stepped out from the front of the Varsity line, swinging a heavy steel chain in his hand. The smile on Sam's face nauseated Gonzalo. The pleasure he took in this was wrong. Baxter probably had that same smile on his face, after he'd locked Gonzalo in that room.

"I could have sworn I heard that," Sam said. "I'm looking, but I don't see one."

Varsity laughed. More of the crowd joined in.

"All I see is nine Scraps with a death wish."

Thup-thup-thup-thup.

Sam signaled to his guys, and Varsity members ran to each exit from the quad, blocking all four hallways. They weren't even going to let them run away.

Varsity began to crack their baseball bats against the ground in unison.

Gonzalo couldn't take his eyes off of this kid, David. He had to be scared, but he was holding it together out there, probably for the sake of those poor Scraps behind him. They were trying to act like savage warriors, but it was clear to everyone that they were terrified. Still, it was moving. He didn't have Gonzalo's size or his reputation or his ax. All he had was sheer will, and it was enough for the whole school to feel its power. Gonzalo felt like a coward compared to this guy. People thought Gonzalo was a monster, but that was a mask he was hiding behind. Just like he was hiding behind his ax and his scarecrows and, truthfully, his own size. He was so scared of the school that he was willing to hide in a mass grave. It all seemed so pathetic now. He thought of Sasha. He wondered if she was watching him right now through some vent. What would she think if she saw him do nothing?

The canopy began to open overhead. This was happening. David turned to his Scraps, and Gonzalo had a strange feeling, like he belonged with that group. He was a Scrap, just like those nine. One of the rejected, the discarded, the ones that go it all alone.

Gonzalo walked. The rush he felt was automatic. He hardly heard the gasps of the crowd or the rhythmic crack of Varsity's bats as he cut across a quarter of the quad to get to David. He knew this was a big move. He was opposing Varsity, and there would be repercussions. He knew it could come back to bite him. He knew he might be throwing away his scary reputation if he fought alongside them, because they might lose. He couldn't beat up all of Varsity by himself. He'd probably get knocked out and the spell would be broken. The whole school would know that the monster was just an act and Gonzalo was just as vulnerable as anybody else. All of that aside, he felt proud in a way that was entirely new to him. He felt full of purpose. He believed this was the right thing.

David's back was turned to Gonzalo when he reached him. He was saying something to the other eight Scraps, who were shaking with fear. The other Scraps noticed him, but David still hadn't. Gonzalo put his hand on David's shoulder, and David turned and looked up at him.

Gonzalo felt a sting of fear that he might not be able to get any words out, that he'd flub his entrance, all because the pressure was too great, but to his surprise, the words flowed freely. It helped that he believed in what he said.

"Heard they tried to hang you in the Market." Gonzalo shook his head. "That ain't right."

David appeared to be in shock. He nodded slowly.

"Is it true you're starting a gang that won't stand for that shit?"

"Th-that's right."

"Then, I'm in."

Gonzalo took his place beside David and faced the school, ax in hand. The crowd was shocked. Varsity cracked their bats faster against the ground. The helicopter lowered the block of supplies through the slit in the wobbling gray canopy above. A kid with a scarred-up face came running up behind Gonzalo and said his name was Ritchie. He said he'd fight with them too.

David seemed touched. So was Gonzalo. They still didn't have enough people to compete with Varsity—they were still going to lose—and that only made Gonzalo angrier. If he was going down, he was taking as many Varsity down with him as he could. He crushed down on the wood of his ax handle.

White heads of hair pushed their way through the crowd. More Scraps coming to lay it on the line. From all over the quad, from out of windows, from out of hallways, they came. White hair converged on Gonzalo and David. Gonzalo had never known there were this many Scraps in the whole school. A lake of white hair surrounded him.

David shouted something to Gonzalo and the rest of them about the fact that they were a gang now, and that the food hanging above was theirs for the taking. Gonzalo decided on the spot that he'd been right about David.

Gonzalo was overcome with a sense of belonging he'd never had in McKinley. All these Scraps wanted to be in a gang with him. The sight of their hair, white like his own, surrounding him, choked him up. When the block of supplies crashed to the ground and they all charged into battle, Gonzalo hoped that Sasha was watching.

17

WILD HORSES GALLOPED ALONGSIDE THE
road. They nearly matched the pace of Gonzalo's van, but
he crept past them. There had to be forty of them, running
together across the plain. He watched the sheen of their coats
dance across their muscles as they bulged and lengthened,
as they shook when their hooves struck the earth. Gonzalo
wondered if they were abandoned horses, left behind by their
owners during the evacuation, or if they were truly mustangs.
Either way, he admired their freedom. He wished he were out
among them, running unbridled through open fields and endless, flat land, but he was stuck with a jackass.

"Bang," Baxter said. He had his hands up like he was aiming through the window with an imaginary rifle. He laughed.
"You know that's how they did it back in the day. They just
leaned out of train windows and took potshots at buffalo."

"Thanks for ruining it for me."

"You know, for such an ape, you're a real sensitive fucker."

Gonzalo did a double-take. Gripped in Baxter's left hand was a half-eaten Fancy Kake—the *last* Fancy Kake. They'd found two individually wrapped Fancy Kakes in the employee break room at an IKEA where they'd slept after the dance-party massacre. They were snack-machine pastries with orange-flavored cake and a frosting center. Gonzalo couldn't take his mask off around Baxter, so he hadn't had any. When Baxter had eaten one Fancy Kake, that'd been fair, but now he'd gone ahead and eaten the second, and it was a slap in the face. Gonzalo craved the taste of that sugary goodness, anything to wash the taste of gasoline out of his mouth. He'd siphoned a good eight gallons out of a delivery truck in the IKEA parking lot to make it wherever the hell they were headed to next.

"Tell me where we're going," Gonzalo said.

Baxter rolled his eyes and said, "After my cake."

Gonzalo mashed the brakes. Baxter flew forward in his seat, reaching his short arms out with splayed little hands as if he were a stretching cat. His voice *guh*'d as his neck strained against the seat belt, turning his face red. The Kake flew out of Baxter's hand and onto the muddy floorboard. The van skidded to a stop, and Gonzalo gripped the wheel like a murder weapon. He stared out the windshield at the clear sky ahead, as if he'd done nothing.

"What the fuck is wrong with you?!" Baxter said.

Gonzalo turned to Baxter with eyes harder than a concrete floor. Baxter eased off of whatever tirade he was about to spew. The little guy knew what was good for him.

"You said if you didn't turn up Sasha after the toy factory, I could ask whatever I wanted. Did you not say that?"

"Why don't you focus on driving and leave the thinking to me, dum-dum."

"I'll throw you out the window."

"No, you won't. I know where to go. You need me."

"You need to know that you dance like a dickhead."

Baxter's eyes were slits.

"Is that what you call investigating?" Gonzalo said.

Baxter sighed. He looked out the window. "Fine, ask your questions."

"Start with where we're going."

"To a hotel in downtown Horlin."

"Why?"

"It's like Grand Central Station for all the different routes through the infected zone."

"What do you mean, routes?"

"Ways to travel through the zone without being visible. There's lots of routes to help you get around Colorado without using major roads, but most of them cross in Horlin."

"And Sasha's there?"

Baxter shrugged. "I don't know, but Eddie might be there."

"You gonna make me ask?"

"Eddie is Sasha's cousin. We caught up with him right after we left Pale Ridge. He introduced the group of us that escaped McKinley to the underground, but then hunters attacked us in Fort Collins, and I got split up from the group. That was the last I've seen any of them."

Gonzalo had a vague memory of Sasha mentioning a cousin named Eddie, so the fact that this had traces of truth made him feel a little better. But somehow, in the past twenty-four hours of being with Baxter, he hadn't thought about the fact that if Baxter was out of McKinley, then of course, he'd escaped at the same time as Sasha. There wasn't any other way for him to have gotten out unless he'd graduated. And he was clearly still infected. It made Gonzalo realize that there had been a time when Sasha and Baxter had been together without him around, outside of the Mice, after the Loners. It was a time he knew nothing about, and it drummed up that nagging awareness that Baxter was as passionate about finding Sasha as he was. Gonzalo shook it off. That didn't help anything now. That was for after they found Sasha.

"It's a good lead," Baxter said. "Eddie has to know something."

Gonzalo nodded and stepped on the gas. Horlin it was, then. They made it there in about two hours. It was a weird, pop-up city, made up mostly of industrial parks and a bunch of tall financial buildings in its downtown area.

"Pull over there," Baxter said and pointed to a covered parking garage.

"Where's the hotel?"

"It's a walk."

"Park on the sidewalk if you want. Doubt we'll get a ticket."

Baxter was looking out the window and up at the buildings above them. "Just do what I say, dum-dum. Things'll go quicker that way."

Gonzalo pulled into the parking garage without arguing. He'd decided that picking his battles was the only way to deal with Baxter. Otherwise, he'd give himself an aneurysm. Gonzalo parked and stepped into the back of the van to get ready. He pocketed three extra filters and his knife, and put his hand on his rifle.

"You won't need that," Baxter said.

The jury was still out on the gun. Yes, it had gotten him in trouble at the water treatment plant, but he might've been better off with it at the dance party. He couldn't help feeling like just being seen with a weapon like this kept danger at bay.

"Have you ever heard of kids that wear hubcaps on their chest and drive dune buggies?"

"Nope."

"Well, I saw a bunch of 'em kill two adults. In cold blood."

Baxter shrugged. "Could be. There's plenty of infected out there that got just as much reason to kill adults as adults got to kill them. Which is why rolling up with a rifle isn't gonna help us get on anybody's good side."

Gonzalo looked down at the gun in his hands.

"Yeah, well, I'm not so sure."

"It's your funeral."

Gonzalo knew that there was a good chance Baxter was right, but his instinct was to oppose Baxter on anything he said. It was the thought of putting his life entirely in Baxter's hands that had him especially edgy. Gonzalo took his hand off the rifle but avoided eye contact with Baxter. He couldn't stand to see the weasel smiling about it.

"You're gonna thank me later," Baxter said. "It's a long walk."

"A long walk for you would probably take me three steps."

"Screw you."

"I bet we could find a baby stroller for you."

Baxter threw open the door and walked off. Now it was Gonzalo who was smiling. He caught up with Baxter at the Horlin Radisson Hotel and Convention Center a block away.

"Is this the place?" Gonzalo asked.

"Yeah," Baxter said, but he kept walking on past the entrance.

"Yeah, wow, this really was a long way. One block."

"You can't get in that way."

Gonzalo looked at the front doors with a frown and yanked on them. They didn't budge. He tried other entrances too with no luck. He jogged to catch up with Baxter one building down.

"I don't get it," Gonzalo said.

"The first floor is sealed off from the rest of the building, and the elevators are broken. To keep people out."

"So, there's another way in?"

He threw Gonzalo double thumbs-up with his tiny, doll hands. "You got it, Stephen Hawking."

They entered an office building two buildings down, at the end of the block. They had to sneak in through a service entrance in the alley, and then take the stairs up twenty-four floors. When they emerged from the stairwell on the twenty-fourth floor, Gonzalo was generally hating his entire existence. He sucked breath slowly through his gas mask. He ached to wipe the sweat that stung his eyes and was dripping from the tip of his nose, but he couldn't get to his face. He didn't like where this was headed, especially since Baxter said they were still less than halfway there. The math didn't make sense.

They were standing in a room full of office cubicles. Baxter pulled something out of his jacket as Gonzalo leaned against a cubicle wall to recover. Baxter kept his back to Gonzalo as he looked at whatever it was. He was trying to keep it secret. Gonzalo popped off the wall and snatched the thing out of Baxter's hands. Baxter jumped up to try to grab it back, but Gonzalo easily held it higher than Baxter could jump. He inspected it with one hand. It was a small, tan cashier's notebook with pages dense with handwriting and hand-drawn maps.

"What's this?"

"Give it back."

"Why should I?"

"Because I need it to get us there."

"Really? Maybe I'll keep it then."

"You can't read the code," Baxter said with a sneer.

Gonzalo inspected the pages as Baxter continued with his desperate grabs. Baxter was right, this wasn't like the dead man's notebook. Every note was gobbledygook.

Gonzalo dropped the notebook, mostly just to watch Baxter scramble for it. When Baxter got his little mitts on it, he scurried a safe distance away and flipped through the pages until he found the one he wanted. He traced his finger down the small page, his lips muttering as he read. At the end, he looked up at Gonzalo and seemed to scan him from head to foot. His hateful eyes started to sparkle. A big smile stretched across his face. Gonzalo had seen that look before, and it had never meant good news.

"Any chance you grew up in a circus?"

"What?"

Baxter laughed. "You're gonna love this next part."

He limped off toward the hall. The next leg of their journey took an hour. There were certain stairwells that had been destroyed or blocked off, so without Baxter's notes telling them which stairs to ascend or descend, Gonzalo knew he would have never found his way to the office with the window that opened to the fire escape where two planks needed to be positioned like a bridge to cross to the fire escape of the Radisson Hotel across the alley.

"Motherfucker," Gonzalo whispered to himself. He peered

down to the alley between the buildings. It was strewn with old newspapers and dark puddles. Lying in the middle of the alley was the decayed carcass of a black bear.

Baxter kept grinning as they put the planks in place. It was seventeen floors down to the hard asphalt of the alley, and Gonzalo wasn't sure those planks could hold his weight. Baxter seemed positive they wouldn't. This was probably the moment Baxter had been waiting for.

"I'll go first." Baxter gave Gonzalo an odd pat on the arm. Like a consolation. "You just worry about not falling and splattering your brains across the alley."

Baxter turned and lifted himself up on the planks, lying side by side. He edged out over the alley sideways to compensate for his limp. His compact shape made the width of the plank bridge seem less horrifying, but Gonzalo couldn't help thinking about the fall anyway. The planks bounced and shifted on the fire-escape rail with Baxter's every movement. The farther out Baxter got, the surer Gonzalo became that there was no way he himself would be able to cross.

Within a minute, Baxter had made it to the other side. He dropped down onto the hotel fire escape.

"Come on. Hurry up," he said.

"Hurry up," Gonzalo muttered to himself.

Baxter waved for him to cross. Gonzalo climbed up onto the planks. They shifted and shuddered more than when Baxter had gotten on, he was sure of it.

"Just do what I did," Baxter said, but the idea of standing up on these things seemed 100% more horrifying. Gonzalo edged out on all fours instead. He felt more stable, and it helped spread his weight out over a larger area. It was very sensible, but as far as Baxter was concerned, it was hilarious.

"You are such a pussy, this is unbelievable," Baxter said and laughed.

Gonzalo ignored him, because his head was swimming each time he glanced down to the alley below and he couldn't afford to get upset. He told himself that this was just like when he'd ventured out into the gym to steal from the Varsity food pile, but it wasn't. He'd been four times smaller back then, and he'd been supported by steel. Gonzalo heard the crack of splintering wood underneath him. It echoed down the building walls. When he was halfway across, Baxter kicked the boards. The planks didn't move but Gonzalo felt the vibration in his hands and knees, and he shrieked involuntarily.

Baxter cackled and crawled through the window into the hotel.

"Where are you going?" Gonzalo shouted. His voice echoed down to the pavement.

"I gotta get you a pass!"

"What pass?" Gonzalo called out, but Baxter was already gone.

It took almost twenty minutes for Gonzalo to edge the rest of the way across. When Gonzalo pulled himself onto the fire escape, he took a moment to calm down. He sat with with his arms wrapped around his knees, staring at his old, battered shoes. When he was ready, Gonzalo pulled himself through the window into a hallway decorated with jazzy, hideous carpeting, artificial flowers in pots in the corners, and textured wallpaper. Baxter stood before him, waiting, holding out a pair of handcuffs, dangling from his fingers.

"What the hell are those for?" Gonzalo said.

"Your pass. Put 'em on."

"Is this a joke?"

"This is how you get in," Baxter said. His lips spread into a winning smile.

"No way."

Baxter shrugged. "Gotta play by the rules."

"This is a rule?"

Baxter nodded. "This is a rule." He waited with a placid smile.

"This is a trick, is what it is," Gonzalo said.

"I feel like I'm being pretty straight-up with you, Gonzo."

"It's Gonzalo. You know it's Gonzalo."

"Yeah, fine, whatever. Here's the deal. Nobody's going to take my word for it that you can be trusted. I don't think you get how secret this place is. The only way they'll be cool with you being inside is if they feel sure that you won't be able to tell anyone what you saw or where this is. Being my prisoner is the only way."

"No."

"Fine. You can go back to the other building and wait. I'll go in and investigate, and tell you what I find out when I come back."

That wasn't going to work for Gonzalo either. He couldn't let Baxter keep investigating alone and take his word for what he'd found. Who knew what they'd already missed because Baxter had been dancing with kids instead of questioning them. No, Gonzalo was going all the way with Baxter this time. He'd nearly died to get this far. He wasn't going to just sit by now. And he never stopped believing that Sasha could be right around the corner. Just like at the toy factory, he still feared that, if given the chance, Baxter might take her and ditch him.

The shiny cuffs glinted as they twirled off Baxter's skinny finger.

"Put 'em on loose so I can slip them off if I have to," Gonzalo said and held out his wrists. Baxter slapped them on quickly and squeezed them uncomfortably tight with a series of clicks.

"Gotta look real," Baxter said. He put the keys to the cuffs in his back pocket and attached a heavy metal chain to the cuffs with a padlock. Holding the long chain, Baxter led Gonzalo down the hall like he had him on leash.

"It's just down these stairs," Baxter said.

Gonzalo plucked out splinters from his hand as he followed Baxter down the stairs and tried to quiet the panic building inside himself. Being led into the biggest infected hub in Colorado handcuffed felt all kinds of wrong. He wasn't pretending to be Baxter's prisoner. As soon as the cold cuffs had wrapped around his wrist, he *was* Baxter's prisoner. Again.

His panic became a cold sweat as they left the stairwell and walked toward the doors of one of the hotel's convention halls. His heartbeat accelerated.

Mistake, mistake, mistake, was all he could think.

Baxter reached for the double doors of the convention hall and gripped their handles. He looked back to Gonzalo and grinned.

"Welcome to the underground, Gonzo."

18

DAVID LOOKED UP AT GONZALO FROM A
couple stairs below, holding onto the railing and looking like
Gonzalo had just punched him in the gut.

"Listen," Gonzalo went on. "I'm just trying to be straight
with you. We had a good run with that first food drop, and
then the last one. You guys got a base now. I made sure it's
good and fortified. You got a solid rep, and Varsity's totally
backed off. You don't need me anymore."

Gonzalo was sitting on the third-floor landing of the Stairs,
the stairwell his new Scrap gang had claimed as their new
base. David took a step up toward him. "It's not about *needing*
you, man. It's about *wanting* you here. I mean . . . can I ask why
you want to leave? Is it something we did? Something I did? Is
it about the smell? Because I'm planning on enforcing daily
bathing."

Gonzalo shook his head. This was exactly why he'd wanted

to leave when everybody was sleeping, but if he was ever going to set foot in the quad again, he knew he'd have to explain himself to David. Except he didn't want to talk anything out. He just wanted to disappear and be done with it.

"I know a lot of kids in the Stairs are a little cagey around you. Or, like, really cagey," David said and sighed. Gonzalo couldn't argue. "It's going to take a while for all of us to gel. I mean, you've gotta remember, we've all been Scraps for a long time. Being alone that long tends to make people a little eccentric."

"Eccentric" was putting it lightly. They'd decided to name the gang the Loners, and Gonzalo couldn't have come up with a better name if he'd tried. Nearly a hundred head-cases cooped up in this stairwell like emotionally disturbed bees. There were these twins, a brother and sister, who were always sniffing each other's pits and picking at each other's scalps. There was a half-blind kid who farted three times every minute. There was a girl whose hobby was peeling off layers of her skin. There was hardly a person in the gang who didn't have a flaw they'd been mocked for. One was fat in spite of a year of starvation. Some stuttered. Some had thinning hair, even some of the girls. Most smelled. Others were so excited to have people to talk to that they never shut up. Voices that honked. Voices that squeaked. It seemed crazy to think it, but he missed the senior lounge. The seniors never made a noise.

"I don't think they like me," Gonzalo said.

As happy as they'd been to have Gonzalo fighting for them, behind closed doors everyone still seemed to be expecting him to snap at any moment and go on a rampage.

"They don't know you," David said.

"Neither do you."

David opened his mouth to speak but then paused. He exhaled and let his shoulders slump. "What I'm trying to say is, nobody's gonna know you as long you're snarling like you do all the time."

"I don't snarl."

"You're doing it right now. I've never seen you *not* do it."

David took a shard of mirror out of his back pocket, framed with layers of duct tape around its sharp edges. He held it up so that Gonzalo could see his own face. He looked away instinctively. He still wasn't used to the cinder-block his jaw had become, or how his brow looked like two stones colliding over a meaty nose. He didn't recognize his new face.

"This is just my face."

"That's not your resting face. You're scrunching it up."

"Am not."

Gonzalo glanced back at the mirror to look for proof that David was wrong, but instead, he saw everything David was talking about. His face was twisted into a knot of anger. He did look frightening, and angry, and volatile. He hadn't even realized he was doing it. He thought that maybe he looked a little upset, perturbed, but not like a furious ogre trying really hard not to eat people.

Gonzalo looked at David and saw him smiling. Gonzalo laughed. David laughed too, except his was more a laugh of relief.

"So, I'm not crazy?" David said.

"Maybe not," Gonzalo said.

"I know it's awkward, but if you just put yourself out there a little more, I don't think people would be so scared of you."

Gonzalo knew that agreeing to this meant he was agreeing to stay. If he retreated back to his lair, he knew for sure that he'd be haunted by loneliness. He didn't want that—not really. But the idea of giving up being the monster scared him because without it, he was vulnerable. If the school and the Loners knew that he was just a normal person who really didn't want to swing an ax into someone's head, they'd stop being afraid.

David's little brother, Will, shuffled up the stairs onto the landing.

"What are you two dick-worms talking about?"

Will got on Gonzalo's nerves. Even in the small amount of time he'd known him, Gonzalo knew that Will talked a lot of shit. It never stopped pouring out of his mouth. Sometimes he was funny, though.

"Could you give us a minute?" David said, waving Will off.

"Don't feel like it," Will said.

Gonzalo saw the anger ripple down David's face. If someone didn't stop them, these two would be yelling at each other for thirty minutes.

"Your bro is saying I always look angry," Gonzalo said.

"You mean, the whole bulldog-fucked-a-gargoyle thing you got going on?"

"Anyway," David said, pushing Will away. "We were just joking. Will, could you go downstairs and—"

"Smile," Will said to Gonzalo.

"What?" Gonzalo said.

"I want to see what it looks like. Smile."

"Will, you can't order people to do something," David said.

"Uh, yeah, I can. It's a fucking smile. How hard is that? I smile literally all the time."

"I told you to stop using 'literally' like that," David said.

"Whatever. You know what I mean. Come on, Gonzalo. Just smile, for Christ's sake."

Will was the only one who didn't act scared of Gonzalo. Will *was* scared of him—Gonzalo was sure of that—but it seemed to be his style to need to project that he wasn't. Gonzalo sighed. This felt kind of humiliating, but maybe this was what David meant by "putting yourself out there." He smiled.

David reacted first. He smiled back, but it was strained and shaky. Will straight-up cringed.

"Maybe don't smile," Will said.

David punched him in the shoulder. "Who talks to people like that?"

"Like that's worse than punching someone," Will said, clutching his shoulder. "You're so full of shit. I can't believe we're related."

"Deal with it."

Will rolled his eyes and turned back to Gonzalo. "So, you're quitting?"

"Will, shut up," David warned.

"What? I heard you doing your whole 'I'm David, I'm a big important douchebag' routine."

"Stop. Now."

Will didn't stop, though. He looked at Gonzalo. "Still, he's right. You might be the weirdest one out of everybody here. You want to go back to living with a pile of dead bodies? What's wrong with you?"

Gonzalo stood up, pissed. He towered over Will. David took a step back. Will flinched but stood his ground.

"Do you talk to them?" Will said.

Gonzalo grabbed Will by the neck and lifted him up with one hand. Will sputtered and clawed at Gonzalo's hand. His legs pedaled an invisible bicycle.

"Put me down!" Will wheezed.

"Looks like you better apologize," David said.

Gonzalo wasn't going to choke him to death, just scare him.

"Apologize for what?"

Gonzalo squeezed down harder on Will's spindly neck. Maybe he'd choke him to death just a little.

"You—*gghgh*—have a visi—*gghgh*—tor," Will said.

"What?" Gonzalo said. He eased up on his grip.

"That's what I came up to tell you. Are you gonna let me down now?"

Gonzalo dropped Will, who landed on two feet.

"What visitor?" Gonzalo said.

"I don't know. Says she knows you."

Gonzalo turned his back on Will. He walked down the stairs slowly, shooting Will a wary look. Will whacked David in the balls with the back of his hand. David's body folded like a jackknife and he nearly fell over. The bustle of the Stairs echoed up toward Gonzalo. He walked down to the lounge level, leaving the sibling dispute behind. Loners backed out of his way.

Downstairs on the kitchen level, a crowd was gathered. He descended the stairs two at a time, scanning the faces on the landing. Everyone in the kitchen went quiet as he neared. Then he saw her. She turned and looked at him, and her eyes went glossy.

She bounded up the stairs toward him. Her hair had grown long, and it wagged side to side behind her as she leapt up the stairs. He wanted to rush down and hug her, but he was scared he'd hurt her. She looked so small. And hot. Somehow, she'd gotten hotter than before, which seemed impossible, since he was practically a boner-factory every minute that they'd hung out together back in the Mice. As she got to the top steps, she slowed. Her expression had shifted from excitement to wonder, with maybe a twinge of fear. She stopped short of him and stared up. His face was probably scaring her. He wanted to smile, but he didn't want her to cringe like Will. So he didn't move a muscle. They stood a stair away from each other, frozen.

"Well," Sasha said, "are you going to hug me or what?"

"Y-yeah. Of course."

He stepped down and leaned over. He hugged her like she was made of feathers.

"What are you doing here?" Gonzalo whispered.

"I just joined! I'm one of you!"

Gonzalo got a swirl of nausea in his stomach, and he searched the faces in the landing below like a hawk.

"Did you join alone?" Gonzalo asked.

"Yup. Just me."

His stomach relaxed.

"Really? You left the Mice? I don't get it. Did they break up?" Sasha blushed.

"Can we talk about something else? Anything else?"

"Oh. Yeah. Totally."

There were so many things he'd been wanting to say to her, but with her standing right in front of him now, his feelings were a giant tangle in his mind.

"Maybe you could introduce me to some people," Sasha said. "All your friends."

"Oh." Gonzalo looked down at the landing below, and every head on the landing turned away in fear at the same time. They'd all been watching. Gonzalo took a deep breath. "No problem."

THE HANDCUFFS DUG INTO HIS WRISTS EVERY
time Baxter tugged on the chain. Baxter led Gonzalo through
the crowded conference hall. It was an astonishing sight.
When Gonzalo had first heard rumors about an infected
underground, he'd expected the epicenter to be something
more exotic. Up in secret tree houses in the mountains, down
in an abandoned mine shaft, something really hidden. Not in
a hotel convention hall, like it was a gem show.

The room was expansive, and the high ceilings disappeared into darkness. Standing halogen work lights, tapped
into the hotel generator, lined the walls and multiple lanes of
booths and tables. It had the look of a flea market at night,
lit by cool beams of bright light. Kids were everywhere, dis-
playing items for sale and trade, and the room rumbled with
voices shouting, singing, arguing. People used long faux-
wood tables and brown, metal folding chairs. The booth

dividers were made of gray fabric and chrome metal trim. There were so many heads of white hair in the room that Gonzalo's black hair stood out like a clump of cigarette ash in a bowl of cream. The gas mask and the handcuffs didn't help much either.

Every conversation Baxter dragged him past quieted. Every head turned. It was impossible for people not to look at Gonzalo, standing nearly a foot over the tallest kids in the crowd. He heard people whispering about him in their wake. Younger kids came up close and poked him in the ribs if they had a chance. A couple pulled on his arms and gave him inspecting looks. Baxter shooed them away, but they hovered like horseflies.

Gonzalo began to notice other gas-masked faces in the crowd besides his own. Adults, all of them chained up like him. Halogen light glinted off the shackles at their ankles and wrists, and if the adults weren't tethered to an infected person by a rope or chain, they were chained to the wall. Most were scary-looking dudes, scruffy men with hard features stuffed in tight gas masks. They were the kind you see at gas stations, who buy single beers in the middle of the day and look like they've come fresh from a sexual assault. Others looked more like parents, and their faces were panicked.

"What happens to these adults? Why are they here?" Gonzalo said.

"They get bought and sold."

"For what?"

"I've heard they get held as hostages. To get ransoms of food and supplies from hunters. Little bit of payback, I guess."

"But they can't be let go. They'll talk about this place."

"Who says they get let go?"

Gonzalo looked at all the infected eyes on him, sizing him up.

"They kill them?"

"Or keep 'em as slaves. Other stuff like that."

Gonzalo craned his head to get a read on Baxter. "What other stuff?"

"You got me. I've never traded in people." Baxter looked back and flashed a charming smile with his stupid handsome face. "Yet," he said.

"You should be a comedian."

"Shut up, slave."

"Jesus. Do you see Eddie yet or what?"

"Slaves don't get to ask questions. Just play the role of a dumb-ass who let himself get captured by a guy half his size."

"Half? More like a quarter."

"A quarter is how much I'm going to sell you for."

Gonzalo wanted to shove Baxter, but if he did, any infected here might kill him in seconds. They walked past tables overloaded with gleaming weapons: push knives, crossbows, bolos, blowguns, night sticks, pistols, rifles, submachine guns, sawed-off shotguns. A group of girls, all dressed in camo, stood around a table piled with grenades. A banner hanging off the table read: "Cervixens." Gonzalo watched Baxter lift a push knife off a table and pocket it.

A blast of fire shot into the air ahead of them, and Gonzalo flinched. It was a vendor showing off a flame-thrower to a potential customer, who held up a box of old porn for possible trade. They walked past a seminar where a kid with sunglasses was grappling a mannequin and instructing a small audience about different techniques to rip off an adult's gas mask. On other mannequins, he demonstrated the weak parts of each mask and where to attack first if you got in close. As Gonzalo and Baxter continued on to other lanes, they saw two guys come to blows over a secret travel route. One kid, who wore an unstrapped, white straitjacket with the words "Batshit Batallion" stenciled on it, claimed that the other had sold it to him and that it had turned out to be no good. In fact, it had gotten all of his friends killed. Gonzalo was surprised to see that two kids wearing white scarves on their sleeves came over to break up the fight, and that both parties agreed to stop.

"What's up with those guys?" Gonzalo asked.

"There's rules in here. They enforce 'em. If you're not game, then you gotta get out. Seems to work."

Cops. Gonzalo wondered why the gangs in McKinley hadn't done something like that in the Market. It probably would have spared a lot of injuries in the long run. They continued to stroll down lanes, passing by traders, Baxter looking for Eddie, Gonzalo on the lookout for Sasha. There were camping supplies for sale, like tents and water filters and rocket stoves. There were people selling bottled water and soda and paper cups full of chili. There were people hawking Bed Maps, which were maps of Colorado that pinpointed safe locations where you could get a good night's sleep. Pink markers pointed you to especially comfortable beds. There were kids calling out that they had schematics to build doomsday bunkers or that they would sell you the location of a suburban bomb shelter where you could presumably live out the rest of your infection if you had enough supplies.

Gonzalo saw innocent stuff as well. Pillows and stuffed animals. Books and DVDs. Phones and walkie-talkies. There were vendors who only sold clothes. A tall, well-built kid in a red union suit, just like Gonzalo had seen at the dance party, was swamped by a crowd of adoring kids, most of them girls. He had two of the prettiest under his arms. Kids screamed for him to look their way, and he laughed, loving every bit of the attention. Life seemed like it could be pretty good for an infected here, and Gonzalo wondered how many of these teens lived in the hotel. Baxter walked Gonzalo over to the wall, and they stopped.

"All right, we gotta start asking around if anybody knows Eddie," Gonzalo said as he kept scanning the room. He felt his hands jerk to a stop. Gonzalo looked at a U-bolt on the nearby wall where Baxter had secured his chain with a pad-lock. "No way."

Baxter stood just out of Gonzalo's reach.

"I'll ask around."

Gonzalo lunged for Baxter but got cut short by the chain.

"You can't do this," Gonzalo said.

"I can. And you let me," Baxter said. He chuckled and walked off.

"Baxter!" Gonzalo was chained up near a standing halogen lamp. The area fifteen feet around him was as clear as day, but past that it was hard to see. Baxter was just limping into the darkness beyond. A second later, the little bastard was gone.

The younger kids, who'd followed them, stood about ten feet away, gawking and snickering. Gonzalo had no one to blame but himself. He'd put his trust in Baxter when he knew he shouldn't. Somehow it had seemed easier than trusting him to come back if he went in alone and found Sasha. Gonzalo had to stop following Baxter and find a way to get back in control. The first step was to get out of these chains. He strained against them until his hands were numb, but nothing gave. The U-bolt buried into the wall was secure.

"Who owns you?" a voice said.

Gonzalo looked up to see an infected girl with frizzy white hair. She had bullets through her gauged earlobes, a chicken-wing bone shoved through the septum of her nose, and a tattoo on her cheek of a skeleton hand giving you the finger. Her skin was greasy, and the purplish rings under her eyes looked like bruises. She had a dented Mercedes hubcab strapped to her chest.

Oh, Jesus.

"No one owns me," Gonzalo said.

Her nostrils flared a little. Like she was excited.

"Your owner gave you away? Why? What's wrong with you? You look strong."

"My owner's coming back soon," Gonzalo said with a wince.

"Is he selling? Is that why you're trying to get free? 'Cause I'll be good to you. Real good. I bet you could do anything for days without stopping."

She reached out with her forefinger and touched his chest. Gonzalo pulled away. Her nostrils flared again. She clearly had ideas of what Gonzalo could do for her. He had no interest in finding out what they were.

"I wonder how much he wants for you. How old are you?"

"Nineteen."

"Young."

"Listen, if you want to buy me, my owner's name is Eddie. Why don't you go find him, and we can sort this out. He's around here somewhere."

The girl smiled and walked off. Gonzalo nodded to himself. For a few seconds he was really proud of himself, until he watched the girl walk straight over to a shivering kid who was looking all around him, like he was about to be attacked.

He was definitely one of the Buggy Boys. A heavy, Mac Truck hubcap hung from his neck, and the weight of it gave him a hunch. A cigarette wiggled between his lips, and he lit it, but he lit the middle instead of the tip. He didn't notice. When the bone-nosed girl approached him, he flinched, and the smoldering underside of the cigarette flared orange. Gonzalo was pretty sure that wasn't Eddie. The girl whispered in his ear, then pointed at Gonzalo. The pair started looking around to see if anybody was watching them. They looked shiftier by the second, and then they started walking toward him. He scanned the crowd for Baxter, or even for those cops or whatever the hell they were.

The nervous boy and the bone-nosed girl approached fast. Gonzalo yanked against the chain. It was no use—the chain held and the pair was beside him in seconds.

"Oh, yeah," the boy said while he stared at Gonzalo. "He could take a beating."

"You know how much Herb would pay for him? He could take on five, maybe ten, at the same time."

"I need my shit, baby."

"I know, I'm thirsty too. This is how we get it."

"I told you, I have an owner," Gonzalo said.

"He ain't here now," the boy said.

The boy took out a pair of paperclips that were bent in different orientations, and inserted them into the keyhole of the padlock. This was bad. If they did unlock him from the wall, he couldn't fight them off and make a run for it. There were too many infected between him and the exit. They'd take him out eventually. Gonzalo searched the room for Baxter and saw no sign of him, but he did spot a face that he recognized. One he hadn't seen since McKinley. A Geek girl who had been friends with Dorothy, one of the Loners. She used to come and visit the Stairs, and she and Dorothy would draw together. Her name was . . . what was it? She was one of the Art Geeks, the ones who painted all the backdrops of the Geek Shows and plastered their art all over the school walls. What was her name?

He heard the tumblers of the lock shift as the kid picked it.

"Pamela!" Gonzalo shouted out. A few people turned, but most ignored him. The room was loud with all the conversations. Pamela looked over. She was wearing a sky-blue ski-instructor jacket and holding a sharpened ski pole. *Please recognize me*, he thought. He waved his hands at the wrist. Recognition clicked into place on her face. She looked confused. She came bustling over.

"Gonzalo, is that you?"

"Afraid so," he said. The boy backed off the lock and hid the paperclip lock picks in his palm. The bone-nosed girl stepped in front of Pamela.

"You're not Eddie," she said.

Pamela looked at Gonzalo, puzzled.

"She's Eddie's girlfriend," Gonzalo said.

Pamela was quick on the uptake. "Afraid so," she said. "What's going on here?"

"They're trying to steal me from Eddie," Gonzalo said.

"Not unless they want me to alert security," Pamela said.

The grubby couple backed off, but they didn't look happy about it. Gonzalo wondered how many times they'd been in trouble with security before.

"Thank you for that," Gonzalo said, once the couple was out of earshot.

"Did I do the right thing? I just reacted."

"It was perfect."

Pamela looked down at his handcuffs.

"How did this happen?"

"Long story."

"This isn't a good place for you to be."

"Yeah, that's coming through pretty loud and clear."

"I thought you graduated a long time ago. What are you even doing in the infected zone?"

"Do you remember my girlfriend, Sasha?"

"Oh, shit. You came back here for her?"

Gonzalo nodded.

"That is so sweet."

"Yeah, thanks. Listen, can you get your hands on, like, a hacksaw or something? I need to get the fuck outta here."

"I've seen her," Pamela said.

He locked eyes with Pamela.

"Wh-what did you say?"

"Sasha. I've seen her. It was, like, three months ago. I talked to her."

Gonzalo felt a rush of emotion, and his eyes welled with water.

"Where was it? Do you know where she is now? Did she seem okay?"

"Aww," Pamela said and dabbed her eyes. "Sorry, you are just too sweet. Yeah, she was all right. Ten fingers, ten toes. All body parts still in place. She said she was heading to a town outside Denver called Razorville."

"Razorville," Gonzalo repeated. "Was she alone? Did she seem safe?"

"She said she'd been having a rough go of it, but she said it would all get better once she got to Razorville. She said . . . gimme a second . . ." Pamela closed her eyes and pursed her lips. "A bakery. That's what she said. The Loners were living at a bakery in Razorville."

"The Loners? Are you sure? Do you know which ones?"

"It was that whole crew that got out when the doors opened. I didn't get to know them very well 'cause I went with the little group that headed into the Rockies," she said, and her face went flat and lost a little of its color. "I probably should've gone with the Loners."

Gonzalo looped his shackled arms around her and hugged her close.

"Thank you so much, Pamela. You don't know how much this means to me."

"I wish I could help you more. I don't have enough to buy a person. Do you know what you're gonna do? Gonzalo, I really don't want you to die or . . . Bad things happen to some of these slaves."

"Get lost, Pamela," someone said.

They both turned to see Baxter pushing his way through the crowd, a bag of caramel corn under his arm. The sight of Baxter limping toward her seemed to repulse Pamela.

"Up yours, Baxter," she said and looked to Gonzalo. "You're stuck with *him*? I feel even worse for you now."

Baxter walked to the wall and unlocked Gonzalo's chain from the U-bolt. "Let's get out of here."

Gonzalo yanked the chain out of Baxter's hand with a hard snap.

"What if I decided I want to stay and talk to my friend here," Gonzalo said.

Baxter shoved a mound of caramel corn into his mouth and chewed. "I guess you don't want to hear what I found out then."

"I already found out plenty," Gonzalo said.

Baxter glanced Pamela's way, "I know where she is, as of two weeks ago. Your info that fresh?"

Pamela gave the slightest shake of her head. Baxter didn't see it because he was already walking off.

"I gotta go," Gonzalo said.

"Good luck," Pamela said.

Gonzalo caught up with Baxter and shoved his chain in the little guy's hand. He couldn't be seen walking by himself. Baxter didn't hesitate to make a big show of Gonzalo being a slave for the entire walk back to the exit, and he stayed in character until they reached the window that led to the plank bridge to the other building.

"Take off the cuffs," Gonzalo said.

Baxter took out the key and held it up.

"You embarrassed me back there."

"I'm sorry, which one of us had to walk around on a leash?"

Baxter huffed, "It was a ruse! An act! Do you want to find Sasha or not? I thought we were partners."

Gonzalo stared at Baxter. He honestly didn't know what to say. He couldn't tell what was real with this guy. Was he actually supposed to feel bad?

"Apologize and I'll take the cuffs off."

He tried to apologize. He really tried.

"No," Gonzalo said.

"Fine. See you on the other side then."

Baxter crawled through the window, out to the fire escape. Gonzalo followed, hands still bound and dragging the heavy chain. He crawled out to the fire escape as Baxter was walking across the bridge. The wind gusted. The sky had gone gray. Gonzalo looked down to the wet alley and the dead bear seventeen stories down.

"Baxter, come on. I can't crawl across with these on." He held up his linked wrists. "I barely made it last time."

Baxter kept limping across. He didn't look down once. He walked across the planks like he was on the ground, like there wasn't a fatal drop waiting for him on either side. Gonzalo grunted and ground his teeth.

"I'm begging you, man," Gonzalo said. It hurt to say it.

Baxter turned around when he was a foot away from the opposite fire escape. There was a small grin, just a tilt to the corners of his mouth, as he chewed. He took a deep breath in through his nose, his eyes closed, and blew it out through a smile, like he was savoring the fresh air.

"First sensible thing you've said all day," Baxter said, and he tossed Gonzalo the key.

Gonzalo's whole body jerked. He flailed his arms out to catch the flying key, aware that if he failed, it would fall straight through the slatted floor of the fire escape. He slapped it against his chest with his palm and was able to hold it sandwiched there. Gonzalo worked it into his fingers and freed himself from the tight cuffs. He rubbed his sore wrists. There was no feeling quite as pure and good as being free again.

Baxter watched him from the other fire escape and chomped his caramel corn. The building was in cool shadow on that side, but Gonzalo's side was drenched in the flat light of the blank gray sky.

"You've had your fun," Gonzalo said. "Are you gonna tell me about this hot lead now?"

Baxter dug a sugary finger deep into his nose and rooted around. "It's a town called Razorville," he said.

Gonzalo nearly bit through his lip.

"You don't say."

20

SASHA SLAPPED THE MEAT OF HIS THIGH.

"Who have you been eating since I last saw you?"

Gonzalo chuckled. Sasha couldn't stop talking about how big he was. She couldn't get over it, and it was starting to worry him. She never said it was a good thing. She only talked about how different it was. He wanted so much to kiss her again, but he feared that something more than his size had changed between them.

She was wearing shoes for the first time that he had seen. Little chunky boots with a five-inch platform. She must have stolen them at some point, either from someone or from the old pile, and secreted them away in case she ever left the Mice. They made her taller, but her head only came up to under his chest. Her crop-top was her only shirt. She was showing a lot of skin, but he didn't mind at all, although he did level a murderous stare at any guy he saw looking. She was like a gift that was almost all the way unwrapped. Her pants were black tights, and that's exactly what they were—tight. He loved it. Leggings told no lies. He could see the exact shape of her, and it was driving him insane.

"Introduce me," she said and gestured toward Belinda, a girl Gonzalo had only met once. "She looks nice."

Gonzalo walked with Sasha down the stairs to the kitchen. A squat kid named Buck, with a peach-fuzz mustache, was heating up his girlfriend's can of sweet corn with his lighter. She had shockingly hairy arms and milky skin. The pair scattered at the sight of Gonzalo, but Belinda didn't notice his approach. She was squeezing three slices of white bread in her hands until it was a compressed ball. She took a bite out of it.

"Hey, um, look at this. I just invented something! It's called a bread-apple. Ooh, brapple! That's bett—"

Belinda stopped mid-word when she saw Gonzalo. Her plump cheeks wobbled.

"Sasha, this is Belinda. Belinda, Sasha," he said.

Belinda quivered, staring up at Gonzalo. She crushed her bread-apple in her hand, and it squeezed out between her fingers.

"Hi," Belinda said. She offered a jittery hand to Sasha. She had a hard time looking Sasha in the face as they shook hands because her eyes kept flicking up toward Gonzalo.

"I'm so excited to be part of the Loners," Sasha said. "I hope we can be friends."

"Yes, of course! Whatever you want. Just tell me what you want."

Sasha looked up at Gonzalo, puzzled. He wanted to smile down at her and reassure her that everything was fine and Belinda wasn't acting like she was meeting the daughter of a mob boss, but he was still trying not to smile around her. Belinda seemed to think Gonzalo would attack her if she made Sasha unhappy.

"She just wants what we all want," Gonzalo said, hurrying through a version of what he'd heard David say, "a safe place to call home, with people we can trust."

"You can trust me," Belinda said. "I swear to God."

"Okay," he said. "Super."

He patted Sasha's and Belinda's shoulders as he said it. Belinda flinched under his touch. She cocked her head at him, as if he was acting like a completely different person—which he was.

"See you around," Sasha said sweetly.

As soon as they were out of earshot, Gonzalo whispered, "She's kind of weird."

Sasha reached out and squeezed his hand, like they'd known each other forever. "I'm glad you said something. That felt so awkward. It felt like you two used to date or something."

"What? No. I barely know her."

She smiled up at him. They moved on to other Loners. Each exchange was more awkward than the one before it. He tried hard to make it seem like he was in tight with the Loners and was a beloved member. Generally, it freaked all of them out. Still, Sasha brought excitement and openness to every moment. As Gonzalo watched Sasha embrace these strangers as new friends, he wondered if he could do it just as effortlessly, if he would only let himself.

They sat down on the bottommost stair, next to the first-floor armory. Clubs made of flag poles and desk legs driven through with nails leaned out from the triangular alcove. She was serious now. The effervescent charm she'd displayed with the others was gone. She glanced at him but avoided looking him in the eye.

"Gonzalo."

"Yeah?"

"I've been hearing things."

"What sorts of things?"

"About you being . . . I guess, a maniac? And living in the lounge with the dead seniors. What's that all about?"

"Uhh, it was more of an act. To scare people off. I never killed anyone."

"And you didn't live in the lounge?"

She was going to be disgusted once she knew.

"I . . . y'know, that was part of the act."

"So you only pretended to live there?"

"No, I . . . did."

Her eyebrows shot up. She took a deep breath and nodded slowly. He cringed.

"I want to see it," she said.

Gonzalo shook his head. He hadn't expected that. "I don't think you do."

"I'm positive I do."

There was no way he could let her see. "Let's just forget about it. It's in the past."

"Gonzalo, I need to know what you've been through."

He argued and argued, but she simply wouldn't let up. She asked until he felt like she was scrubbing his eardrums with steel wool.

"Just show me. I promise I can take it."

"Fine, Sasha, I'll take you. Jesus Christ, you're like a weed-whacker."

She laughed, happy that she'd won. She nearly skipped all the way to the lounge. He knew she'd said she could handle it, but the closer they got to the lounge, the more he began to sweat. She didn't know what she was talking about. He'd lived with the dead seniors for so long that he no longer saw it all, but he remembered when he'd first walked in how it had made him sick. She was going to think there was something wrong with him. Like, really wrong. And he guessed that was what this was about. That was why she wanted to see this place. This was the closest thing to a background check she could get.

They made it to the scarecrows. Two had been knocked down since he'd left. Gonzalo resisted the urge to fix them. Sasha walked past them without caring, and sooner than he would have liked, they were at the double doors to the lounge.

"Are you absolutely sure that—?"

Gonzalo didn't get the chance to finish because Sasha pushed the doors open and walked inside. He wiped the sweat from his forehead and went after her.

She stopped a few steps into the room and stood still, looking at it from behind her hands, which she now held in front of her face. She wasn't speaking. He could hear his footsteps as he walked to her.

The lounge looked different to him now. So much worse. The bodies seemed twisted in greater agony. The dry wax of their flesh, the stains on the floor, the crust on the carpet, the teeth, the bones, the hair, the death all around him was repellent. He felt sure that Sasha's opinion of him had changed forever.

She didn't make a peep. She stared blankly at the room. She was probably thinking of what she'd have to do to distract him so that she could run away.

"I chose it *because* of how awful it is, you know? To keep people away. You get that, right?"

She cringed at the sight of one of the corpses and looked away.

"Let me show you the back rooms. That's where I stayed. I didn't hang out in here. This is more like a moat. Does that make sense? Just come back here. I need you to understand."

He realized how creepy that sounded.

"I get it," she said.

Gonzalo stopped walking. "You do?"

He was afraid she was saying it like she was on the verge of running, like she'd say anything to get away. But she wasn't. Her face didn't show fear. In fact, she was nodding, almost with appreciation.

"Yeah. I don't know if I could do it but . . . I actually think it's really smart. You do whatever you have to do to stay safe and stay fed, that's what I say. But . . ."

"But what?"

She looked around the corpse-strewn room.

"This is what you wanted?"

"I wouldn't say I *wanted* it."

"But this is why you left? I thought we had something going, but you apparently wanted this more and . . . I'm trying really hard to understand."

He was so taken aback that he couldn't respond at first. He could see the pain and confusion in her eyes.

"I didn't leave," he said. "Baxter locked me in a bathroom for three months."

The change in her was immediate. Her posture went straight as a ladder, her chin raised, and she held her fingers crooked into claws. "That little—ohh. I can't believe . . . Do you know how long I looked for you?"

"No."

She palmed her forehead, and her eyes flitted left and right.

"It had to be about that same amount of time. Two months, at least. I can't believe him."

She told Gonzalo that she'd searched for him whenever she could, and slowly, over time, she'd lost hope. She thought he'd gotten tired of her. Baxter had told her repeatedly that he had probably died. And she said he never let her alone either, hanging around her constantly, even following her until he found out where she slept. Gonzalo's heart hurt as he heard her talk of her hope dwindling, about her doubt in him growing. She said that during the time Gonzalo must have been living in the senior lounge, Baxter had locked all the Mice in a room until they conceded to appoint him leader. He said that he wasn't getting tied to a tree and humiliated again just because none of them knew how to keep a gang running. Everyone had fallen in line, except for Sasha. When she resisted, he isolated her from the rest. He kept her locked up in a room for weeks by herself, and he visited her daily, coaxing her, then badgering her, until eventually she realized that Baxter didn't just want to be her leader.

"He was obsessed with me. He wanted me to say that I loved him as much as he loved me. But he treated me like a dog."

"Did you tell him you loved him?"

"I escaped. I was on my own for almost a week before I heard someone say your name and heard you were in the Loners."

"I'm so sorry," Gonzalo said. "You don't know how bad I wanted to see you. I thought it would never happen again."

Sasha grunted her disgust. "It's not fair. All that time. I can't believe he . . . he tricked us. That's so evil."

"I want to hurt him," Gonzalo said. It was the best he could manage on short notice.

Sasha wiped the tears that were gathering in her eyes now.

"I'd be fine if I never thought about him again." Sasha said.

"Let's talk about something else."

"Yeah, and no offense, I'm not judging you or anything, but can we go somewhere else? I think I've had a lifetime full of this room too."

Gonzalo smiled. "Yeah. Come on, let's go."

She took his hand, and he walked her to the quad. At night, the quad was a completely different place. During the day, sunlight shone through the gray canopy that obscured the sky. It was dim, maybe 30-40% as bright as actual sunlight. At night, the moonlight barely made it through the barrier at all. Night in the quad was murky and dark, and you could barely see a thing. When the sun went down, it became a place to do things that you didn't even want your gang to see.

As they strolled out of the hallway and onto the dirt of the quad, Gonzalo looked up. The entire canopy glowed a weak, dark gray. Sasha's face barely emerged from the darkness, like an egg yolk in a puddle of orange juice. He could sense other couples out in the quad, vague figures holding hands and embracing. When they got closer to them, he could make out some details but not faces. Based on the darkness of their hair, how they stood, what they wore, he could make educated guesses about what gangs they were from. So many couples were in cross-gang romances. He spotted a Pretty One and a Slut walking hand in hand. Nerds with Freaks. A Varsity with a Skater. Varsity with . . . Varsity. The quad was a dark haze, but slowly Gonzalo's eyes adjusted to the whisper of moonlight that survived the canopy.

He started to see more people across the quad, far more than he'd assumed were there when he'd first walked out. Sketchy deals were going down. People handed each other things, looking all around while they did it, as if they were scared of getting caught. Groups huddled together, wrapped up in hushed conversations, plotting. People had definitely been killed out here in the dark. That was the rumor. The other rumor was that there were lots of bodies buried in the dirt. People said that murderers came here at night to bury their victims. Some even said that if you walked out here late enough, on a night with no moon, you might witness a burial taking place.

Sasha gasped, then whispered, "Gonzalo, look!"

She pointed to a couple making out by the tree at the edge of the quad.

"What? There's people hooking up all over the place."

"That's Wiggles!"

"No . . ."

Gonzalo strained his eyes and saw that she was right. The

girl-half of the couple was Wiggles, and she was tongue-kissing the scraggly Skater boy she'd always watched through the vents.

"I'm so happy for her," Sasha said. "I want to go say hi."

She started to walk over, but Gonzalo held her arm.

"No, leave her alone. She's busy."

Sasha groaned, but she came back to him. She gave one last try to get Wiggles's attention by waving and giving her double thumbs-up, but Wiggles didn't see.

"I never stopped looking for you," Gonzalo said.

Sasha forgot about Wiggles and turned back to face him. She walked up close to him, until she was nearly touching and had to crane her head all the way back to look in his eyes.

"You're like a mountain."

"Keep talking."

Sasha laughed and leapt onto him. "I want to climb the mountain!"

With her legs clamped around his body, she began to crawl up him like he was a jungle gym. Some people nearby watched, but most ignored them. Sasha snaked around to his back. It tickled.

"What the hell are you doing?" he said, cracking up.

"Oh, my god, have you felt your own muscles? You're like a bull or something."

"No, I don't feel my own muscles," he said.

That was a lie. He did that all the time.

Sasha grunted with effort as she climbed Gonzalo's back. "It's like I'm on Mount Everest. I believe in myselfffff!"

She threw out her arms as she rose up onto his shoulders. She lost her balance and flopped sloppily over his shoulder. Gonzalo caught her as she slid down his front, stopping her from falling on her head. Her knees were on either side of his head and he held her in a bear hug around her waist.

"Easy. Jesus. Let me help you down."

"No! I have to climb it."

Sasha writhed around, half letting Gonzalo hold her up and half pulling herself up. She climbed back up him until her arms were wrapped around his neck They were eye to eye, and he held her. Gonzalo smiled widely. He couldn't help it. He forgot all about how bad he looked when he did it.

"Ah, he finally smiles," Sasha said.

He frowned. "Do you wish I hadn't?"

"No. When you smile, you look just like you did on our date, right after you kissed me."

He doubted he'd get a clearer signal than that. He kissed her, and he felt something relax within him that had been held tense all these months. Sasha flirted with passion and energy, but her kiss was slow. Her lips were soft, and they moved with his, and she seemed delicate, and it made him kiss her more softly. She made little noises that he could barely hear, little groans as she slid her hands down his chest.

21

"ONCE WE GET TO THE INFECTED COMMUNITY
in Razorville, I'll see what I can do to get you access," Baxter said.

Gonzalo stayed silent. He gazed at the flat landscape around them and the infinite road ahead.

"I'll come up with something different than the slave routine," Baxter continued. "I know that gets you all bitchy."

Bitchy? Gonzalo kept his mouth shut. He couldn't get sucked into Baxter's head games. He didn't buy this "infected community" business either. Baxter had to know there were Loners in Razorville, and he was choosing not to tell. He must have thought it would give Gonzalo an unfair advantage. And it probably would. If Sasha wasn't in Razorville, Gonzalo could still fall in with the Loners, and they could vouch for him from here on out. He wouldn't need Baxter at all.

"I could really go for a croissant," Gonzalo said.

"A croissant? You been seeing a lot of those lately?"

Gonzalo shrugged. "Nah, but people are coming back to Colorado. Maybe there's a bakery in town."

Baxter didn't have a comment. Gonzalo grinned. The idea of being rid of Baxter was warming his heart.

"If you're nice," Gonzalo said, "maybe I'll grab you a mini-croissant."

Baxter responded with a raised middle finger.

"We got another one," Gonzalo said, nodding toward the road ahead.

Baxter clicked open his seat belt and slid off the seat. He balled himself up on the floor, small enough that no passerby could see him unless they were in a big rig and on the right side of the car. Gonzalo always stayed in the right lane so that wouldn't happen.

The car was a matte-gray Range Rover, heading in the opposite direction. It passed so fast Gonzalo barely got a chance to see who was inside. He saw sunglasses and a beard. There was a passenger as well, but he only saw a blur of blonde hair. No gas mask on either one. No gas mask might mean they were infected. It wasn't hard for an infected with a heavy beard to dye it brown as a disguise. No gas mask might also mean the driver had his Range Rover sealed airtight like this van. If Gonzalo didn't have Baxter in the passenger seat, he'd be able to enjoy that same freedom. Whether they were infected or not, their gray vehicle shrank in his rearview mirror until it was gone.

"Is it gone?" Baxter said from below.

"Almost," Gonzalo said. He liked Baxter better when he was crouching in fear on the floor.

"Did they turn around or what?"

"Hmm?"

"Can I get up?"

"Oh, yeah," he finally said. "They're gone."

Baxter didn't climb back up. He glared at Gonzalo from down there, still hunched over, arms still wrapped around his shins.

"What are you so smug about?" Baxter said.

"Oh, nothing," Gonzalo said. "You just make me laugh."

"I have to go to the bathroom."

"Again? You just went a half hour ago."

"And now I have to go again. So what?"

Last time he'd refused to pull over, Baxter had pissed in an empty Gatorade bottle, and the thing was still sloshing around in the back.

"I'll pull over, but make it fast," Gonzalo said. "I don't like sitting out in the wide open."

Baxter shook his head. "I gotta go number two."

"Shouldn't make a difference."

"I don't like squatting out in the wide open."

"But you'd rather walk into a dark room where the shitter's been backed up for years?"

"Better than you watching me."

"I'd rather watch a hospital fire."

Baxter climbed up in his seat.

"Just stop up there."

"Your funeral."

Ahead was a cluster of fast-food restaurants. When they got nearer, Gonzalo navigated toward the closest one, a Carl's Jr. It looked surprisingly pristine, not just for a building in the infected zone, but for a fast-food restaurant.

"Go to the Long John Silver's," Baxter said, rapping on the window. The Long John Silver's up the street looked like a smoker's lung.

"Got a hankering for some fish?"

"No, I worked there for a summer. I hated my boss. Fucking drunk. He picked on me 'cause I was the smallest." Gonzalo watched Baxter's top lip curl. "If I ever see a Long John Silver's, I go out of my way to shit in their deep-fryers."

"You got problems, man," Gonzalo said and pulled into the parking lot. He circled the van to point it toward the parking lot exit, out of habit. "You got five minutes before I drive off."

Baxter's face scrunched up like he was mad, but then he smiled.

"You won't do that. You still need me," he said.

He opened the door and hopped out of the van, slamming the door shut behind him. Gonzalo couldn't see Baxter for a few moments—that was how short he was—his head didn't clear the bottom of the window. Then he saw Baxter climb through a broken window of the restaurant. Gonzalo's nerves were buzzing. Baxter didn't have to do anything to get under Gonzalo's skin. He had already shoved needles under his skin long ago, and now all it took was for Baxter to brush his fingers against them to reignite the old pain and anger. He was sick of Baxter being in his van, in his head, in his life at all. He started to wonder why he was doing Baxter the courtesy of even waiting now. The inevitable was coming, and probably soon too. Baxter would ditch him once he didn't need Gonzalo anymore, or Gonzalo would ditch *him*. So why couldn't Gonzalo ditch Baxter right now?

Gonzalo placed his hand on the gear shift and pulled it into drive. He punched the gas. Nobody needed to go that fast through a parking lot, but once Gonzalo had made his decision, he wanted out. He could feel Baxter's vampire grip on him slipping away as he sped forward. The van began pulling right, and Gonzalo fought with the steering wheel to keep the rig straight.

"No, come on . . ."

The van wobbled slowly, dipping toward the front right corner. He had a flat tire—he knew it. Gonzalo took his foot off the gas and eased the van over to the side of the road. He pushed open the door and stepped onto the baking-hot road. He was right. The front right tire was rim to the ground. There was no saving it. There was a jagged tear in the rubber tread. A push knife with a bent, four-inch triangular blade hung out out of the ruined tire. Scratched into the molded plastic handle in razor blade cuts were the words, "Absolutely Stabulous." It was the same knife he had seen Baxter steal at the Radisson.

He looked back to the Long John Silver's. Still no sign of Baxter, but he'd have to hurry if he wanted to get the spare on and get out of there before Baxter was done defiling the deep-fryer. He found the tire iron and jack in the back of the van, along with a dinky spare tire. He got the jack under the van and cranked it until the van was high enough that the tire spun freely. Then he fumbled to get the iron onto the first lug nut. He couldn't get the stupid angle right. The iron slipped onto the nut, and he twisted. The wheel rotated, giving him no leverage. He tried to hold the wheel still with one hand and crank the tire iron again, but the nut stayed put.

"Stupid."

He was in such a rush that he'd forgotten to loosen all the nuts before he jacked it up so the weight of the van on the road would keep the wheel still. He lowered the jack and got all the nuts off, even though he had to stomp the tire iron a few times to do it. Once he jacked it back up, it was quick work to change out the spare and lower it back down. Gonzalo was sweating and cursing like mad. With the final twist of the last lug nut on the new tire, Gonzalo fell back on his ass, beat. His breath was loud in his head, blasting against the dewing face shield of his mask.

"Well, this is awkward."

Gonzalo instinctively pushed off the ground, away from the direction of that voice. Baxter stood in the shadow of the van with his head at a tilt.

"You boobytrapped my van?" Gonzalo said. He reached down and picked up the push knife.

"Gee, I just got this feeling that you might try to up and ditch me. I don't know where I get these kooky ideas."

Gonzalo hucked the knife into the high grass. "Well, now I have to drive on this thing."

The van leaned toward the front right corner. The tiny tire looked like a dinner plate compared to the others.

"You mean, *we* have to. You still need me, Shrek."

"Why's that?"

"Because there are things I haven't told you."

"Like that the Loners are living in Razorville?"

"Like that Sasha's not living there with them."

"Bullshit."

"Afraid not. I know where she is now, though. I was going to tell you, but you went and fucked everything up again."

Baxter opened the passenger-side door, climbed inside, and locked it shut. Gonzalo wanted to reach down, grab the underside of the van, and flip it over. He could pull him out of the van if he didn't mind risking that Baxter might have more knives hidden on him, and throw him out, and be done with it all. He wanted to, he was dying to, but he couldn't walk away without finding out whether Baxter was telling the truth. He could be walking away from the key to finding her. Gonzalo kicked at the spare like he was testing the air pressure, but he just wanted to kick something.

He got back into the van without letting Baxter see that the situation bothered him, at least not too much. Baxter wouldn't look at him. Gonzalo started the van up and pulled onto the road. They crept toward Razorville, the van slumping down the highway, leaning on its miniature spare.

"Faster, dum-dum, we're wasting time."

Gonzalo suppressed his urge toward violence.

"You seem pretty eager to get to Razorville for someone who knows Sasha's not there."

"Well, I didn't say we couldn't learn things there."

"Uh-huh."

He was probably lying, as usual, and playing Gonzalo once again. All Gonzalo wanted was for Sasha to be there with the Loners, and for that to be the last time he ever saw Baxter.

"Do you wish you were normal?" Baxter said.

"I am normal."

"You know what I mean. Not so freakishly big."

"Doesn't bother me."

"Really? Because you can't hide. Everybody stares at you. They all think you're dumb."

"No, they don't," Gonzalo said, and then felt stupid that he fell for the bait.

Baxter cracked a smile. "Of course not. Don't worry about it, buddy."

"Does it bother you that you're the size of a large grade-schooler?"

"*You* bother me."

"Have you ever had a friend? I'm being serious," Gonzalo said.

"I've had plenty," Baxter said.

"Really. That is hard to imagine. When was this? Please don't tell me you mean Kent."

"I always have friends. I'm not the school weirdo who fucks dead bodies."

"No one ever said that about me."

"Are you kidding? Everybody said that."

The van jolted. The road was in awful shape, cracked and littered with debris. The van was so heavy that Gonzalo felt every crack and bump they rode over.

"They said that's why you didn't want anyone around. 'Cause you humped a different one every night."

"At least people knew who I was. The only way anyone knew you was as the naked kid tied to the tree. Did you think I forgot that? How could I? So many people took pictures of you doing some pretty rough stuff."

Baxter bristled in his seat. His nose wrinkled and a vein on his temple pulsed.

"I remember a video," Gonzalo went on, "where you got on your knees and kissed a Skater's boot 'cause he said that he'd make his friends stop beating you up if you did. Do you remember this?"

Baxter turned away and looked out the passenger window.

"Right when you kissed it, his friend kicked you in the balls from behind, and they all laughed. I think they went on kicking you around for a bit after that, if I remember right. I miss the old days sometimes."

Baxter turned back to face him. His face was flushed wine-red.

"I know something too, and I know it for a fact," Baxter said.

"Oh, yeah? What's that?"

"I don't think you'll like it," Baxter said.

"Are you gonna say it or not?"

Baxter said it, but it would be the last time he spoke for the rest of the long slog to Razorville, no matter what Gonzalo said to provoke him.

"I know she won't pick you," Baxter said.

22

SASHA HAD A BIRTHMARK ON HER BREAST.
A dot of chocolate. Her shirt was off, and for the first time, he was soaking in the sight of her naked. The two of them had been making out in this empty classroom, with Gonzalo holding the door shut behind him because there was no lock. Then Sasha had pulled away with a sparkle in her eye and whipped off her shirt.

He walked toward her.

"No, don't let go of the doorknob." She reached out as she said it, and the rest of her jiggled.

Gonzalo took a step back and grabbed the knob again.

"Then you come over here," he said.

"You're not the boss of me."

"This is cruel."

"Well, maybe if you're nice." She took a step toward him. "And you tell me how I'm the most important thing in your life." A step closer still. "And you look at me real mean and do that growling thing you do . . . I'll come a little closer." She paused with her foot hanging in the air, toes pointed. He was already as far away from the door as he could get without letting go of the knob. If she took another two steps, she'd be close enough for him to touch her.

He let a growl rumble up from deep within his chest, as menacing as he could muster.

She giggled and put her toes to the floor.

"Ooh, Mister Monster, please don't hurt me."

She cowered in mock terror as she took another step closer. He reached out to take hold of her, but his fingertips only grazed her warm skin. He wanted to make fun of her for calling him Mister Monster, but he couldn't force himself to care when she was naked from the hips up and almost within reach.

"Come here," he said.

"Tell me how you feel about me."

"Are you serious? Sash, you're killing me."

How could she ask about emotions when she had her breasts out? How was he supposed to think of anything but how they would feel in his hands, on his lips, against his cheek?

"You better not be saying you don't feel anything," Sasha said.

"Definitely not. Get real."

"Okay, great. Then, elaborate."

"I like how passionate you are."

"Like or love?"

"Love."

"Correct."

Gonzalo laughed.

"What else?" she said.

Gonzalo sighed. "You're pretty, you're sexy, you're—"

Sasha silenced him with a snore.

"Put a little effort in."

"I . . ."

She started stretching, reaching her hands toward the ceiling and arching her back. It wasn't fair. He couldn't think when she did that.

"I'd do anything for you," he said.

Sasha stopped stretching. Her flirty tone grew more serious, and she looked him in the eyes.

"Do you mean that?"

He hadn't thought before he'd said it. Would he really do anything for her? He thought for a moment, because the answer seemed crucially important to her. He couldn't think of what he *wouldn't* do to keep her in his life after being separated from her for so long, or to save her if she were in trouble.

"I do," Gonzalo said.

She closed the distance and pressed herself into him. He wrapped his arms around her and they went at it. They could have only been devouring each other for a minute or so, before someone opened the door.

Sasha jumped and bolted for her shirt on the floor. Gonzalo turned and saw Lucy, an ex-Pretty One, backing away from the doorway with her hand over her eyes.

"Sasha said you'd be here, sorry. It's about to start. Wanted to tell you," Lucy said. She turned and hurried away. When Gonzalo looked back to Sasha, her shirt was back on and it caused him pain. She headed for the door.

"Wait, that was going so well," Gonzalo said.

"Moment's passed. Come on, let's go. You heard Lucy."

They left the room and walked the halls, back toward the Stairs.

"We gotta get our own place on the side," Gonzalo said.

"I'm not messing around in the lounge."

"I never said that. There's just no privacy in the Stairs."

"I said I'm not hooking up in the lounge."

"I'm not talking about the lounge," Gonzalo said, throwing his arms up.

"Oh, my god, stop trying to get me to have sex with you in a room of dead bodies!" she yelled.

Her words reverberated down the hallway, and he saw a few passing Geeks and a Varsity at the hall's end turn and stare.

"I hate you so much," Gonzalo said with a grin.

Sasha giggled about it all the way back to the Stairs.

As much as Gonzalo craved being alone with Sasha, he didn't exactly begrudge their time with the rest of the gang. She thrived in the Loners, and Gonzalo loved watching her.

It had only been a week since she'd joined, and she was already friends with half the gang. When they walked through the door to the bottom landing of the Stairs, they were welcomed by a chorus of cheers. Mostly for Sasha, if he was being honest, but they were sort of meant for him as well. People simply liked hanging out with Sasha, and since she and Gonzalo were always together, they'd become more comfortable with him too. He was even having actual conversations with them now, some as long as a minute. Sasha told him that she'd heard Loners bragging about him in the halls, that they had the biggest, strongest kid in the entire school. He thought about that every day.

When they reached the dining level, they found it transformed by explosions of color. Streamers of intertwined, dyed toilet paper hung along the walls. Old T-shirts had been molded on basketballs, hardened with glue, and shaped to resemble balloons. The T-shirt fabrics were all pastels, like baby blue, chick yellow, sunset pink, and mint. Loners crowded the landing, but Gonzalo towered over them all. He put Sasha on his shoulders so she could have a better view. She peered up the flight of stairs.

Lucy stood nearby, and she blushed when she saw Gonzalo.

"How'd you pull it off without David seeing?" Gonzalo said.

Lucy looked relieved to not talk about the scene she'd just walked in on. "I put Will on the job," she said.

Shouts echoed down the Stairs, and Lucy winced. They

heard feet pounding down steps. Something crashed. Will pounded down the stairs, snarling.

"Hey!" David's voice came from one floor up. "Don't walk away from me. We're not done here."

Will reached the bottom of the stairs and spun around to look up, like the rest of the gathered Loners were doing.

David came storming down. "You asshole! You're going to listen and listen good! You cannot . . ." David's voice trailed off as he soaked in his view of the dining area covered in decorations. "What's going on here?"

Will busted out with a hooting laugh. "Surprise, dickless!"

David's face was still pinched in anger.

"What do you mean, 'surprise'?"

The Loners broke into a boisterous round of "Happy Birthday," and as they sang, David slowly unclenched his jaw until his mouth hung open. When the song was over, David stumbled down to Will and put his hand on his shoulder.

"So," David said, "you didn't punch Violent in the face then?"

"Afraid not."

David sighed. "And the Sluts and Varsity aren't teaming up to take us down?"

"I could go punch her if that's what you want."

"Oh, thank god," he said. "Thank god." He slapped Will's shoulders as he turned away. "If you do that, I will kill you."

Lucy was the first to clap, then other Loners joined in. Some laughed, and someone cranked a playlist. David walked down the stairs to the dining level and was swept up in congratulations and conversation with the gathering Loners.

After the party was done, and they'd each had their square of instant cornbread, Sasha and Gonzalo made their way to the beds on the third flight of stairs. Technically, they were supposed to each have their own stair to sleep on, but for most Loners that was a tight fit. For Gonzalo, it was cartoonishly impossible. Lucy was leading the charge to widen the stair beds, but in the meantime, he simply didn't fit. He slept on the landing of the bottom stair in the flight. Sasha slept on the stair above him. If anyone had a problem with it, they didn't say anything.

He looked up at her, and he felt grateful to have her in his life. If she'd never walked into the Stairs that day, he probably would have gone back to the senior lounge. He wouldn't feel any of the security, the love, the respect he received on a daily basis now. There certainly wouldn't be anyone making him cornbread.

"Hey, Sash," Gonzalo said.

She looked down at him. He wanted to tell her that he loved her. He wasn't even sure what it meant, other than that he really, really liked her and wanted to be around her all the time, but he thought she wanted to hear it. That was probably what she was hunting around for back in the classroom with her top off. He did feel all those things. He did love her. He just didn't know why it felt so scary to say.

"I, uh, I just wanted you to know that . . . ever since we met in the Mice, I—"

"Shhhhhhh."

Gonzalo paused, puzzled. Sasha hadn't shushed him. He looked around. Two Loners on the stairs above were still awake, but they weren't paying attention to Gonzalo and Sasha.

"Did you hear that?" Gonzalo said.

"What?"

"Someone shushed me."

"Who?"

"You didn't hear it?"

"I guess I wasn't paying attention."

"Huh."

"What were you saying?" Sasha said.

Gonzalo looked around him, still confused. "That you should pay attention when I'm talking."

She laughed. "I'm sorry. I was thinking about tacos."

"You don't care about anything I say," he said, overdoing it for effect.

"I do, I do!" she said, and tugged on his arm.

Gonzalo supposed he could tell her, but the emotion of the moment had passed. If he was going to say it, he was going to do it right.

"You're my girlfriend, right?"

She smiled.

"Is that a yes?"

"Uh huh." She leaned off her step and kissed him. "I pretty much assumed so, but I'm glad you said it."

"Okay, girlfriend. Let's go to sleep. I'm tired."

She giggled. "Me too."

She fell asleep before he did. Sleep didn't come that easily for Gonzalo. He stayed up for a bit, watching her drool and marveling at how she made it cute. The Loners who hadn't already gone to sleep stepped silently over the others and settled in for the night on their steps. Eventually, he drifted off to sleep with the rest of his gang.

He woke up feeling like death. He was tired, his mouth was dry, and the crystals of sap that he picked out of the corners of eyes were big enough to dangle off an earring. His vision was blurry at first, but when it cleared, he noticed a piece of paper next to his head on the floor.

Gonzalo picked up the paper and blinked away the last of the blur. It was a handwritten note on three-ring-binder paper. The handwriting was tight and angular and written in red permanent marker. It read:

Keep your hands off her or I'll use a knife.

Gonzalo tensed. His eyes shot to the nearest vent. Then to the next. He could see three from where he sat. Baxter had come here. He'd always known it was possible, but he didn't think he'd dare. Baxter had stood over Gonzalo while he slept.

"Sasha, wake up," Gonzalo said, shaking her shoulder.

Her eyelashes fluttered and her eyes opened. She looked at Gonzalo, then groaned and turned over on her side.

"No, baby, get up. You have to look at this."

Sasha propped herself up on one arm.

"Did you just call me, 'baby'?"

"Yeah, but listen—"

"Awww. That's the first time you've called me something sweet like that, even though 'baby' is kinda weird. What about 'goddess'?"

"Look at this note," Gonzalo said.

He held Baxter's note out in front of her. The sight of it leeched the sleepy happiness from her face.

"That's not good," she said.

"He was here."

Sasha's cheeks burned red, and he could see fear creep into her. He almost wished he hadn't told her.

"What's going on with your neck?" She said.

Sasha reached out and traced her fingertips across his Adam's apple.

"What? What is it?" Gonzalo said.

"He . . . drew a dotted line across your neck."

"Let me see your compact."

Sasha grabbed it out of a bag hanging off the banister above her stair and handed it to Gonzalo. Her compact was a faux-leather wallet with a clear slot for an ID. She'd shoved a shard of mirror into that slot instead of a card. Gonzalo flipped the wallet open. He saw a dashed line drawn across his neck in the same red marker as the note.

Gonzalo spent the whole day furious. There wasn't much he could do. There was no way he could ever make it into the vents again. Instead, he had to try to satisfy himself by throwing hateful glares at every air vent he passed. For a minute, he thought about blocking off all the air vents to the Stairs, but he couldn't put the others through that kind of torture. They'd get no fresh air and the place would be a sauna in a day. It would start to smell worse than it already did.

He refused to let Sasha out of his sight. At first she liked it and found it cute that he was always by her side, but by the end of the day, he could tell she was getting irritated.

"You're not coming in the bathroom with me," Sasha said. They stood outside a girls' bathroom in a second-floor hallway

"I have to."

"Trust me. You don't."

"It's not safe."

"I'm not okay with it. We aren't at that place in our relationship." She smiled.

"What?"

"I like how that sounds. Re-la-tion-ship."

"I still don't want you going in alone."

"Well, I have to go, and boys aren't allowed in the girls' room. That rule's older than, like, the Bible."

Sasha ducked into the bathroom. Gonzalo wanted to follow, but she called out, "Don't be a pervert!" as the door swung shut. He hated it, but he stood guard. Gonzalo twisted his ax around in his hands and smoldered with anger, thinking of all the ways he wanted to hurt Baxter.

He heard half a scream from the ladies' room—a scream cut short. Gonzalo swung around and kicked the door in. As he flew in, he saw Sasha's limp arms disappear into the open duct low in the tiled wall. He rushed across the bathroom and threw his arm into the wall, but she was already out of reach. He could hear Baxter scrambling behind the wall, then up and overhead. Gonzalo frantically followed the sound until he was back out in the hall, still staring up at the ceiling. In that moment, Gonzalo had a flash of how the air ducts were laid out on this floor, a memory from his time in the Mice. He knew there was no way for Baxter to escape without using the main duct running the length of this hallway. So, Gonzalo took his ax, broke through the foam-board ceiling panels, and smashed in the duct until it was impassible. With one move, he'd trapped Baxter in a dead-end stretch of hallway and the rooms that branched off of it.

It was at this point that Gonzalo scared a lot of people. When you're a foot taller than the tallest kids in school, built like a bear, and you run down a hallway jumping up in the air and hacking at air ducts with a fire ax, you tend to look a little mental, but he knew what he was doing. Section by section, room by room, Gonzalo hacked into the ceiling and tore open the ducts with his ax. He didn't care that this was Geek territory—he destroyed every square foot where Baxter could hide, slowly working his way down to the end of the hall, and the Geeks got out of his way. He was forcing Baxter to either retreat into the last possible corner or reveal himself. He devastated the thin metal of the ducts with his heavy ax, until entire sections of eviscerated duct work were falling to the floor.

In the last classroom on the left, Gonzalo found him. Baxter's handsome face was coated in sweat and cobwebs. He'd dropped out of the vent in the wall and was struggling to carry Sasha with his little body. She wasn't moving. There was blood on her face. When Baxter saw Gonzalo, he knew he was screwed. He didn't even try to run. He already knew he wouldn't get away. For a split second, Gonzalo had the itch to swing the ax into Baxter, but he tossed it to the side.

Gonzalo charged forward with all the rage he'd felt toward Baxter for kidnapping him, for threatening his life, for taking Sasha and making her bleed. Gonzalo shoved him to the floor and stomped on him.

Baxter's scream was octaves above any noise he'd ever heard from him. It shocked Gonzalo, but not as much as what he'd done to Baxter's leg. Both bones in Baxter's shin had snapped under Gonzalo's foot, and now the lower half of his shin hung down off his leg like a sock full of meat.

Gonzalo staggered back. He didn't know he could do that. He'd forgotten his strength.

Sasha gasped on the floor behind him, like she was waking up from a nightmare. He rushed to her side and held her face in his hands. She clung to him.

"Are you okay? What did he do to you?"

"He came at me in the bathroom. That's all I remember."

"You're bleeding."

"I am?" she said, and touched her face.

He inspected her forehead and saw that all the blood was coming from a small cut near her hairline.

He glanced back toward Baxter, but he was already being carried off on a folding table by panicked Nerds. They tried to yell into the hall about first-aid kits, but it was hard to hear. Baxter was screaming like he'd been set on fire.

23

GONZALO TURNED OFF THE IGNITION. HOPSCOTCH
Bakery sat across the street from them, a one-story, canary-yellow building on a block of gray, slumping structures. The sun was setting behind it. It had taken them fifteen minutes, maybe less, to find the place once they'd crossed the city limits into Razorville. Gonzalo and Baxter sat in the van in tense silence, staring at the tinted glass front doors of the bakery.

Baxter was his enemy. Always had been. They hadn't even been trying to fake that things were fine for the last forty miles. They'd sat in silence, and Gonzalo had had lots of time to think about what would happen if they found Sasha here, what Baxter might do, and he couldn't figure it out. He never knew what Baxter was going to do.

Gonzalo hopped out of the van and clicked a new filter into his gas mask. Baxter opened his door and took off toward the bakery. Gonzalo was a second behind him. He took big strides across the street, and Baxter hustled in a short-legged limp to beat him to the front doors. He gave the handles a pull. As soon as Gonzalo saw the doors were locked, he cut a path around the building to the back loading dock. He heard Baxter behind him, clomping in a crooked run. Gonzalo spotted a garage-style door where the bread must have been loaded onto a truck once upon a time. The door was closed except for a six-inch gap close to the ground. Gonzalo leaned down, gripped the bottom, and strained to lift the heavy door. It budged, but only moved up a foot. Baxter slipped under the door and disappeared. Gonzalo threw all his strength into heaving the heavy door the rest of the way up. He ran after Baxter, through a packed storage room full of cardboard boxes and metal racks stuffed with bakeware and white plastic buckets. Golden afternoon light flooded the room. He saw a game of "Chutes and Ladders" laid out on top of a box, with buckets arranged around the box like stools.

Gonzalo's pulse quickened. He followed Baxter into a large industrial kitchen lit by a dirty skylight above. Pots and pans hung neatly on the wall. Stainless steel worktables filled the space, and a third of the room was one massive oven. Everything was clean and organized, like it was still in use. Baxter ran straight through the room and into a short, dark hallway. His eagerness made Gonzalo wonder if maybe the guy did know something more than he did after all. Was it that Sasha was here? He ran through the kitchen like an amateur, knowing that moving this fast into uncharted territory could get him shot. But he couldn't be beat by Baxter.

Gonzalo barreled through the short hallway and skidded to a stop when he emerged in the storefront of the bakery. It was bathed in a dull blue light from the tinted front windows that looked out onto the street. Baxter stood perfectly still in front of him with his hands up. Two Loners stood on either side of Baxter, each holding kitchen knives to Baxter's throat. Gonzalo recognized them instantly. He'd hoped to see any Loners other than these two nasty hillbillies. The twins.

Gonzalo had never gotten along with the twins. Everything they'd done in McKinley had been gross. They were always touching each other. They were pale and gaunt, and oily. Their skin was as gray as the moon. Their looks hadn't improved. Their long, stringy hair was slathered with some sort of clumpy grease, and it glistened in the tinted light. The brother had red scratch marks over his neck and collar bones. He wasn't wearing a shirt. He had his free hand down the back of his pants. His mouth hung open when he saw Gonzalo. His sister was wearing two shirts, one of which was too big, her brother's size, with a picture of peanuts on it that said, "Deez nuts." She had a scab covering most of her nose.

"Hey, guys," Gonzalo said, breathing hard. "How you been?"

"Gonzapo," the brother said, his mouth full and cheeks stretched. He was chomping on something.

The sister just giggled, like she always did. Standing there, tittering with a vicious-looking butcher knife pressed into Baxter's Adam's apple, she looked like an escaped mental patient.

"Can you call them the hell off, please?" Baxter said, his hands reaching for the ceiling.

Gonzalo ignored Baxter. "Is Sasha here?" he said.

The twins blinked at him. They cocked their heads and stared at each other.

"Y'all thirsty?" the brother said. He lowered his knife, but the sister didn't. Her focus on Baxter was unflinching. "We got flour."

The brother walked over to an opened one-pound bag of flour on the bakery counter, shoveled out a handful, and stuffed it in his mouth with a poof.

"I'm good," Gonzalo said, scanning the room seriously for the first time. "Is there anybody else here with you two?"

"Yeah, uh-huh," the brother said. Suddenly, his eyes went wide and he raised one finger like he'd just been struck with a brilliant notion. The kid hurried over to an unplugged refrigerator. He opened the door with a yank and revealed mostly empty shelves speckled with black mold. The brother scooped up something sitting on a paper plate and shut the refrigerator door.

The sister, still holding Baxter hostage with the knife scraping his jugular, giggled again and started jumping up and down with excitement. Baxter's eyes bugged out in a panic.

"Whoa, easy! Calm down," Baxter said.

She leaned into his ear and spouted off ten seconds of giddy gibberish. Baxter's eyes locked onto Gonzalo's, looking for him to offer some kind of mercy, but seeing Baxter this vulnerable and scared was one of the few happy moments Gonzalo'd had since teaming up with the asshole.

"What the hell's she saying, man?" Baxter said.

"She wants to know if you're an actual dwarf."

"Go to hell."

Baxter tensed up when the brother twin sidled up to him. The kid held up what he'd pulled from the fridge, a Hot Pocket that had five bites already taken out of it. It was a ham and cheese pocket, by the looks of it, but it was hard to tell because the cheese was dry and the bitten-away parts were caked in a fur of white mold. The brother pointed to a section of one side of the Hot Pocket where no bites had been taken, and held the half-eaten Dumpster delicacy out in front of Baxter's mouth. Baxter didn't dare recoil with the sister at his neck.

"No, thanks," Baxter said.

The door to the bakery's restroom swung open.

"Okay!" a voice said. "Who's ready to find the cure to this darned virus once and for all?"

Nelson, Gonzalo's old gang-mate from the Loners, stepped out. He wore camouflage hunting overalls and a waffled blue longjohn shirt, and was carrying two packed bags and a plastic baking funnel. If Gonzalo had to guess, the funnel was probably Nelson's new ear trumpet.

"Nelson," Gonzalo said, a warm grin cracking his cheeks. He'd always liked Nelson.

Gonzalo's old friend came up to him, stammering and confused, and dropped everything on the floor.

"Gonzalo?"

"Hey, man," Gonzalo said and patted Nelson on the shoulder. The kid wrapped him in a surprising hug.

"I am so glad to see you," Nelson said.

"You too, Nelson. You too."

"No, we don't have YouTube. Are you telling me other places have internet?"

"No, I said, 'You too.'"

"The old band?"

Nelson had always been hard of hearing, but this was impossible. Gonzalo leaned down and picked up Nelson's baking funnel. When Gonzalo handed it to him, Nelson put it to his ear. Gonzalo repeated himself loudly and slowly, making sure to enunciate every syllable. "Nice to see you too!"

"Oh. You too. I guess I already said that. What are you doing here?"

Gonzalo started to answer, but Baxter interrupted with a shout. "Did you say 'cure'?"

Nelson peered over at the weird hostage scenario going on between Baxter and the twins. Baxter had managed to swat away the Hot Pocket. It sat on the cement floor, a crumbly mess. The twins gawked at the moldy meal like Baxter had just hit their family dog with his car.

"I know you," Nelson said and shuffled in Baxter's direction.

"Yeah, yeah, we all escaped McKinley at the same time," Baxter said. "Get back to the cure."

"They're working on the cure in Minnesota."

"Who is?" Baxter said skeptically.

"Doctors at some famous hospital. My girlfriend told me."

"Your girlfriend better be a nurse at that famous hospital if you expect me to believe that."

Nelson shook his head. "She's a Loner. Her name's Trisha."

Baxter guffawed.

"I remember Trisha," Gonzalo said. "Is she here?"

"She's with the other Loners in Gunbarrel. Me and the twins got separated from the Loners ages ago in a hunter attack, and I haven't seen her since. But her dad was a trucker who was really into ham radio. She taught me how to use it. So soon as I found one, I started scouring the airwaves for her."

"Ugh, write a book about it," Baxter said. "Get to the point."

"A few days ago I found her," Nelson said to Gonzalo, ignoring Baxter. "She'd been searching for me the whole time too!" Nelson's smile stretched to his ears.

"You expect us to believe there's a cure to the virus that's killed half of Colorado 'cause your dork girlfriend said so?" Baxter said.

"Trisha wouldn't lie to me," Nelson said. "She just wouldn't. If she says there's a cure, it must be true. She convinced Ritchie and the others to wait three days for us to get there, before they all head out for Minnesota. We're leaving as soon as it gets dark."

Gonzalo was happy for Nelson. To search for his girl for so long and finally find her . . . it almost brought a tear to Gonzalo's eye.

"Hey," Nelson said, still smiling, "you should come with us. It'll be like old times."

"Thing is, I'm looking for Sasha. Is she here with you guys?"

"Oh." Nelson's voice dropped. "She was here for a while."

Gonzalo tried not to let his disappointment show, but he felt his shoulders sink. His hope that Sasha was in this bakery had secretly grown into something solid.

"She left?" Gonzalo said.

"Was she bereft?" Nelson said. "She was crying when she decided to go—a lot actually. She felt really guilty for leaving us, but I didn't blame her. I would have joined Thunder too if they'd wanted me."

"Wait, what's Thunder?"

"It's a gang. They all wear red jumpsuits and—"

"I've seen them," Gonzalo said, thinking back to the dance party and the Radisson. "Why would she want to join them?"

"Everybody wants to join Thunder. They drive around in food trucks slingin' pizzas. They literally make fresh pizzas for anyone who wants them. For free. No one knows how they have so much food, but they're all about sharing. And they're brave too. They drive around in those big trucks like they aren't afraid of getting shot. They say their leader, some guy named Zeus, keeps them safe and provides all the food. They talk about him like he's magic, like he can do anything."

The pit in Gonzalo's stomach swirled. Popular or not, he didn't trust Thunder, or this Zeus, with Sasha. They probably only chose her because she was pretty, which only meant trouble.

"Where did they take her?" Gonzalo said

"I guess back to their home base in Denver."

"Where in Denver?"

"I don't know."

"Great," Baxter said as he elbowed the sister in the gut and slipped out of her grasp. She fell. "Thanks for nothing. Later."

He hopped over the top of the glass pastry counter, unlocked the front door of the bakery, and ran out.

"I gotta go," Gonzalo said to Nelson in a rush, hurrying around the counter after Baxter. Gonzalo yanked open the bakery doors and walked out onto the streets of Razorville, a little wearier than before. Night had fallen quickly, and it was cold. Baxter was standing across the street near the van, facing Gonzalo.

"You should probably turn back now," Baxter said.

"Is that a joke?"

Gonzalo crossed cautiously, but Baxter stayed still.

"If you try to take on Thunder, you'll die. Me, I can get in undercover and not get noticed. I could even join."

"I'm not stopping."

"Look," Baxter said, putting his hands up. "I'm just trying to help. Even if you got there alive, same time as me, it's still gonna end in heartbreak for you."

"What makes you think for a second that Sasha would pick you over me?" Gonzalo said, marching toward Baxter.

Baxter held his ground with eerie assurance, and Gonzalo caught up with him at the van. "I never did tell you what happened after you graduated."

"I'm all ears," Gonzalo said, trying not to sound nervous.

"You remember when you left me with this?"

Baxter pointed to his bent shin.

"Well, I couldn't do too much sneaking around like I used to once you gave me this, now, could I?"

Gonzalo felt a stab of guilt.

"I had to come up with other ways of getting by," Baxter continued. "After I got messed up, the Mice had all bailed on me, and I was getting hungry. That's when I had one of my greatest strokes of good luck in McKinley history. I found a pair of bolt cutters in a janitor's closet off the basement. You know what bolt cutters are good for cutting through? Padlocks on lockers. All of a sudden I had the key to everyone's personal safe—all their stuff that they kept locked away."

"Is there a point to this?"

"Yes, dipshit. The point is . . . I was rich. I was doing better than I ever did in the Mice. I'd even claimed a stretch of ten lockers as my own and used some tinsnips to cut away the metal walls between the lockers so they were all one, big, ten-locker-wide locker. That's how much space I needed to keep all my loot."

"Yeah, ya know, now's as good a time as any to part ways."

"No, wait, you're gonna like this. I was riding high, but some people found out I was the one robbing all the lockers. A lot of people found out, actually, and they locked me inside a locker and left me there to rot. I'd bang on the doors to be let out, but nobody cared."

"Finally, it's getting good."

"Sasha was the one who let me out."

A coyote cackled in the distance. Baxter paused to let it finish, never breaking eye contact with Gonzalo. Gonzalo hated giving Baxter the benefit of an audience, but now he was hooked.

"She found out about me and came by the locker to talk to me."

"No, she didn't."

Baxter nodded. "I told her where I'd hidden the bolt cutters. She was the only one who cared. She cut off the lock, and I'd never been so grateful in my life. It was a life-changing moment for me. I came out of those lockers with an entirely different perspective than before. The lights went out and the food drops stopped, but I didn't care. I was so happy to be alive, and to have her back. It took her a little while to understand, but everything I'd done to her, to you, it had come from my passion for her. From my love."

"You're unbelievable."

"After we escaped McKinley, we were inseparable. And one day, she finally told me that she loved me as much as I loved her. That was the day before the hunters ambushed us. But I gotta tell you, man, it was the best day of my life. When she was lying in my arms—"

"Shut up."

"—we made fun of you. How big and stupid you were, how ugly your big face was. I brought up how you two used to date just to see her cringe and try to shake off the memory. She'd be like, 'Me and who?'"

"You're lying."

"I'm definitely not. You might have been thinking about her this whole time, but I guarantee you she hasn't thought about you in a long time, Gonzo."

Gonzalo got close. There was no getting back in the van together after this. He could feel the potential for violence like static electricity between them.

Baxter leapt up, surprising Gonzalo with how high and far he could jump with his gimp leg, and grabbed hold of Gonzalo's gas mask. Before Gonzalo could get a hold of him, Baxter tore his mask off.

Gonzalo held his breath. Baxter was on the ground and getting up. He had the mask in his hand. Gonzalo lunged for the mask and snagged his finger around one of the straps as Baxter tried to run away with it. Gonzalo yanked, and the mask popped out of Baxter's grip. Baxter ran off, his limp causing him to bob up and down like a hopping rabbit.

Gonzalo dashed in the opposite direction and around the corner. He didn't stop moving until he crashed into a tipped baby stroller in front of a cell phone store. He had to be more than fifty feet upwind of Baxter. He peered back. Baxter was nowhere to be seen. Gonzalo sucked in a breath of fresh air, and his lungs didn't liquify.

He got his mask back on and headed back to the van. Baxter was long gone. The moon highlighted Denver's dead skyline ahead. The black cutouts of the skyscrapers looked like the painted backdrop of a silent movie. Unreal and evil. He needed to get there fast. Faster than Baxter.

24

RED PAJAMAS. HE'D BEEN DRIVING THROUGH
Denver all night in search of kids wearing them. He'd tried
to keep his headlights off as much as he could so that he
wouldn't scare anybody off, but it had made his task next to
impossible. The moonlight was feeble that night because the
sky was congested with clouds. The whisper of light that fell
on the road was just enough to keep him from crashing into
a lamppost. Where the buildings were tall on either side, he
couldn't see the street at all. He'd passed a McDonald's, just
south of the I-70 freeway where the train tracks crossed the
South Platte River, and thought he'd spotted some activity
behind the restaurant. It turned out to only be a pack of dogs,
ripping into a freshly caught cat, but the commotion had gotten Gonzalo out of the van. And outside the van, he was able
to hear voices echoing across the river.

He scrambled down to the rocky shore of the river and found

a quick hiding spot behind the pillar of the railroad trestle. The river was no more than twenty yards wide in this section. Gray moonlight shimmied down the surface of the flowing water and lit up the opposing shore. Four white-haired figures on that shore were tugging on ropes that disappeared under the water. Their union suits were dripping wet, and the red fabric looked nearly black in this light.

He'd found the Thunder members without Baxter. Just that felt good. He'd only spent a couple days with the guy, but in that time, Baxter'd managed to mess with Gonzalo's confidence plenty. He'd started to believe that he'd never find Sasha without Baxter's help.

Gonzalo puzzled over what these Thunder kids were doing. All four boys pulled on the same bolt-straight rope at the same time, like they were playing tug-o-war. They dug their heels into the soft earth of the riverbank. Gonzalo guessed that they'd set traps for fish, but what came rising out of the water wasn't a barnacle-covered cage full of fish. It was a shopping cart full of plastic bottles.

Once the Thunder crew had the shopping cart all the way out of the water and dripping dry in the grass, they moved on to another rope that was rigged the same way. Gonzalo noticed that there were three other ropes disappearing into the water, all under high tension and secured to rebar stakes driven into the ground. The boys muscled against the current of the river to pull another shopping cart full of bottles out of the water. They seemed exhausted after the second cart. One paced around with his arms on his hips, his belly inflating and deflating. Two of them dropped to the ground, and the fourth grabbed four bottles from a cart and tossed one to each of them. They twisted off the tops and took long chugs.

For ten minutes or so, while the Thunder guys lounged on the other side of the water, Gonzalo stayed perfectly still. He had to be patient. Finding out where Thunder lived, and hopefully where Sasha lived, was his only priority. After their break, the Thunder guys pulled up the other two carts. Each of them pulled a shopping cart up to the paved walkway that cut through the grass beyond the river. Once they were on a smooth surface, life got easier for them, and they pushed their carts off ahead of them as they walked.

Unless he was going to run to his van, jump on the highway, cross the river, get off the freeway, and try to find those four Thunder again, he was going to have to cross this river. He hated to abandon his airtight, virus-free van. All of his extra filters were in there, along with his weapons, but his only lead—well, four of them—were strolling away. The Thunder boys were almost out of view.

"Goddamn it," Gonzalo said.

He hurried down to the shore and charged into the rushing black water. Immediately, his nuts attempted to relocate to his ribcage. The farther he walked into the water and the deeper he dipped, the more the cold attacked him. His breaths grew shallow and quick as the frigid water pressed in on him. The current pushed against his chest. Halfway across, his shoes were still on the slippery rocks of the silty riverbed and his head was still above water. He was grateful when his next steps allowed him to rise out of the water, but the whipping wind iced his sopping clothes.

For a moment, he stood at the water's edge and shook. Sitting in the grass at his feet was a sixteen-ounce plastic bottle of Squirt soda. It was unopened. It must have fallen from one of the carts. Gonzalo picked it up. It was cold. Now he understood. They used the river for refrigeration. He shoved it into his sopping-wet pocket. It was late, and he might need the sugar rush. Gonzalo ran in a crouch, trying to cover some of the ground between him and the four members of Thunder. He realized the grassy field that abutted the river was a park, which ended up ahead at a massive parking lot. The four boys in red pushed their carts onto the flat asphalt of the parking lot and picked up speed. Gonzalo was careful not to close the gap between them too much, but the rattle of the carts ensured he wouldn't lose them. The parking lot was a behemoth, the size of two or three football fields, dotted with abandoned cars.

Not all of them were cars, he realized. There were other bulky, dark shapes in front of him, and he didn't realize what they were until he heard them moo. Cows meandered between cars in the parking lot, and some munched on grass at the park's edge. The dull aroma of manure hung in the air. An abandoned stockhouse was nearby, a long warehouse-style building. Beyond it a bigger building, impressive enough to warrant so much parking. He hadn't noticed it at first because he'd been too concerned with staying undetected. The shape of its arched roof was unmistakeable. The Denver Coliseum loomed before him.

The Thunder guys pushed their carts toward the freight doors at the back of the Coliseum. Gonzalo ran from car to car, dodging cows, until he caught up with them at the building. He took cover behind a big-rig trailer that was still parked against the concrete loading dock of the warehouse. He was only twenty feet or so from where the Thunder crew had gathered at a Coliseum freight door. It was as close as he was going to get for now. There was no place else to hide. He'd have to hang back and watch until it was safe.

That turned out to be a long time. Taking breaks was evidently a big part of being Thunder. The boys pushed the carts up onto the loading dock and plopped themselves down for a smoke, which was just about the cruelest thing they could have done to Gonzalo. Since teaming up with Baxter, Gonzalo hadn't been able to have a cigarette because he'd had to keep his mask on. On the drive to Denver, finally alone, he hadn't been able to find his last pack. With the clock ticking to beat Baxter, finding cigarettes wasn't exactly his top priority now.

But with the wind pressing his soaked clothes to him, transforming him into the world's biggest popsicle, he would have killed for a drag. A large part of him wanted to walk over and bum one.

Gonzalo was shivering so badly he was afraid the Thunder crew would hear his teeth chattering over the droning moos. When the boys lit up their second round of cigarettes, he threw up his hands in frustration. He dipped his finger in a puddle at his feet and held it up to test the direction of the wind. He was less than twenty feet from them, but the wind was blowing pretty strongly toward the Thunder guys. He pulled his gas mask up on top of his head so that his face was exposed and pulled out the bottle of Squirt. He cracked the cap slowly to lessen the noise. He took a sip, careful to keep his eye on the four Thunder, then downed the whole bottle. Hopefully the sugar would keep him alert as he waited.

A roll-up door at the Coliseum's freight entrance opened with a metallic screech. A dim, warm light flooded out. A new Thunder member, also in red pajamas, stood silhouetted under the door. The four smokers rolled their soda carts into the Coliseum. The guy operating the door pulled the segmented metal door back down.

Gonzalo ran up to the loading dock and tried to pull up the door, but it was already locked. There was a second freight door beside it. As he moved to check it, the first door he'd just checked screeched open again. Gonzalo plastered himself up against the second door. Four more Thunder kids exited, again pushing shopping carts full of soda bottles, as well as bottles of milk, chocolate milk, orange juice, six-packs of beer, and sports drinks back toward the river. None of them noticed him there in the dark.

This was his best shot at getting inside. Gonzalo stepped into the doorway. Immediately the Thunder boy inside the Coliseum, with his hand still on the bottom edge of the door, took a sharp breath in, but before he could use that breath to scream, Gonzalo hit him on the jaw, and the kid hit the ground, unconscious.

Gonzalo whipped inside and yanked the garage-style door down just as one of the shopping-cart-pushers was starting to turn around. He spotted an open padlock dangling beside the door and wasted no time putting it in place and locking it. He didn't think the guy had seen him, but better to be sure.

He turned and took in his surroundings. An antique pewter candleholder hung on the concrete wall. Its three candles were the only source of light in the high-ceilinged room. It was an empty loading area. A forklift was parked near a wall of stacked pallets. Gonzalo turned to the unconscious Thunder boy on the ground. He took off his high-tops and used the laces to tie the Thunder's left wrist to his right ankle and his right wrist to his left ankle, all behind his back. He gagged the guy with one of his own socks and carried him to a dark corner behind the pallets. The kid was bound to wake up soon. He had to get moving.

He took the candleholder off the wall and moved toward the heart of the Coliseum. He was careful not to walk too fast and extinguish the three candles. The darkness surrendered to the light he cast, for at least six feet in front of him. Whenever he forgot to hold it straight, hot wax would spill onto his arm. He walked through the dark room and found a dormant escalator leading up. The metal teeth of the stairs gleamed like rows of knives in the light of the three candles. At the top, he stepped off into a long hallway that appeared to run the length of the building, the end disappearing as it curved left around the stadium center. It was sectioned by concrete arches, and he felt like he was inside the ribcage of a dead dinosaur. Random torches and more candleholders illuminated the hall, dotting the dark corridor with spots of warmth. The concession stands were empty, the gift shops closed, and the kiosks knocked over. The high ceiling sloped at a forty-five-degree angle, giving the corridor a triangular shape.

He could make out the distant sound of people. A lot of people. But it was faint, and he couldn't see them. The sound echoed off the bones of the Coliseum.

Movement ahead startled Gonzalo. He darted behind a concrete wall and put out his candles with three quick, stinging pinches since blowing them out was impossible in a gas mask.

He snuck a look around the wall and watched a group of girls exit a bathroom, cross the hall, and walk up the stairs that led to seating section C-11. They wore red, full-body pajamas, just like the boys he'd seen. The outfit looked better on girls. It looked best on one girl in particular. Sasha.

25

IT WAS HER. GONZALO COULDN'T BREATHE.
After months of imagining where she might be, how she might be, what she would look like if she was even alive . . . now he was within shouting distance of her. And it took every square inch of willpower he had not to scream her name so that it bounced off the cold concrete walls and up the stairs to where she was just turning the corner out of sight. He yearned to see her stop, for her head to turn slowly, for her mouth to drop when she saw him.

Gonzalo started after her, but a group of seven Thunder boys appeared at the top of the stairs, tromped halfway down and sat in the middle. They blocked his way. They were a bee sting to the balls. He had to find another way up.

Gonzalo stuck to the shadows and snuck past the stairway. He moved down the hall in the direction he'd seen Sasha go. She was inside the arena, and he was just below her in the hall that wrapped around the arena. His hope was that he could beat her to the next stairway. He ran. Charged up with a fizzing cocktail of adrenaline and love. He'd never felt anticipation like this. He was a bolt of lightning, ready to strike a wet tree.

He slowed when he reached the next staircase, and peeked around the corner. He gritted his teeth in frustration. Thunder kids were gathered at the top of the stairs, their backs to Gonzalo. He pushed on, hoping that maybe the next staircase would be clear, but the farther he moved away from where he'd first seen Sasha walk up, the more anxious he became. What if he was wrong about where she was headed? What if every step he was taking was actually *away* from her?

The next stretch of hallway had a long window running down the outside wall, nearly the entire length of this end of the building. Hundreds of empty black folding chairs sat lined up, basking in the moonlight. The area must get plenty of sunlight in the day, and he imagined that it was a pretty luxurious place to lounge if you'd been used to running for your life every day.

His mind skipped back to seeing Sasha when she'd walked out of the bathroom with those other girls. She'd looked healthy and unharmed. She had seemed upset, though. In the short flash he'd had of her face, he could've sworn that she'd been furrowing her brow. She certainly hadn't been joking around. In fact, none of the girls around her had been smiling. His heart rate was galloping. His head felt stuffed up, congested almost. This was too much. His brain throbbed with one thought: Sasha is here. Sasha is here. Sasha is here.

He passed under one tall archway after another, deeper into the dinosaur's guts. The next staircase, the next opportunity to ascend to the level where Sasha was, had people milling about at the top as well. He hid behind a column, looking up. Gonzalo's heart teetered over a pit of despair, threatening to ruin him, but then he saw Sasha again.

She was with that same group of girls. They walked past the top of the stairs with long, purposeful strides, going the same direction as Gonzalo was. He hadn't lost her, he was dead on track with her, and the synchronicity had him feeling like their reunion was destined.

Gonzalo wanted to cry, to yell out. He was feeling so much all at once. He ran on to the next set of stairs, aiming to intercept her, but the floor was covered in empty plastic soda bottles, and crunching them would have called attention to himself. He had to hop from one clear patch of floor to the next, knowing it was slowing him down and helpless to do anything about it. At the next staircase, he arrived just in time to see the last of Sasha's crew disappear past the top of the stairs.

At least the stairway was clear. As he took the first step up, Baxter crossed the top of the stairs above, wearing a red union suit with a sagging crotch. His compact body and limping creep were unmistakable. He was only a few paces behind Sasha and the girls.

No-no-no-no—

Gonzalo was about to rush up the stairs, but a cluster of Thunder members stepped into view behind Baxter. Gonzalo sprinted down the hall, past lunch tables, and slid to a stop at the candlelit bottom of the next staircase, sending a spray of plastic bottles scuttling across the floor without even caring. He'd moved so fast he figured Sasha should walk by at any second, and he would do something to get her attention. He didn't know what, but he'd come up with something. It had to happen. It was going to happen.

Seconds passed. And more seconds. Sasha didn't come walking past the top of the stairs with her crew. Neither did Baxter. Finally, for the first time, there was no one at the top of the stairs.

Gonzalo climbed the stairs on legs that felt like taffy melting in the sun. The fear of what awaited him was making him woozy. One foot after another. The stairs felt soft.

He heard people in the stadium. The sound grew with each stair until it filled his ears. Another couple of steps and he'd be visible to anyone who passed or looked in his direction. He kept going.

Sasha is here. Sasha is here.

A steady drumming arose in the arena. The beat punched at the air. It was hypnotic. Gonzalo poked his head up until he could see the arena clearly for the first time.

"Jesus, Mary, and Joseph," Gonzalo said.

The place was gargantuan. Bigger than his memory of it as a kid. Red pajamas crowded the stadium seating below him and the Coliseum floor down below that, like a field of crimson clovers. Sixty or seventy fires burned in fire pits across the Coliseum floor, stairs, and box seating, pulsing like stars in a planetarium. Together, they provided a warm raspberry and honey glow in the huge space. Where Gonzalo stood remained dark enough that he had a good chance of traveling through the arena unnoticed.

He kept moving. The threat of Baxter's voice in Sasha's ear still drove him. He could only be so cautious. When he looked more closely at the Coliseum floor, he saw that Thunder were gathered in a semicircle on a half-constructed stage. Guys were baring naked chests, keeping their red pajamas from falling down by tying the sleeves around their waists. They pounded on the floor with rhythmic slaps while others flailed and danced before them.

Past the stage and the drummers, half of the Coliseum floor was taken up by a bed. Not one giant, seamless mattress, but countless mattresses with white fitted sheets that had been pushed up against each other. The collective bed was half the size of a basketball court, filled with Thunder, all lying down in a circle. There was an outer ring of boys, containing circular rows of lounging girls, and at the very center, with girls clutching his legs, draping themselves over him, and nuzzling up next to him as they slept, there was a guy in a gas mask.

26

GONZALO CREPT IN A CROUCH, JUST ON THE
edge of darkness, trying to make sense of what he was seeing,
when he saw something he couldn't believe. A shotgun lying
in one of the seats, one row in front of him. Firelight from a
distant flame gleamed off its cold metal barrel. He blinked
once in disbelief, then reached over the seat and took it up
in one hand. He gripped the chestnut stock and cracked
open the single-fire chamber. One unfired shell gleamed. He
clicked the barrel back into place. The sound was sweet. For-
tune favored him.

Gonzalo scanned the stadium. There were hundreds upon
hundreds of Thunder kids. He hated the idea that he might be
looking right at Sasha and have no idea.

He had to get out of the dark section of the bleachers and
head toward the light. That was the only way he'd be able
to see. They might be able to see him too, but he was out of

options. He edged toward the nearest fire, about two hundred feet away, in the next seating section.

As he got closer, his skin rose into goosebumps. He saw a pair of red pajamas draped over the back of one of the seats. His gas mask was a dead giveaway, but maybe the pajamas would allow him to blend in somewhat. Gonzalo struggled to pull them on over his clothes. The pajamas were too tight around his body. He could feel stitches ripping and fabric splitting, but the flannel was so soft he couldn't stop running his hands up and down it, enjoying the sensation against his palms. It was softer than anything he'd worn in years. It felt so good he didn't want to stop. Then he caught himself.

What the hell was he doing?

He felt a bolt of panic when he realized he didn't know how long he'd been rubbing the flannel. What was he doing focusing on the feel of his pajamas like there was nothing else in the world?

Gonzalo's gaze went back to the guy in the center of the bed on the Coliseum floor, surrounded by dozens of prone Thunder girls and boys—although the Thunder closest to him seemed to be all girls. That had to be Zeus. His face was obscured by the glaring shield of his gas mask. What kind of uninfected person in their right mind would lounge in a den of poison?

Gonzalo's eye caught movement nearby. Sasha was charging down the stairs toward the Coliseum floor, flanked by the same group of Thunder girls. She looked angry. They all did.

"Baby, what are you doing?" Gonzalo muttered.

When Sasha and her crew hit the Coliseum floor, they headed straight for Zeus. The girls walked on the mattresses. They stormed toward the man in the gas mask, stepping over sleeping people, stepping *on* some of them by accident. The closer they got to the man in the mask, the more the sleeping Thunder seemed to notice. They lifted their heads off the beds to glare at Sasha and the others.

Gonzalo's anxiety rose as Sasha cut through the inner circle of girls and finally reached Zeus. She stood over him and stuck her finger in his face, an inch from his gas mask. The affront created an agitated ripple through the surrounding Thunder.

"Get outta there, girl," Gonzalo said softly.

Sasha kept wagging her finger in Zeus's face. She was giving him a piece of her mind. It made Gonzalo anxious. Zeus stood up to face Sasha. She gave him an angry push. The drumming stopped dead, and all the Thunder across the entire expansive mattress jumped to their feet. The standing crowd swallowed up his view of Sasha.

Gonzalo's stomach dropped. He charged forward, bounding over rows of seats until he reached the walkway of the next level down. He ran to the nearest stairs. He pulled the shotgun to his shoulder, and his finger found the trigger. He prayed that he wouldn't have to kill anybody.

Thunder boys and girls sat on the stairs below him. Gonzalo barreled past them, knowing they were watching him now. He knew this was a grave mistake, but he didn't have a choice. Sasha was in trouble. When his feet hit the Coliseum floor, he heard a storm of whispers saying, "Look, look!" A muffled yelp cut through the air from the bed. It sounded like Sasha. He broke into a full sprint, and the stadium came alive.

Shouts and howls. Fire pits being knocked over and burning logs pouring down the stands. A girl sang high and fast. He heard dogs bark. He swore he heard his grandmother's distinctive snore, a noise he knew by heart because her room had been next to his when he was a kid and the walls in his family's house had been thin. He staggered in his run.

He knew that every member of Thunder was watching him now. The shotgun in his hands was his chance. He had only one shot, and they would probably eat him alive right afterwards. The thought washed over him that he wasn't getting out of this.

His feet hit mattress, and the soft ground changed his stride, slowing him down. Twenty feet ahead of him was the crowd of Thunder who'd surrounded Sasha. They were watching him approach. He lifted the shotgun and pressed his cheek against it. Wherever he turned his head, the gun turned with him. The mattress felt gooey underneath him, like he was sinking deeper into melted marshmallow with every step.

For some reason, maybe because of the gun, the crowd parted in front of him, making a passageway lined with bodies. Zeus appeared deep within the cavity of the crowd and came walking calmly down the passageway they'd made for him. With each step, Zeus grew taller. Gonzalo stopped. He couldn't believe what he was seeing. Zeus closed the distance until they were two feet apart, and Zeus stood at least three feet taller than Gonzalo.

Gonzalo kept the shotgun aimed at Zeus's chest. "Everybody keep their distance," Gonzalo shouted through the muffle of his gas mask. He hoped he didn't sound as scared as he was.

Zeus raised his hands up, and it seemed to be a signal because all the Thunder moved back. Gonzalo stood perfectly still, but he felt like the mattress underneath him was bobbing him like a milk jug on top of the ocean. He kept his eyes on Zeus looming over him. He wore the same style gas mask as Gonzalo, and he wore his red union suit unbuttoned to mid-belly. His face was obscured by the reflection of fire stretching across his face shield.

"Why is he here?" someone said.

"Are they coming for us?" someone else said. "Do we have to leave?"

"No, no," Zeus said. "Be calm."

Zeus was bigger than any human being Gonzalo had ever seen. He had to be nine feet tall, maybe ten.

"Sasha!" Gonzalo called out, but he didn't hear her voice. The crowd of Thunder gasped and tittered at Sasha's name. Gonzalo thrust the gun at Zeus. "Where is she? Bring her out or I'll blow a hole through your chest."

Laughs spouted out of the crowd.

"Are you sure about that?" Zeus said, and he pointed at the shotgun.

Gonzalo let his eyes drop to the gun in his hands. The shotgun was gone. In its place was something closer to a toy gun. Stuffed in its big, clear plastic barrel was about nine inches of pink fabric. It was a T-shirt cannon. Gonzalo looked back up at Zeus. He saw his own confused and frightened face reflected back at him amid fire.

Gonzalo pulled the trigger, and the pink fabric wad thumped Zeus in the chest and dropped to the mattress.

Zeus laughed, and the Thunder echoed him with peals that bounced off the walls and ceiling. Someone picked up the clump of fabric and spread it to reveal a T-shirt with the Arby's logo on it. Gonzalo stumbled backward, staring again at the T-shirt cannon in his hands, trying to understand. It had been a shotgun. He'd felt the heft of a wood stock, of cold steel. He hadn't taken his hands off it since he'd picked it up. He was losing his mind. This was how it happened. People aren't born schizophrenic. They grow up normal until one day, from out of nowhere, their brain cracks in half.

Gonzalo swayed on the gooey mattress, trying to keep his balance, but he toppled over and landed on his back. Hands converged on him. Grabbed him. Pinned him down. Fingers hooked through the straps of his mask.

Zeus stepped into view, towering even more over Gonzalo

now that he was pressed down to the mattress. Thunder stepped in too, and he felt like he was looking up from the bottom of a deep pit. Their pajamas were gone. They were all nude, but their skin was red all over, the same red as the pajamas.

"Where's Sasha?" Gonzalo said. He could hear his voice trembling. "She was just here. I saw her."

Multicolored light sprang from Zeus's head, as if Gonzalo were viewing him through a series of prisms. He tried to focus on the guy's face, but again, he only saw his own frightened reflection, small and stretched.

"You shouldn't have come here," Zeus said.

"Will he bring others?" one of the Thunder asked.

"Yes," Gonzalo said, panting, trying to swallow his fear. "There are others. If I'm not back outside in five minutes, the rest of my team will come in. They've got guns. You hand Sasha over, and you'll never see me again."

Zeus stared at him again, reflecting Gonzalo's confusion back down at him. He'd never felt smaller in his life. Zeus sang a high, clean note. Other Thunder kids sang in harmony, and then more. Gonzalo heard the sound of their chorus travel around the whole Coliseum, like the wave at a football game. Eventually, it became softer and more distant, until he could barely hear it. All the Thunder looked off, as if they were waiting for something. A moment later, the sound traveled back through the room, except lower now, voices picking it up and passing it to each other like an Olympic torch, until the stadium was filled with that low tone.

"There's no one else out there," Zeus said. "What other lies do you have for us?"

Gonzalo tried to struggle to his feet, but hands still held him down. He felt like he was sinking deeper into the mattress, like his bones were softening, like his muscles were dying.

"Let go of me," Gonzalo said.

"Take him away," Zeus said.

Thunder hands lifted Gonzalo to his feet. His mind swirled like a flushing toilet.

"My power protects us all," Zeus said to his followers. With his next sentence, every Thunder in the stadium spoke in unison. "Trust in Thunder. Believe in Zeus. Be free."

Blazing-red Thunder shoved Gonzalo away from Zeus, walking him toward the edge of the bed. What had to be twenty pairs of red hands were pushing him, gripping him, as the ground wobbled under his feet and the crowd hissed.

"Where is she?!" Gonzalo shouted. He wrenched his arms from the Thunder's grasp and threw them off. Nude red bodies toppled away from him. He whipped around to face Zeus again, but to his horror and shock, Zeus had grown. He was taller than a telephone pole now. His head was so high that the surrounding fires' light didn't even reach it. Everything above his shoulders was darkness.

Zeus's voice boomed from up high: "You'll never find her."

I will, Gonzalo thought in spite of everything he was seeing. *I will.*

Gonzalo mustered his last ounce of bravery and stepped forward, but the ground began to tilt like a seesaw. It was as if he were walking up a forty-five-degree incline, and the angle grew steeper by the second. Gravity betrayed him. Before he knew it, the mattress floor was now a wall and he clung to the edge of a mattress for dear life. His feet dangled.

Mattresses around the one he was clinging to began to fall away and whip past him. Thunder members were stuck to some, oblivious to what was happening. He heard splashes below, and when he looked down, he saw a lake of blood. The blood bubbled and frothed into a pink foam, its surface swept by a wind he couldn't feel.

Gonzalo started to scream. Zeus laughed at him. Gonzalo looked up and saw that gravity still functioned normally for Zeus. He stood perpendicular to Gonzalo, his huge feet only inches from Gonzalo's fingers.

"Do you see how he trembles before my power?" Zeus said.

Gonzalo was convinced now. Zeus was doing all of this, somehow. He was making the world go haywire. He really was magic, like Nelson had said.

"Make it stop!" Gonzalo said.

"No."

Zeus stepped on Gonzalo's fingers, and his precarious hold

on the lip of his mattress gave out. Gonzalo fell. He plummeted across the room, or down—he couldn't tell anymore—spinning and tumbling through the air. His scream was silenced when he plunged headfirst into the blood.

Down into the thick red plasma he sank. Deeper and deeper, into the dark and cold, until all he could see was black, until the blood seeped into his mask and filled his mouth with a cold syrup that tasted like copper and chalk. He couldn't feel anything but the cold, and he was left alone with the knowledge that he'd come within a hair of getting the only thing he'd ever wanted, and failed.

27

GONZALO'S GUMMY EYELIDS PEELED APART
and he found himself lying on frigid concrete. There was no blood inside his mask. No blood anywhere inside the small room. An LED camping lantern with solar charging panels sat in the corner and shone a thin light on the area. Gonzalo shivered. He was surrounded by half-open boxes of Denver Cutthroats souvenir jerseys, caps, and earmuffs, and stacks of twenty-four-ounce clear plastic cups, each emblazoned with a cartoon bull rider. Every stack was enclosed in crinkly plastic wrapping. There was a wasp on the face shield of his gas mask, rubbing its legs together and moving in twitches too fast to see. It flew away.

"You shouldn't have come here."

The voice had come from behind him. Gonzalo twisted around to see Zeus. He stood in the hall outside with the door only open a foot. He wasn't twenty feet tall anymore. He was normal-sized, about six feet. Torchlight flickered in from the hall behind him, leaving his face cloaked in shadow. Gonzalo scrambled away from the door. He didn't want the ground to start tilting again or the lake of blood to reappear. He could still feel the cold blood on his skin, the way it had tasted in his mouth, the sick feeling of it flooding into his lungs when he couldn't hold out any longer and inhaled. Zeus had been responsible somehow. He'd reached into Gonzalo's mind and pulled it apart like slow-cooked pork.

"I'm sorry that you're going to die here," Zeus said, "but you brought it on yourself."

The hint of regret in his voice sounded genuine. Or maybe it was shame. Gonzalo strained and was able to make out a face behind the mask for a moment, but then Zeus shut the door. The lock engaged with a heavy metallic clunk.

Gonzalo sucked in a breath. He hadn't realized he'd been holding his breath, but now he noticed that each inhale came easily. Too easily. His hand went to his mask, and he felt the plastic latching mechanism. Someone had taken the filter off of his mask while he was unconscious.

Gonzalo shuddered. Zeus hadn't been bullshitting. Without a filter, Gonzalo's death was imminent, and it wouldn't be slow. He eyed the crack of firelight from the hall lining the bottom of the closed door. The light ebbed and flowed. Not only would that crack let in the virus, but the Coliseum beyond was teeming with infected. He could crumple up the plastic sleeves that

278

were sealing the cup stacks all around him and stuff them into the crack. But how long could bunched plastic protect him? The virus would seep in somehow, like it did for the seniors in McKinley, accumulate in his lungs particle by particle, and destroy him from the inside out.

This was the end of the road. In a souvenir closet. Just another body in some dark corner of Colorado. He'd pushed his luck way too far. All those near-death experiences had been warnings to turn back, and he'd been too stupid to listen.

His family had told him the same. They'd said he was insane to head back into the infected zone. His father had called him a fool. His mother'd said it would be the biggest mistake of his life. He'd ignored them. They just didn't understand—that was what he'd thought. They couldn't understand because they didn't know Sasha. They didn't know how much she meant to him. As soon as his family had gotten word of his plans, when his cousin had snitched on him, they'd tried to stop him. They wouldn't let him be alone for even a minute. There was always a family member with him. Every time he thought he'd escaped their watch, he'd realize another family member was following, ready to tackle him if they saw him try to get in a car or make any effort to leave the neighborhood.

They'd been living in a temporary community with hordes of other displaced Colorado residents about five miles outside of Chapel, New Mexico. They lived in a drafty modular house provided by the government, just like all the other families in the area. Even though they were all reeling from the upheaval of leaving their home and the virus paranoia, it had been the first time that his entire extended family had lived together in the same place. His uncles, aunts, grandparents, cousins he'd never met before—they were all living, sleeping, and eating within a one-hundred-foot radius of each other. Despite the fear and death and tragedy, it had been good. When he'd made it out of the infected zone, they threw him a Welcome Home party that was more enthusiastic than any birthday celebration he'd ever had. It was like he'd won a gold medal at the Olympics and brought honor to the family name. He'd known how much they loved him in that moment, and he'd felt the same toward them. Now, he felt idiotic for ever leaving them.

He should have stayed. He'd be in the family kitchen at this moment. His mother would be working her magic, turning what supplies they had into the closest imitation she could make of old family recipes. He'd have to live with the uncertainty of not knowing what had happened to Sasha. His pride would have been wounded, he would have battled with guilt, probably would have sunk into depression over it off and on for the rest of his life, but he'd have been safe, alive, around other uninfected people. He wouldn't be waiting to die.

Finally he understood what his parents had been trying to tell him. He'd been so defensive, he'd thought they'd been attacking Sasha's character. But what they had really been saying was that maybe Gonzalo was more swept up in high-school love than he should have been. He and Sasha hadn't actually dated that long, and Gonzalo had been acting like people didn't move on. Sasha was one of the Thunder now. She had adapted. That didn't mean that she'd never loved Gonzalo, but plenty of time had passed since he'd seen her last. She could have fallen for someone else. The infected zone was hard, and the littlest bit of comfort went a long way out there. For all he knew, what Baxter had told him was true. And if it was, who could blame her for wanting some comfort when there was so much harshness around? Sasha never knew that Gonzalo was tearing up Colorado trying to find her. It wasn't her fault that he was so naïve.

How much anguish had he put his family through this whole time he'd been gone? Had his mother gone to sleep even once without fearing he was dead? When he died here on this floor, would they ever find out? Or would they still think he was alive somewhere, and would his dad promise his mother that he'd come looking for him? Gonzalo sobbed.

Something dropped from above and landed with a harsh clang on the floor between his legs. He reached out and touched it. It was a metal vent cover from an open air duct high on the wall.

The duct was barely visible in the gray light. Another object came flying out of the open duct and skittered across the floor, stopping a half foot from the door. Gonzalo instantly recognized what it was—a gas-mask filter sealed in a plastic pouch. He grabbed it, tore open the bag, and jammed the filter onto the front of his mask until he heard a click. His next inhale had that familiar drag that meant he wasn't going to die.

A moment later, Baxter poked his head out of the wall with a small flashlight held between his teeth. He spit the flashlight into his hand and pointed it at Gonzalo.

"As usual, you're useless without me," Baxter said.

Gonzalo squinted in the flashlight's harsh beam. After what he'd experienced in the stadium, he didn't feel sure about anything. He could've been staring at an electrical socket. He spoke cautiously. "Are you here?"

"Uh, yeah, dumbfuck. What kind of question is that?"

The anger that flared inside him helped convince him that Baxter was real. No conjured-up version of Baxter could be as grating on him as the real thing.

"Are you crying?" Baxter said.

Gonzalo moved his hand to wipe the wetness from his cheeks, but the barrier of his gas mask prevented it.

"Oh, my god!" he said. "You were!"

"It's sweat."

"What a pussy!"

"Why are you here?" Gonzalo snapped.

"I came to let you out."

"And why would you want to do that?"

"I need your help."

"You want me to help you? After you tried to kill me in Razorville?"

"You're paranoid, man. I didn't try to kill you. I just needed to get away from you."

"How dumb do you think I am?"

"You don't want me to answer that."

Gonzalo studied Baxter's pale face in the white glow of the flashlight and frowned.

Baxter sighed. "Thunder took Sasha and those other girls to Zeus's quarters. I know where it is."

Gonzalo's heart jumped at the mention of Sasha's name. She was real too. He hadn't imagined her. Still, he hesitated. Baxter always had a way of forcing him into vulnerable situations. Once again, though, Gonzalo didn't see any other choice.

"If you already know where he is, what do you need me for?" Gonzalo said.

"I need you to beat people up."

Gonzalo stood up.

"That I can do."

28

GONZALO'S KNUCKLES WERE SPLIT. HE'D
already knocked out three Thunder boys on the journey down
to the subterranean levels of the Coliseum. While he got the
thankless job of walking the halls, Baxter crept along in the
safety of the ducts. For the last twenty minutes, Gonzalo had
been following Baxter's taps and whispers. He'd tap three
times on the metal of the duct somewhere ahead so that Gonzalo would know which way to turn. It'd been five minutes
since he'd heard anything.

His only relief was that the hallway ahead was empty. The
LED camping lantern swung from his fingers as he walked
on, and the sweep of its meager light kept him from tripping
over fallen chairs and stray cardboard boxes. The hall ended
at a set of stairs to his left, and a glossy door to his right. The
stairs probably led to some sort of boiler room or the guts of
the Coliseum. Gonzalo listened carefully for directions from

Baxter. Maybe the guy was playing catch-up. Gonzalo remembered from being in the Mice that you had to spread your weight out as much as you could to not make noise. Forearms were better than palms. To slither on your stomach was best, but it was slow.

There was a soft thump behind Gonzalo, and he turned back to see Baxter crouched in the hallway. Baxter motioned for him to come close, and he did.

"Now what?" Gonzalo said.

"Behind that door is a hallway. There's three offices on either side. At the end of it is another door. That's where Zeus is."

"Okay, so . . ."

"So, all the offices on the way down are guards' quarters. They're the biggest and toughest kids in Thunder, 'cause they protect Zeus. I can get into Zeus's room, but if anything goes wrong, those guys are rushing in. And some asshole gave me a gimp leg awhile back, so I can't do much. So, you gotta take care of them."

"What do you mean, 'take care of them'?"

"Do your thing."

"I don't have a *thing*. I'm not Wolverine."

"Just do whatever you have to do. We've got the element of surprise right now. We've got to use it so that they can't stop me once I drop out of the vent into his room."

"Yeah, and what exactly is gonna happen once I 'take care' of all those guards for you and you're nice and secure inside Zeus's room? What's stopping you from getting Sasha to crawl into the vents with you and just get the hell out of here without me?"

Baxter's face was grave. "'Cause she's not there."

"What?"

"I already went ahead and looked through the vent. Zeus's there, but she's not."

Gonzalo shook his head in frustration. He wanted to be mad at Baxter, but he didn't have good reason to be. Baxter had said she was there, but that was awhile ago. Who knew what Zeus had done with her in the meantime?

"Look," Baxter said, "if we get to Zeus and we hold him hostage, he'll have to take us to wherever Sasha is, and Thunder will have to lay off. It's the only way we're getting out of this. There's too many of them."

"I never trust you when you're being nice."

"Don't worry," Baxter went on. "I'm not gonna kill you till we get out of here."

Gonzalo did a double-take.

"I thought you weren't trying to kill me."

Baxter shrugged. "I lie sometimes."

"So, it's like that, huh?"

"It's always been like that, Gonzo," Baxter said. He flicked his fingers toward the end of the hall, like he was dismissing Gonzalo. "Chop-chop."

Baxter pushed a swivel chair under the vent he'd just dropped out of and climbed back up.

"Baxter," Gonzalo whispered. Baxter paused and looked back at him.

Before he faced Zeus again, Gonzalo needed answers about what'd happened before in the arena, but could he really bring himself to ask Baxter if Zeus was actually some kind of sorcerer? Or was he more than that? Was he some god on earth who'd perverted the laws of physics inside that arena?

He couldn't do it. Baxter would just use it as an opportunity to mess with his head.

"See you on the other side," Gonzalo said.

Baxter nodded. "I'll be waiting."

Gonzalo rounded the corner and faced the door. Piled up on either side of the door was office equipment. Computer monitors, broken printers, broken chairs, spools of ethernet cord, extension cords, filing drawers, and hole-punches. Gonzalo let out a heavy breath and turned off the camping lantern. All kinds of trouble waited on the other side of this door. A weapon would have been nice. He placed his hand on the knob, twisted it, and pushed the door slowly open. At the end of the torchlit hallway was a door with the large "Z" burned into it, and just like Baxter had said, there were six offices lining the hallway, three on either side. Every door was closed. If Gonzalo could have it his way, those doors would stay closed. A crazy idea came to him. He stepped back and looked at the piles of office junk. He eyed three coils of extension cord. He looked back at the doors running the length of the hall. The door hinges were on the inside, so if he tied the doorknob of one door to the doorknob directly across the hall, then neither door would be able to open. If he did this for each pair of doors, the guards would never be able to get out of their quarters, as long as his knots stayed secure.

Gonzalo bent over and picked up a coil of orange extension cord. He set to work tying the cord around the first knob. He took great care to be slow and make as little noise as possible as he cinched the first knot tight. He doubled and tripled the knot and tied the cord tightly to the door across the hall. He was sweating and breathing a little harder, but the cord was on securely. The knobs had barely even creaked through the process. He heard an occasional murmur from behind two of the doors, but no sign that they knew what was happening. He moved on to the next two doors, and everything went perfectly like before, except for the fact that he couldn't stop staring at the door with the "Z" burned into it. With the second set of doors tied off and a high-tension cord between them, he knotted the third extension cord to the first knob of the final pair of doors.

He was stretching the cord across the hall to the last doorknob, just about to secure it, when that door opened. A Thunder boy with a jagged pink scar across his throat stepped into view, holding a hunting knife. His long face bunched in hatred, he bared his rotten, blackening teeth and charged.

"Shit," Gonzalo said.

The Thunder maniac lunged at him with the hunting knife. Gonzalo fell back as the gleam of metal whizzed past his mask.

The door he'd just tied off opened behind him, and he yanked the door shut again with the cord in his hand.

The knife-wielder swung at him again. Gonzalo grabbed his arm with his free hand and wrenched it clockwise, hard enough to send the kid head over heels. He heard the guy's shoulder pop, and a scream.

A weird sound rose up from behind the door he was still holding shut with the extension cord. It was a grunting kind of sound that came in short bursts, like a pig rooting for slop under its trough. The grunt morphed into a mechanical roar so loud and terrifying it made Gonzalo's nuts shrivel.

Chainsaw, he thought.

The guy on the other side managed to pull the door open half a foot, and a bluish poof of exhaust burst out. Gonzalo wrapped the cord around his fist and tugged the door shut again. He pulled on the cord like he was dragging a plow. The four doors he'd already tied shut began to rattle, and the cords between them wobbled. The other guards were trying to get out. Gonzalo's knots were holding.

A piercing pain in his thigh made Gonzalo drop the cord entirely. He looked down to see the other Thunder's knife buried into his leg. The popped-out shoulder hadn't stopped him. Gonzalo palmed the back of his head like a basketball and held it in place as he smashed his other fist into the Thunder's face. Gonzalo felt the nose shatter under his knuckles.

The chainsaw revved behind him. Gonzalo dove to the side, and the pain from the stab wound throbbed. He rolled onto his back and saw a wiry Thunder boy in an adult diaper, holding a chainsaw over his head. Why did he have to go and drop the cord?

Gonzalo ripped the blade from his thigh. The chainsaw wielder charged toward him, with the chainsaw out in front of him like a spear and smoke spitting out of its exhaust. Gonzalo was barely able to get up on two feet before the guy was on him and the roaring blade was swinging down.

He threw the hunting knife up to block with it, as if he were in a sword fight. He didn't know what else to do. The spinning teeth of the saw ripped the knife from Gonzalo's hand and severed his pinkie and half of his ring finger.

But his attacker had too much momentum for his swing, and he flew forward with his arms stretched out to brace for a hard landing. And he did land hard. The chainsaw hit the floor first, kicking the spinning saw back at the kid. It sliced through his skull like wedding cake. The kid's whole body shook as the chainsaw ground through bone and brain until his finger fell off the trigger and the blade stopped.

Gonzalo stifled a scream and fell to his knees. His pinkie finger was on the floor in front of him. He didn't know where the half of his ring finger had gone. Twin streams of blood squirted from his stumps in synchronized pumps. The pain burned. The chainsaw rumbled at a low idle next to him, still nestled in the boy's skull. The four doors he'd tied off rattled as the inhabitants of the rooms tried to open the doors and find out what all the commotion was about.

The Thunder guy who had stabbed him in the leg had regained consciousness. His head rose, face in a pained grimace and nose flattened. He blinked as he took in the bloody scene. Gonzalo put his tough face on again. He let the blood pump from his stumps and reached over and took hold of the chainsaw. With a syrupy tug, he pulled the blade out of the kid's head. He squeezed the chainsaw's trigger and let the saw roar.

"Get back in your room!" Gonzalo said.

The Thunder guy's eyes vibrated with fear. Gonzalo walked toward him revving the engine, and the kid scrambled backwards, his dislocated arm dragging on the floor. Gonzalo sped up, and the kid popped to his feet and stumbled back into the room. He slammed the door shut before Gonzalo could get to him.

The next second, his facade of confidence crumbled. He slumped and whimpered. He couldn't look at his fingers yet. Gonzalo put the chainsaw down and snatched the fallen cord from the ground. He tied it to the knob of the final door, having to use his good hand to get it as tight as he could. He even revved the chainsaw a few times in the middle of his work to keep the guy scared.

He couldn't think about what had just happened. He had to keep moving. He stole shoelaces from the dead Thunder guy's sneakers and tied them around his gushing stumps to stop the bleeding. Then came the hard part. He didn't want to do it, but he'd seen too many people die from infected wounds in the infected zone. He walked up to the torch that hung on the wall next to the door with the burned "Z" on it, and pushed his stumps into the flame. The pain was more severe than any he'd ever felt, but he held his fingers there as long as he could. When he jerked his hand away, the stumps were sizzling, and he fell to the floor.

It took him a minute to realize that lying there and thinking about it wasn't going to make it hurt any less, and certainly wasn't going to reattach his fingers. He had to keep going, but the "Z" burned into this last door scared him. What Zeus had done to him had been worse than the worst nightmare he'd ever had. A hundred times worse. But the fear of what Zeus might do to Sasha dwarfed that. Gonzalo got up and walked to the end of the hall. He raised his good hand and knocked on the door. No one answered.

"Baxter!"

He knocked again. And again. And with every rap of his knuckles, he became more and more certain that he'd gotten screwed.

29

GONZALO PUSHED THE CHAINSAW'S BLADE
through the door. Two cuts, making a triangle around the knob.
One solid kick, and he was in. The door swung wide to reveal
a control room. The far wall was stacked with black-and-white
TV monitors over a long desk, ten monitors wide by four high.
All the monitors were switched on, and every one showed a different angle on the Coliseum. Together, they cast a blue glow
across the room and the only two people in it—Baxter and Zeus.

Zeus was lashed to a swivel chair with what looked like USB
cables. He was still six feet tall. He still wore his gas mask, but
his union suit was torn open and his chest was slashed up like
a tree in Zorro's backyard. Baxter held a six-inch Buck knife
in his hand.

They barely acknowledged Gonzalo, even with the chainsaw
crackling and sputtering. He couldn't hear what they were
saying, so he shut it off.

Baxter cut a deep wound across Zeus's chest.

Zeus shouted in pain, "Stop! Please! Just stop!"

"Make me . . . Zeus," Baxter said with a crazed fierceness. He raised the knife again. "I thought you were all-powerful."

"I'm not!" Zeus shook his head. For the first time, Gonzalo could see his face behind his gas mask. He was young, maybe eighteen or nineteen. He had a doughy face and prominent eyebrows that seemed to move with every thought.

"But can't you just make me disappear in a puff of smoke?" Baxter said with a smug, self-satisfied smile. "Isn't that what they say about you? That you're magic? Let's see it."

Zeus groaned through gritted teeth. "It's not true. All right? There's no magic."

Gonzalo kept his distance and just listened. He felt sure this was some kind of grand trick by Zeus. How could there be no magic after what Gonzalo had seen? He felt sure that Baxter had the wrong guy, that this guy had been planted here as a decoy.

"Where do you get all the food and drinks that you send out into the zone?" Baxter said.

Zeus hung his head. "It's a long story."

"Then make it quick." Baxter dug the tip of his knife into Zeus.

"The government gave me the food!" Zeus screamed.

"Say what?" Gonzalo said, taking a hesitant step forward. Zeus's eyes flicked to Gonzalo. Gonzalo shrunk a little, by reflex. What'd happened in the arena still haunted him. His mind felt like a paper target riddled with bullet holes. "Why you?"

"I wasn't in Colorado when the virus hit," Zeus said. "I was recruited. I was in military school, and the government needed recruits."

"To do what?" Baxter said.

"To get food to the infected in hiding."

Gonzalo and Baxter both let surprised scoffs slip, almost in unison. They glanced at each other.

"Since when does the government care about infected?" Gonzalo said.

"Just because they messed up handling the virus doesn't mean they don't want to fix stuff. You got the wrong idea about the government."

"We got plenty of reason to have the wrong idea," Baxter said. "The military abandoned the school where we came from. Left us locked in to die. So—"

"Everybody makes mistakes, even the people in charge. But I'm telling you, they're trying to set it right. Look, that's the point. You don't believe me about them. Neither would kids in the infected zone. So, to get food to the infected who needed it, the government had to send it through channels kids would trust."

"You?" Gonzalo said.

Zeus nodded. "The government gave me the virus and

dropped me here. They stockpiled the Coliseum and put me in charge of the food. My mission was to—"

"Get it to the infected," Baxter said.

"It wasn't hard," Zeus said. "Unlimited resources made me a god here. I had food, and I didn't have to explain how I got it. No one cared. They were just hungry. And maybe it was growing up in military school, but I've always been really good at giving orders. Making people fall in line. It's part of why I got selected for this mission."

"So, you told kids you were magic?" Baxter asked. "I'm not sure I would've gone with that."

Zeus gave the tiniest grin, even through his haze of pain, and glanced at Gonzalo. "I didn't tell anybody I was magic. I'm not nuts. Kids just started saying it about me 'cause I never revealed my sources. I made food magically appear out of nowhere. And—"

"You've got kids driving on highways patrolled by hunters, wearing red for chrissakes, and claiming your powers keep them from getting shot," Gonzalo said. "How do you explain that?"

"Sounds like you actually believe in magic, big man," Zeus said and coughed out a laugh.

Baxter swiped at Zeus with his blade, leaving behind a fresh red diagonal line down his chest. He howled through his gas mask.

"Goddamn it, stop!" Zeus screamed.

"I told you no more bullshit," Baxter said. "Not one word of it. Now, spill everything."

"Okay, okay. Thunder isn't invincible. Plenty have died on the road, all right?" he panted. "Shot up and killed by hunters. We just do a damn good job of covering it up. I might not have come up with me being magic, but this whole operation depends on them believing it. It's why I make everybody dress in red. It's bold. Infected shouldn't draw attention to themselves, but all that red makes it look like we're unafraid. Like we can't be hurt. Some collateral damage, a casualty here and there, is worth it if it makes the rest of Thunder feel that they're safe. Besides, I got no end of replacements. Infected can't wait to join Thunder, to be a part of what we've got going here in Denver, if they make the cut."

"You mean, if they're desperate enough to believe your lies," Baxter said.

Zeus shrugged in agreement. He grinned up at Baxter. He seemed to like that there was someone to finally appreciate his story. And if there ever was a perfect audience for a story about manipulating large groups of people, it was Baxter.

Gonzalo shuffled forward. Zeus was so unlike the reality-warping sorcerer he'd been before, and it still had Gonzalo confused. "I saw things in the arena. Things . . . that don't happen. How'd you do that?"

Zeus's eyes traveled to Gonzalo and narrowed.

"You were drugged. When you came running at me upstairs

the first time, I could see it in your eyes. Your pupils were blown out. I knew you'd drunk some Squirt."

Squirt, Gonzalo thought. *All of that because I drank a Squirt?*

"I call it dream juice. It's a nice little cocktail of muscle relaxants, two kinds of acid, and a dash of DMT. Two capfuls and most kids are in heaven for hours. You looked like you had a little too much, though."

The answer staggered Gonzalo. His reaction seemed to please Zeus, even though he was being held at knife-point by a stumpy psychopath.

"Where do you get the drugs?" Baxter said. It seemed like an odd question to Gonzalo. It had nothing to do with why they had Zeus as a hostage. In fact, barely any of this had to do with Sasha, but Gonzalo had gone along with it to fill the holes made by what'd happened in the arena. Things were starting to make a lot of sense now that magic was off the table.

"Early on," Zeus answered, "I made a visit to the evidence room at Denver's abandoned DEA headquarters. Didn't take much to get in, and then it was like shopping at WalMart."

"Dosing sodas and spreading them through the infected zone was part of your mission?" Baxter said.

"Hold on," Gonzalo said. "The sodas aren't just here at the Coliseum?"

Baxter and Zeus ignored him. He was one step behind, but he was putting things together quickly. Gonzalo had seen sodas everywhere he and Baxter had been together. At the sewers in Longmont. At the dance party. At the Radisson. He hadn't given them a second thought.

"The sodas were my idea," Zeus said. "Nothing gets kids' attention like getting high. And sugar makes it easy to swallow. Pepsi's a good gateway. It's got a little weed in it, some anti-depressants. Sprite kicks things up a notch with a little speed. Root Beer makes you numb, Tab is like ecstasy, and Cream Soda will make you feel invincible. I make sure all my Thunder guys on the road get Cream Soda."

"You're a sick bastard," Gonzalo said.

"Hey, people need a little inspiration out there. They're dying to forget how bad it really is. I just give them a little medicine to help."

"And help you get laid, right?" Baxter said. There was more envy in his voice than disdain. Zeus hesitated before he answered.

"Look, man," Zeus said. "I went to an all-boys school for a long, long time. Just 'cause I'm here to feed people doesn't mean I have to be a saint. I'm the most popular kid in the infected zone. I'd be stupid not to take advantage of that. Girls, they just want me. It's human nature for them to shoot for the top—I can't help that."

Baxter smiled a little too wide. He flicked the face shield of Zeus's gas mask. "Your bosses outside the zone know you phased out?"

Zeus shook his head. "No, and I'm not leaving." He stared into Baxter's eyes as he spoke. "Do you have any idea what it's like for people to believe every word you say? No matter what you say? Do you know what it's like for people you've never seen before to show up, after traveling through hell just to meet you, just to have you say their name? I'd do anything to keep that feeling. It's the best drug you've ever had. I was just some kid named Matt before, but here I'm Zeus. You can be a god too, man. If I tell them you are, they'll just accept it. I don't mind sharing the wealth."

Baxter lowered the knife. For once, he didn't have a question at the ready. In fact, it seemed like he might be ruminating on an answer. Gonzalo didn't want to give Baxter another second to consider Zeus's offer. There was a way-more-pressing issue.

"Where's Sasha?" Gonzalo said.

"I already told your friend here," Zeus said. "She doesn't want to see you. She doesn't want you to take her away from here. This is heaven."

Gonzalo looked at Baxter, who confirmed with a nod that he'd heard this.

"There's no way she said that," Gonzalo said.

Something caught Gonzalo's eye on one of the monitors behind Zeus. He saw multiple views of the Coliseum halls, and in every one Thunder were gathering in throngs, running, shouting. Gonzalo had a sinking feeling they were coming to save their leader.

"He's working you," Gonzalo said to Baxter. "Killing time."

Baxter raised a hand to silence Gonzalo. "Shut up."

"We've gotta go," Gonzalo said. "The others know we're here!"

"If you stand with us," Zeus said to Baxter, "you have nothing to fear from the Thunder coming for me now. I'll tell them to accept you. Don't listen to this oaf."

Gonzalo watched the conflict on Baxter's face. He couldn't let him get sucked into Zeus's tractor beam of bullshit.

"I know you hate me," Gonzalo said to Baxter, "and even if any of what this guy is saying is true, that doesn't mean that Sasha's on board with it. I saw her. She was upset. She was screaming at him."

"You also thought a T-shirt canon was a real gun," Zeus interrupted.

Baxter looked at Gonzalo with distant eyes. Gonzalo put his hand on the pull-start of the chainsaw, ready for anything. His eyes flicked to the monitors. The Thunder were coming fast, but that wasn't what had Gonzalo worried the most. On a monitor labeled "Room E-12" Thunder members were forcing Sasha and her girlfriends into a room against their will.

Gonzalo shouted at Baxter, "Cut him loose. He's taking us to E-12. Now!"

30

AN OVERSIZED KEY RING, WITH ITS COLLAR
of a hundred keys, jingled in the hands of Zeus as Gonzalo
shoved him down the hall. The red of his pajamas looked like
charcoal by the wan light of his camping lantern. Only when
Baxter swung his flashlight beam across Zeus did he see
flashes of the suit's true red.

"Do you ever think about your place in history?" Zeus said.
Neither Gonzalo nor Baxter answered. Since they'd left his
quarters, Zeus had been preaching in one way or another
about the importance of what was happening here at the Coliseum. "I guess it's not something people our age usually think
about, but have you? Do you figure anyone will think of you
twenty . . . fifty years from now?"

"Keep moving," Gonzalo said.

"I'll be remembered," Zeus said. "They will know my name."

Gonzalo gave him another shove using his bad hand, and

pain shot from his severed fingers up his arm.

Baxter walked close to the wall, ahead of Gonzalo and Zeus by a few feet. He had his arms outstretched, one palm skimming the wall, the other flicking his flashlight beam everywhere he looked. His head swiveled back and forth, like he was trying to look both ways down the concrete hall at the same time. His eyes bulged from his handsome, little head. Gonzalo could see Baxter would have preferred to be crawling through the ducts. The only reason he was braving the halls was because he knew what Gonzalo knew. They were close.

Gonzalo had lost track of what part of the building they were in. His mind was too consumed with anticipation. He'd have Sasha back soon. Zeus's lie about Sasha wanting to stay in Thunder had already been exposed. They wouldn't have been locking her up if she'd been on board with what was happening here. No, one way or another, they'd be walking out of here, probably using Zeus as a hostage, like Baxter had planned. It was the rest of Baxter's plan that Gonzalo still had to worry about, but most of that would be resolved depending on whose arms Sasha ran to when they finally saw her. It wouldn't be Baxter. It couldn't be.

Zeus stopped in front of the room they'd seen Sasha forced into, Room E-12. His trembling fingers sorted through the clinking keys, making a sound like metallic rainfall. He gripped one key and let the others fall. Gonzalo stood directly behind

Zeus, with Baxter at his side. He knew there was a possibility Baxter would try to kill him right now, in the moment before the door opened, before Sasha could see it. He could feel the potential of it down the right side of his body. His skin tingled in anticipation of an attack, but Baxter stayed still, eyes fastened on the locked door.

Before turning the key, Zeus hesitated. His back was to them, hunched, rising and falling to the rhythm of his raspy breathing.

"Do it, or I'll cut you a new butt crack," Baxter said with the Buck knife outstretched.

Gonzalo heard the key sink into the tumblers of the lock. He heard the lock disengage. Zeus remained still. He wasn't opening the door.

"Last chance," Zeus said, "to be part of history."

Gonzalo gripped Zeus's shoulder and pushed him aside before Baxter could answer.

"Enough already," Gonzalo said.

He grabbed the knob and turned it. The metal was hot, painfully hot, and he let go the moment he swung the door open. Black smoke billowed into his face shield, swallowing him up as it surged into the hall. His vision was a swirl of black.

"I smell gasoline," Baxter said with a cough.

Gonzalo strained to see through the black. He saw the dull glow of fluorescent ceiling lights in the room beyond. He saw the smoke clear in spots, for moments. He saw water dripping off sprinkler pipes that ran along the ceiling. He saw a burned wooden chair, missing a leg. The more he squinted, the more he saw burned objects. A folding table. A singed couch. Part of it was still burning, just a single tongue of flame on the armrest. Large, dark masses that he couldn't quite make out lay strewn across the floor.

Gonzalo reached out to grab Zeus with his free hand. Instead, he felt a cold metal blade slide into him, between his ribs. Pain assaulted him. The blade was yanked out before he could get his hands to it, and Gonzalo fell onto his ass. He heard Baxter grunt, in his distinctive, nasal tone, and then he heard the slap of a body hitting concrete.

Through the haze of smoke, Gonzalo saw Baxter writhing on the floor, only three feet away. Zeus stepped through the thinning smoke and stood over Gonzalo with a blade in his hand.

"Where is Sasha?" Gonzalo mustered.

"She had a big mouth," Zeus said.

"Where is she?!"

"With her friends," Zeus said with a wave toward the room. "I had them burned."

Gonzalo's eyes snapped back to the dark masses on the floor, and with the smoke blowing out through the open door, he could see it all. The drips from the emergency sprinklers splashed into puddles on the floor, the sound delicate, musical, and all too pleasant for the abominable sight before him. A dozen carcasses lay scattered across the floor, all burnt to a black char, all still steaming. His eyes traveled to a corpse by the wall. He watched smoke slide across the burnt ribcage. The girl was small, and that was all there was left of her to recognize. Her curves, her beautiful brown eyes, her perfect lips—they'd all been burned away.

Evil. It was all he could think. Gonzalo pulled himself up, overpowering the jabbing pain in his side. Baxter sprang up too, and drove his knife into Zeus's stomach to the hilt. Zeus's face clenched and his eyes bugged in confusion. Gonzalo charged and whipped his entire body into a heavy punch. His fist busted through the clear face shield of Zeus's mask, shattering it. When he withdrew his fist, it was like he was pulling the plug out of a drain. Lung blood poured out of Zeus's mouth, raining down on the knife in his belly.

Zeus crashed to the ground on his back. The knife was still planted in his stomach like a flagpole. The blood and lung continued to flow out of his mouth, like a baking-soda-and-vinegar volcano, until it filled his broken mask and began to spill out the sides.

Gonzalo fell to his knees. He was . . . he was . . . he didn't know. He felt like he should scream, or claw at his skin, or destroy something, but he felt nothing. He wasn't even there. Baxter began to trudge away. There was a long gash running up the right side of his chest. As vicious-looking as it was, he ignored it and limped away. He didn't say a word to Gonzalo, or even glance at him. He walked off with his crooked gait and didn't look back. Gonzalo watched Baxter climb atop a vending machine in the hall, tear off a vent cover, and crawl into the wall.

31

THEY WERE CALLING IT THE LOVE OVEN.
It was in Geek territory, and run by three Geek girls, and
Gonzalo had told Sasha that he didn't want to go. The Geeks
had looked at him like he was a psychopath when he'd broken
Baxter's leg, and that had only been two weeks back. Sasha
had insisted. If they were going to sleep together for the first
time, it had to be in the Love Oven.

Two Art Geeks and one Fashion Geek had gotten the idea
for it, because they wanted a nice, private place to have sex
with their boyfriends. As Sasha explained to him at length,
the girls in McKinley were "sick and tired of getting taken
to dark corners of dirty classrooms, or sweating in a closet."
They wanted to make a place where a girl and her boyfriend,
or girlfriend, or whoever, could have a nice time together
in a safe, pretty place that locked from the inside. And they
also wanted to charge for it. Sasha had paid them two cans of

stew and a rattail comb for three hours in the Oven.

"Are you ready?" Sasha said.

"You have no idea," Gonzalo said.

She giggled. The door before them looked like any other classroom door. The Geek girls had given them the room's location and told them it would be unlocked for fifteen minutes. The Geeks also had said that if they stayed for more than three hours, they'd owe the Geeks more stew.

Sasha pushed the door open, and Gonzalo was assaulted with pink. Every wall had been painted pink, along with the ceiling and two chairs in the corner. Thin ribbons of tinfoil hung from the ceiling all around the fluorescent ceiling lights. They twisted and swayed and twinkled, bouncing the light around the room. More tinfoil had been cut into confetti-sized squares, and it was spread all over the pink walls, like they'd thrown handfuls of the shiny squares at the walls and ceiling while the paint was still wet. The bits of tin glittered like sequins. The whole room sparkled.

"Oh my god," Sasha said and ran inside.

Gonzalo followed and locked the door behind them. Sasha spun around.

"This place is so me!" Sasha said.

"You never wear pink."

"Yeah, but this is what it looks like inside my soul." She gasped. "Is this bed real?"

She bounded across the room and dove onto the mattress.

The bed frame was made out of pallet wood. Sasha lifted up the pristine white bedsheets to reveal that the mattress underneath was made of winter coats, wall insulation, and rolled-up socks, all held together in a mattress shape by the walls of the bed frame. Gonzalo walked over and sat down next to her. The mattress had zero springiness, and it was lumpier than a mogul field, but it was soft. The sheets were clean and smelled like springtime. Folded paper flower petals made from neon pink Post-It notes had been sprinkled across the sheets and piled atop the Miss Piggy bicycle helmet full of condoms that sat on the pallet-wood side table, along with a stack of white hand towels and a jelly jar full of cooking oil.

Gonzalo lay down on the bed and pulled Sasha down with him. As soon as they were on their backs, they started laughing. A mirror from one of the bathrooms had been mounted on the pink ceiling over the bed. Hundreds of hearts had been scratched into the glass all around the edges like a frame.

"You told me once that you'd do anything for me," she said.

"I did."

"Well, I'd do anything for you too."

His hand found hers and he held her slender fingers like they were made of glass. Girl bones were probably hollow, he thought, and he wanted to say it out loud because he knew Sasha would swat him for it and get all riled up, but he didn't want to ruin the moment. Her warm breath flowed over his neck. Her eyes were closed. She looked ready to fall asleep. He understood. Neither of them had felt an actual bed in over a year, and locked in this room was the safest and most private he'd felt since he'd lived in the lounge. And a tad prettier.

If Sasha wanted to nap, that was okay. He'd let her sleep and wake her up after a bit. They had this room for three hours, and they'd only just walked in. There was still plenty of time left.

32

SASHA WAS DEAD, AND YET HE COULD FEEL
her hot breath on his neck. Gonzalo stomped on the gas.
Trees. Shopping centers. Tipped and flipped cars. They all
blended together as they whipped past his periphery. He'd
barely made it out of Denver alive. Thunder had chased him
all through the Coliseum, then through the parking lot full of
cows and across the river. When he'd finally reached his van
and fired it up, Thunder kids were slapping at the windows,
kicking the doors, and screaming like apes. They wanted his
head. He peeled out of there.

His wobbling spare tire finally gave out near Pale Ridge.
David was actually still working with the parents at McKinley, and Gonzalo was surprised to find Will there too. He
traded them his van for an old pickup truck and patched up
his wounds. He couldn't bear to tell them about Sasha. He
wasn't ready to hear those words out loud. But David and Will

were so bright-eyed and goddamn hopeful that they wanted to know everything he'd seen out in the zone. He told them about the cure, and their minds exploded. They didn't ask him about Sasha again. It should have been good to see them, but he felt like he wasn't really there. His body was, but everything that made him human was still back in Room E-12.

Gonzalo slowed when he saw the border fences ahead as he crept up on the Colorado–New Mexico state line. The land on either side of the highway was filled with abandoned vehicles. The cars weren't organized in any way. They'd just been driven to a spot anywhere off the road where there was space and left there. Piles of bicycles and tipped motorcycles dotted the road closer to the border.

To prevent the smuggling of infected across the border, no cars were allowed to leave the zone. So once someone got to the border, to one of the gates in the wall, like this one on Interstate 25, they had to ditch their wheels and pass through the gate on foot if the guards let them through. Gonzalo left the key in the ignition and climbed out of the truck. He abandoned it about two hundred feet from the gate because he couldn't find a place to park that was any closer or that wasn't in the middle of the road.

Gonzalo approached the border barrier. There were rows upon rows of chain-link fences, topped with razor wire. The fences stretched as far as he could see. Breaking in or out of the infected zone was no small effort. Military drones patrolled the border, and their response was swift and merciless. Based on what Gonzalo had heard from different people's accounts, outsiders spotted breaking into the zone were dealt with on a case-by-case basis. It seemed that the military didn't want or need any controversy as a result of killing civilians who were already hellbent on getting themselves killed in the infected zone (or planning to do some killing of infected). It was a different case with people trying to get out of the zone. Anyone caught leaving the zone through an unauthorized, unmanned exit would be shot on sight.

Gonzalo approached the cement-block command post that had been built in blockade fashion across the interstate. It was a single-story, gray block, featureless except for a door that sat squarely in the middle of the building, right where the cement median of the road ended. Gas masks sat in piles on the ground by the door. Giant, industrial-grade fans were mounted along the roofline of the building, angled down toward the front door. Soldiers stood on top of the building behind a concrete and razor-wire barricade. One of them manned a mounted machine gun that looked like it could tear someone in half in the blink of an eye. The others held assault weapons and wore futuristic gas masks that would have made him drool days ago. Didn't matter now, though. Once he was on the other side of this building, he wouldn't need a gas mask anymore. Hopefully, he'd never have to see one ever again.

Twenty feet from the building, the fans kicked to life and blasted him with powerful, steady gusts of hot air. He was sweating in seconds. Soldiers were aiming the fans at him, operating them by some unseen handles.

"Remove your mask," a voice said through a gray PA speaker on the roof.

Gonzalo pulled off his mask.

"Approach the door."

The door was steel, and as he neared it, the sun glinted off scratches in the metal. They were names, etched with keys or knives. The door had a little window in it, and a steel plate that covered it. Scratched to the right of the plate was a big name in cursive: Buddy.

Gonzalo sighed softly. At least there was room for one happy ending in the zone. The steel plate slid up, revealing a metal oval, big enough to fit someone's face. A padded cup was mounted to the bottom of the oval to act as a chin rest. He didn't love the idea of sticking his face into some unknown hole. At least when he'd graduated from McKinley, it had been his hand. That seemed a little less unsettling than this. But leaving McKinley had been terrifying. He'd felt like he was leaving everything that mattered behind, and the freedom he'd earned had only brought on bigger and more complicated problems.

As he looked into this metal oval in the door now, he began to wonder what kind of life he was about to cross into. He would have his family, but without his search for Sasha, who was he? Could he really go back to "normal" life? Leaving the infected zone meant finally closing the door on all the trauma he'd endured since the day his high school blew up. It also meant closing the door on Sasha.

This was the end, and he didn't know if he wanted it.

Gonzalo thought of Sasha's face before he walked out of McKinley, how twisted with pain it was. The tears glistening on her cheeks. He remembered her yelling that it wasn't fair, that after everything they'd already been through, she couldn't lose him too. That was when he'd promised her that they'd be together again.

"Place your chin on the cup and open your mouth," the voice said from the speaker above.

Gonzalo squatted to fit his face into the opening and opened his mouth. Some sort of brace lowered onto the crown of his head and squeezed tightly, holding him in place. He panicked and wanted to pull away, but between the headpiece and the chin brace, he was stuck. A mechanical arm unfolded from the back of the cubby in the door and grabbed hold of his tongue with a plier-like clamp. Another miniature arm unfolded and pushed a thick needle into his tongue until it popped through. He screamed.

The image of the steaming carcasses of the burned girls in Room E-12 rushed to the front of his mind. Their gleaming white teeth inset in charred flesh with no lips, eyes melted, fingers twisted in on themselves like black snakes. The memory was so crisp it was like he was there all over again. The clamp let go and retracted into the wall. As soon as the brace on his head rose up, he yanked his head out of the door.

"Please remove your head and—Thank you. No virus detected . . . Congratulations."

The door to the gray building slid open, disappearing into the wall. Beyond the door was a long hallway that ended at an officer in a booth, behind a glass window, waiting like a Customs official.

Gonzalo took a step forward. He wanted this walk back to the real world to bring him some sort of peace or closure, but how could it? How would he ever forget what had happened? What he'd seen?

Another image burst into his mind. Sasha's burned rib cage, butted up against the wall. Skin shrunken around her ribs, going from black flakes to bubbled brown flesh to dead gray dough. A coffee-brown stain on the floor where her insides had boiled and poured out. Steam rising from her ribs and then snaking sideways across her ribcage. Errant water droplets hitting her flesh and sizzling. One of her fingers had still been on fire.

His whole body jerked. He stood, tense, in the doorway.

The man in the booth at the end of the hall had a deadly bored look on his face. He was propping his jaw up on one arm, his cheek squishing up into a ball in his hand. With his other hand, he tapped something in front of him. A static hiss sprang from an unseen speaker.

"Please enter," an automated voice said.

She's gone, Gonzalo told himself. *Just forget it.*

The automated voice bounced down the featureless hall toward Gonzalo. "Re-entry into the infected zone is prohibited by law."

He couldn't bring himself to step through the doorway. It was irrational, but letting the door shut behind him felt like a betrayal of Sasha.

He saw that burned ribcage in his mind again, saturated and sharp. The tendrils of smoke from the smoldering parts and the haze of steam rising up from the whole ribcage and flowing over the ribs into the wall.

Into the wall.

Gonzalo gasped. He turned away from the hall and ran out of the building. He scooped his gas mask up off the ground and hightailed it to the truck. The key was still in the ignition where he'd left it. The truck's tires spit dirt into the air, left rubber on the road, and rocketed him north, up the dirty interstate.

Toward Denver.

33

A FUNERAL BY THE RIVER'S EDGE. GONZALO
peered through binoculars over the lip of the elevated highway, a few hundred feet east, where the highway was level with
the arched roof of the Coliseum. His truck idled behind him.
There was a herd of Thunder crowded close to the river. Some
had removed their red and wore normal clothes. Some wore
all black to mark the occasion. Some had gathered wildflow-
ers, white, pink, and yellow. Some were wandering around on
the outskirts, clearly not as invested as the rest, but the great
majority was focused on the body of Zeus, as it was carried
through the crowd on a raft made of lashed-together pallets.
They'd swaddled him in golden fabric, with only his young
slack face exposed. Rouge tinted his gray cheeks.

There were so many Thunder. Gonzalo had hoped that their
numbers had been part of his hallucination, but there were
hundreds and hundreds of them. Thunder kids laid the raft

down next to the flowing water. A boy, who wore a plaid suit jacket over his red union suit, stepped out in front of the raft and began delivering a speech from a wobbling sheet of paper. His voice was swallowed up by the wind. Countless others in the crowd held sheets of paper, or notebooks, or scraps of cardboard. A lot of Thunder intended to say their piece. That was good for Gonzalo. The longer they mourned, the more time he'd have.

Gonzalo edged back to his truck and eased it in reverse, away from the funeral. He got off at the first available exit and navigated to the Coliseum as fast as he could, making sure to brake gradually when he came to a stop alongside it. The river was still close enough that the mourners might hear if his tires were to screech or his brakes squeal. Other cars were abandoned along the road, so his truck would hopefully blend into the scenery.

There was no one on the street with him, as far as he could see. His pace quickened as he approached the loading docks where he'd entered the Coliseum last time. The rolling door on the loading bay was almost closed, with a two-inch gap between the door and floor. He got his fingers under the cold door and tugged up gently. The screeching wasn't that bad when he only pulled it up a little at a time. He kept looking over his shoulder, but he saw no Thunder sneaking up on him—only moaning cows meandering through the parking lot.

Once he had the door up to hip height, he ducked inside. The place was dark. A kerosene camping lantern hanging from a nail in the wall was the only illumination in the big room. He forced the bay door shut, being just as careful as before to keep the noise down. He made his way through the dim building and up the dormant escalator by the light of the lantern. When he reached the hall that ran down the length of the Coliseum, he found it empty. Gonzalo walked fast. He never saw a soul. He was sprinting by the time he reached the burned room.

The door was closed but not locked. Everything inside was just as he'd left it, except for streaks of dried blood on the floor from where Thunder had dragged Zeus off. The lights were still on, and the bodies scattered, charred, and shrunken like forgotten burgers on the grill.

The burnt ribcage was still butted up against the wall as he remembered it. Clothes burned away, revealing broiled skin. He tripped as he rushed to it, and skidded on the heels of his palms until he stopped face to face with the blackened skull. He forced a wave of nausea down. He'd known he was going to have to get close to her. He'd known he was going to have to touch her too.

Gonzalo placed one hand on the side of her burnt hip bone and one on the rough side of the ribcage. He took a breath and hoped he was right.

The corpse didn't want to budge when he pulled gently,

so he closed his eyes and put some muscle into it. The body detached from the floor with a dry crack and scraped across the concrete, like sandpaper on a brick.

Low in the wall, by the floor, where the corpse had been, was an open air duct.

Gonzalo's heart jumped into his throat.

He held his hand in front of the open duct, and felt cool air flowing between his fingers, sucking into the wall. A bent vent cover lay on the floor next to the corpse. Gonzalo stuck his head into the duct.

Please...

He saw something in the dark. His eyes took a second to adjust. He was staring at the bottom of a pair of boots.

He grabbed the cold leather boots. He could feel the firmness of ankles inside. Gonzalo pulled. With a soft hiss of cotton on duct metal, Sasha's limp body slid out of the vent.

"Oh no," he said.

Gonzalo pulled her up close to him. Tears were already streaming down his face. He touched her forehead. It was cold. Her eyes were closed. Her face was smeared with soot. Her mouth hung open. Her skin had no color.

"I'm sorry, Sash," he said.

Sasha's eyes fluttered.

Gonzalo nearly died.

"Baby," Gonzalo said.

Her eyes stayed open, but they lolled. She wasn't looking

at anything in particular, certainly not his face. She opened her mouth and hacked out a cough instead. The coughing wouldn't stop. It clenched her whole body, until she curled up on his arm like a shrimp.

"Stay with me," he said.

Gonzalo stood, holding her tight, and hurried her out of the room. He didn't want her to come to, surrounded by the brutal picture of what she'd survived. Also, he had an idea. As Sasha hacked and groaned, slipping in and out of consciousness, Gonzalo hunted room by room for soda, until he found what he was looking for stashed in a pair of hanging pantyhose—a bottle of Cream Soda. Zeus had said it made you feel invincible.

Gonzalo lifted her head and placed the opened Cream Soda bottle to her cracked lips. He tried to give it to her in sips, but Sasha grabbed it and chugged like a calf drinking from its mother. She inhaled some of it and coughed up a storm. When the coughs subsided, she lifted her head and her eyes were clear.

"Whoa," she said.

"You okay?" he said, an uncrushable smile stretching across his face.

Her eyebrows bunched. "You look like my boyfriend," she said.

"It's me, baby. But you have to whisper, okay?"

She scrunched her eyes shut and moaned.

"I'm dreaming again," Sasha said.

"It's not a dream."

Her eyes went round like a hoot-owl's. She reached out and pinched his arm hard.

"Ow!" he said. "What are you doing?"

"Trying to figure out if this is real."

"You're supposed to pinch yourself, not me."

Her eyes glittered in the lantern light.

"It's really you, isn't it?!" she said.

"Goddamn right it is," he said, keeping his voice low, and hoping she would too.

She kicked him in the knee with her boot.

"Hey, what the fuck?" he said. "We've already settled that I'm real."

Sasha's eyes began to pour tears. "Just making sure," she said in a paper-thin voice.

Gonzalo's eyes flooded too. "I thought I'd never find you. I thought you were dead."

Sasha wrapped her arms around him and squeezed like a boa constrictor.

"So did I," she said.

At first he felt incapable of anything more than tears and hugs, holding her and stroking her hair, but he knew they had to hurry. "I think we'd better go," he said.

"Okay," Sasha said, looking around for the first time. She didn't look healthy, but she was alert and full of energy. She wiped the tears from her soot-smudged cheeks and massaged her temples. "What happened?"

"Zeus tried to kill you."

Her eyes darted around with a surge of panic. Gonzalo put his hand on hers.

"You don't have to worry about him anymore."

Sasha's eyes came to rest on Gonzalo. "I figured out where he got all the food."

Gonzalo nodded. "From the government. He told me. Come on, baby, we have to go."

Gonzalo pulled her forward, but she pulled back.

"Not the government," Sasha said. "The hunters."

Gonzalo paused. "The hunters? That makes no sense."

"They set him up here with an unlimited supply of stuff and told him to distribute it to the infected underground. In return, they left him alone here."

"Why would they do that?"

"They put little tracker chips in the soda caps."

Gonzalo's mind reeled. He'd bought Zeus's story about the government, but this made more sense. It also made Gonzalo nauseous. With trackers hidden in the drugged sodas that kids couldn't get enough of, hunters could find infected hideouts easily. Gonzalo had even seen the plan in action at the toy factory when the hunters had attacked the dance party. And now it made sense that Thunder wore red. It wasn't a bold statement of defiance at all. It was a signal to any hunters that saw them: "Don't shoot us! We're on your side!"

"Do Thunder kids know what they're doing?" Gonzalo asked.

Sasha shook her head. "No. I don't even know if Zeus knew exactly what the hunters were having him do. All he knew was that he'd lucked into a goldmine and he wasn't going to give it up."

"And you confronted him," Gonzalo said, touching her cheek softly.

"Wouldn't you?" Sasha said, her voice hoarse. "Just like when you stepped up against Varsity with David on the quad."

"I think you outdid me," Gonzalo said with a little smile.

Sasha shook her head. "Zeus's guards dragged me away before I could get it all out. They shoved me and the others I'd told into a room," Sasha said. "They had knives. They started pouring gasoline everywhere. On the furniture. On us. And when they got to the door, they . . . they just dropped a torch and locked us in."

Sasha's eyes welled up. Gonzalo saw the cold reality of her friends' burning deaths enter her brain. He knew that once that soda wore off, it would feel so much worse.

"There was fire everywhere so fast. I couldn't save the girls," she said. "When I saw the vent, I just went for it. I knew I could fit and—"

"Shhh."

"It was awful, Gonz. It was—I should've tried to—"

"There was nothing you could do," he said.

"Maybe I should'a kept my stupid mouth shut."

"Don't say that," Gonzalo said. "You did the right thing."

She took a deep breath. Her lip wobbled, and her chin tremored. The memories were clearly returning with a vengeance, and it scared Gonzalo. He couldn't have her break down right now. Not yet. The silence all around was making him nervous. They'd talked for too long as it was.

"Here, finish that," Gonzalo said and helped guide the bottle to her mouth. She downed the rest of the Cream Soda. "Let's go."

Now that she'd finished the bottle, her reaction to the drugs was nearly instantaneous. Her pupils expanded as a smile stretched across her face. The stuff was strong, no doubt about it. He stood and helped her to her feet. Her mood was fully reversed, and she leapt onto him with a giggle. She clamped her legs around his middle and looped her arms over his neck, so that they were face to mask.

"I feel pretty good," she said.

"I'm glad."

He started hustling through the Coliseum, carrying her like that, with his hands interlaced under her butt, and her staring into his eyes. Her gaze was strong. She crinkled her eyebrows in amazement. "You came for me," she said.

"I promised I would."

She squeaked and rained kisses all over the face shield of his gas mask. He'd never once wanted his gas mask to not be separating him from an infected person before, but in that moment, with Sasha's pink lips smushing against the plastic, he wanted to rip his mask off and die kissing her.

They reached the long hall that ran the length of the Coliseum and once again found it empty. They made their way down the escalator to the rolling bay door that led to the loading dock. They were so close. He turned and looked at Sasha, just to see her. He touched her cheek and she leaned into his touch, closing her eyes. The fear of losing her again was nearly crippling, but they had to move. The funeral wouldn't last forever.

"I . . . missed you," Gonzalo said. His words were so completely inadequate.

"I missed you too," she said, her voice rising a note. Sasha hugged him with fierce strength, then let go and slid down to the floor.

Gonzalo took a deep breath and tugged the bay door up. The screeching of the metal wasn't that bad, but the blaring sunlight revealed that they weren't alone anymore. Baxter was in the process of climbing up onto the loading dock, and when he saw Gonzalo and Sasha, he nearly fell off.

"Sasha?" Baxter said. He stared in disbelief.

Gonzalo wanted to yank the door down between them, shut Baxter out, and find another exit, but he didn't get the chance.

Sasha pushed past Gonzalo and wrapped Baxter in a hug.

34

GONZALO WATCHED SASHA WITH A TERRIBLE mixture of fear and disbelief. It didn't take a genius to see that she cared for Baxter, but Gonzalo never thought he'd see this day. He'd never really believed it could be true. Even after Baxter's story about dating her after Gonzalo had graduated. But there Baxter was, with his arms around Gonzalo's girl.

"You're alive," Baxter said softly, gently squeezing Sasha's arms. They were nearly eye to eye, standing "this close." Jealousy flamed up inside Gonzalo.

"Yeah," Sasha said, then stepped back and turned toward Gonzalo. "Gonzalo found me."

She smiled at Gonzalo, and he closed the gap between them. He put his hands on her arms right where Baxter had just touched her. He kept his face as hard as ever.

"She hid in a vent," Gonzalo said. His voice was as steady and cold as a snowplow.

"That's my girl," Baxter said.

Gonzalo squeezed her harder.

"So I guess you think you won?" Baxter said.

Sasha looked up at Gonzalo, puzzled.

"What does he mean, 'won'?"

"Me and Gonzalo have been travel buddies for a few days now. He's got it real bad for you, Sash," Baxter said and smiled.

Baxter was trying to make Gonzalo look desperate while he acted nonchalant.

"Sasha," Gonzalo said, and then he froze. It seemed crazy how much land he'd crossed, how many doors he'd kicked down, how many times he'd nearly died to be this close to her, and still he might lose her to the person he hated most in the world.

"What's wrong?" she said.

"Yeah, use your words, big fella." Baxter's grin spread wider, and it made the gears in Gonzalo's head grind.

He wanted to tell her how serious he'd been when he'd said he would do anything for her. He wanted to tell her how long he'd searched, but she already knew all that. If she still wanted Baxter despite everything he'd done, there was nothing more he could do.

"I don't want you to pick him," Gonzalo blurted out. "But I can't stop you. I just want you to know that I'll never stop loving you, and in a week, or a year, or whenever he turns out to be the lying piece of crap I know he is—"

"Oh, that's real nice," Baxter said.

"I'll be waiting."

Sasha stared at Gonzalo like she was really weighing the meaning of his words.

"What the fuck are you talking about?" she said.

Gonzalo stood still with his mouth hanging open. Baxter shook with laughter.

"But . . . ," Gonzalo said. "You and Baxter . . ."

"Me and Baxter, what?"

"Oh, this is too perfect," Baxter said.

"He said you guys dated after I graduated," Gonzalo said.

"Ew, Baxter!"

Baxter sighed. "Well, I guess the fun is over," he said.

Gonzalo fumbled to speak. He'd been put through so many ups and downs because of this asshole, and he was weary. "I knew you were lying."

"No, you didn't. That's what made it so fun."

Gonzalo's face burned. Baxter was right—he'd never been able to tell whether Baxter was telling the truth. Still, there was one thing he needed to know.

"So you're not in love with Sasha?" Gonzalo said.

"Hey, I care about her." He looked Sasha in the eyes. "You saved my life. I don't want anything bad to happen to you, but you're not why I came. Yeah, sure, I know I went a little bonkers over you in the Mice, but that was high-school shit. I'm not like you two morons. I don't think love lasts forever and unicorns hump rainbows."

"Well, what the hell was all this for then?" Gonzalo said, his voice rising.

"Zeus," Baxter said, as if it was obvious. "I'd heard so many rumors and crazy-ass claims about him. That he'd keep you safe, that he was a wizard, that he had a harem of girls. One guy getting all these people to do what he says and believe what he says. It was inspiring. I mean, I knew he was bullshit—had to be—but I was dying to see how he did it. And then you showed up. You had a van, you could get me past hunters, and I needed a ride here."

"But we didn't find out Sasha was in Thunder until Razorville."

"No, *you* didn't find out till then. I'd heard that two months ago."

"You're lying again."

"Afraid not."

Gonzalo and Sasha exchanged skeptical looks. "I *have* been here that long," Sasha said.

"Then why the toy factory, why the Radisson?" Gonzalo said. "If you already knew everything, why not have me drive you straight to Denver?"

"That dance party was once-in-a-lifetime. I'm gonna tell my grandkids about that. And the Radisson? I just really love that caramel corn they sell there, and I figured I'd run into some people I know, shoot the shit a bit. I actually was about to leave you chained up there when I saw some Thunder there, but I couldn't convince those assholes to take me with 'em."

Gonzalo felt like he needed to sit down. His mind did a back-stroke through the last few days.

"You took me to places where you knew I might get killed."

"And I got to watch you squirm. Watch you be afraid that you were going to die. I got to chain you to a wall and make you think you were being sold into slavery." Baxter was overtaken with laughter. "I got to see you doubt Sasha's feelings for you. That was my absolute favorite part of all."

"That's fucked up, Baxter. Even for you," Sasha said.

"I don't think it is," Baxter said.

"No?" Gonzalo said.

"No," Baxter said. He limped one step forward. "I can never run again. I'll never walk like a normal person. I think about what you did to me every time I take a step. Do you understand? You think I'm ever going to forgive you for that?"

Gonzalo wasn't proud of what he'd done to Baxter's leg. His guilt kept him from arguing.

"Great, I hope you had a whale of a time. Sasha, let's go," Gonzalo said.

"Nu-uh," Baxter said.

Baxter reached into his Thunder pajamas and pulled out a handgun. The black finish had been worn down to raw metal in spots, like the exhausted pistols at firing ranges.

"Back inside. Now," Baxter said. He directed them with a

flick of the gun barrel, but kept the weapon leveled at Gonzalo's chest the rest of the time.

Gonzalo and Sasha looked at each other. Sasha was in just as much shock as he was.

"You know I'll shoot," Baxter said.

For once, Gonzalo believed him. Gonzalo backed into the dark of the Coliseum, pushing Sasha behind him.

"Baxter, you're taking this too far," Sasha said.

Baxter followed them into the building, gun held out in front.

"What more do you want?" Gonzalo said.

"You," Baxter said.

The cold light from the outside sprayed off of Baxter. Gonzalo and Sasha stood just beyond the light's reach. Baxter smiled as he glanced out the door.

"Killing me won't heal your leg," Gonzalo said.

"Believe me, you'd have been dead a long time ago if it could."

"Then let us go. Let it be over."

"Over? This is just the beginning. I'm taking over Thunder. See, I found where Zeus hid all the food and drugs. I found his notebooks. I understand his whole operation now," Baxter said. "I'll just tell them Zeus is speaking to me from beyond the grave. Hell, I'll say I'm Zeus reincarnated."

"You can't be serious," Gonzalo said.

"They won't believe you," Sasha said.

"I think they will. You should see the way they're carrying on down by the river. They worshipped him. They really believed he was a god. They're pounding sodas left and right, I mean, they're really broken up about it. I think they're dying to believe in someone else as soon as possible. I just need a grand gesture, to introduce myself with, y'know? I think bringing them the man who killed Zeus should do the trick."

"We both killed him," Gonzalo said.

"That's not what I'll say. Who are they going to believe, another infected or the adult they saw charge in and attack their leader yesterday?"

"They'll kill him," Sasha said to Baxter.

"They better," Baxter said with a smile.

"If you ever had any real feelings for me, if you ever cared like you said, you'll let us go," Sasha said.

"Why do you even want to leave with him in the first place?" Baxter said. "I don't get it. You know he can't take you out of the zone yet. You'd be looking over your shoulder all the time, hoping the big guy doesn't attract attention, never getting to mix with your kind. You'll be on the run nonstop. Here you're safe. You know that. Especially with Zeus gone."

"If I stay, will you let Gonzalo go?"

"Sasha, no," Gonzalo said.

Baxter raised an eyebrow. "You'd do that?"

"I'll say you brought me back to life."

"Sasha!" Gonzalo said, but she was already walking to Baxter.

Baxter grabbed her wrist and pulled her over the rest of the way. His gun stayed on Gonzalo.

"Gimme a kiss," Baxter said. He grasped her hair by the back of her head and mashed his lips into Sasha's, his eager eyes looking only at Gonzalo. He cared more about seeing the anger and disgust on Gonzalo's face than he did about her lips.

Hatred. Gonzalo had never known it as acutely as in that moment. He could feel his capacity for clear thinking, for logic and common sense, evaporating in the steam of his anger. The sight of his girlfriend being molested by that grinning jackal in pajamas was like a white-hot branding iron being dragged across his face.

Sasha looked at Gonzalo, but it wasn't the violated-victim look he was expecting. Her eyes were hard and angry, like his. He felt a bolt of connection between them, and that's when he knew. Sasha was going to try something.

She chomped down on Baxter's lip and grabbed for the gun. Gonzalo charged Baxter, and the gun went off. Gonzalo felt a plunging pain in his inner thigh and fell to the floor. Baxter and Sasha crashed to the floor in a tangle. Baxter screamed. His bottom lip was mostly missing, and blood fountained from the torn flesh. It coated his exposed bottom teeth with red. Sasha spit Baxter's lip chunk on the floor as she tried to wrestle the gun from him. Gonzalo scrambled toward them. The screaming pain in his thigh swelled.

Baxter yanked his wrists free of Sasha's grip and pointed the gun at Sasha's face.

"You don't win," Baxter said through a froth of red spit.

Gonzalo whacked Baxter's hands with his forearm as fire blasted from the gun's snout. The handgun spun into the air and soared across the room, into the shadows.

Gonzalo jerked his gaze over to Sasha. She looked rattled, and she was patting her body and examining herself, but Gonzalo saw no wound, just flecks of Baxter's blood on her chin.

Baxter scrambled to his feet and tried to run, but Gonzalo grabbed him by his pajamas and yanked him back to the ground. Gonzalo shot up despite the searing pain in his inner thigh, and promptly lost his mind. He stomped Baxter once, twice, again, and then again, ignoring the howls of pain and the sounds of bones snapping like celery stalks. He wasn't in control of himself anymore. The restraint he had exercised every day because of the destruction he knew his powerful body could create—Gonzalo let go of that completely. The rage felt freeing, satisfying, like a shower after a weeklong camping trip, and it wasn't until he was out of breath that he stopped.

Gonzalo peered down at the ruin he'd created. Baxter's other leg was broken, as were both forearms and one upper arm. He squirmed on the floor in shock, arms and legs bending in unnatural directions, like he had extra joints. Lower lip missing. Eyes shivering. Whimpers belching out of a wet throat. It was just like the last time. Gonzalo had snapped and caused irreparable damage to Baxter's body. Exactly the same, except for one thing. This time, he felt no remorse.

"They're coming back. Gonzalo, we have to leave," Sasha said. She was at the open door, peering out.

Gonzalo hopped to her side, keeping weight off his wounded leg. His inner thigh was screaming. He looked back over his shoulder at Baxter before he hopped out the door.

"Convince 'em you're a god now," Gonzalo said.

35

HE'D THOUGHT THAT BAXTER MIGHT'VE SHOT
his dick off, and he'd feared it was actually true as Sasha cut
away the leg of his jeans in the bed of the truck by the side of
the road. His thigh was covered in a candy-apple-red glaze. In
that moment, he'd been sure that Baxter had been aiming for
his crotch, to wound Gonzalo in a way he would never recover
from. Baxter's final revenge. Luckily, Gonzalo was wrong. The
bullet had entered his inner thigh and exited the back of his
leg, just under his butt cheek. His manhood remained intact.

Gonzalo sat on a tree stump ten yards away from the truck. It
was a clear day. The wind blew hard and steady off the nearby
mountain lake, but still the sun warmed him. He stared down
at the square mound of gauze taped to his bare right thigh, a
blossom of red in the center, like the flag of Japan. His jeans
had been cut down to short shorts so that no fabric irritated
the dressing of his wounds.

The gauze had come from one of Sasha's backpacks. She'd stashed backpacks full of supplies all over Denver so that if she ever had to flee Thunder or get out of the city, she could grab the nearest one and go without missing a beat. He was impressed. The pack they'd grabbed had a first-aid kit, and they'd used all the gauze to bandage up his gunshot wound, the knife wound in his other thigh, the one in his ribs, and the burned stumps of his pinkie and ring finger. He'd thought the pain he'd felt during his growth spurts in McKinley had been the worst he'd ever experience. He'd been so naive.

The pain was so debilitating that he could barely think. Thank God Sasha was together enough to drive. They were somewhere in the Rockies now. He didn't know where exactly. The last couple hours had been a blur.

"This place had a generator, like I thought," Sasha said, pointing to the A-frame cabin behind her. She carried a red plastic gas can and set it on the ground as she unfastened the truck's gas cap. "I siphoned off enough to get us near the border, I think."

"You shouldn't do stuff like that without me," Gonzalo said and grimaced in pain.

Sasha laughed. "You just need to rest, big boy. Here—"

Sasha opened the truck and pulled a bottle of Cream Soda from her emergency backpack. She tossed it to Gonzalo and he barely caught it. The wind whipped against his back.

"Drink up while I'm downwind. We got a long drive," she said, and hoisted up the gas can to fill up the truck.

Gonzalo looked at the full soda bottle in his damaged hand. It had a dense wad of paper towel shoved in the top like a stopper. Sasha had destroyed the bottle cap back in Denver. As for the rest of the bottle caps in the Coliseum, Sasha had left their destruction up to the Thunder. Before they'd left Denver, Sasha had told a few trusted Thunder members about the hunters and the tracking chips inside the bottle caps. They vowed to convince the rest of Thunder to head back out on the road while the hunters still thought Zeus was in charge. They would spread the word about the hunters' plan from infected hideout to infected hideout. Gonzalo was proud of Sasha. Countless lives would be saved because she'd had the courage to speak up.

He uncorked the Cream Soda in his hand. After what that bottle of Squirt had done to him, he didn't want to hand his reality over to chemicals again.

"I need to stay sharp," he said. "We're still not safe."

"It makes you sharper."

"I don't trust it."

"Do I seem like I'm out of my mind?"

Sasha was having no trouble holding up the full, super-sized gas can as it emptied slowly into the truck. Her posture was straight, her eyes alert, even though she still looked like she'd just crawled out of a chimney.

"No," he said.

"Then, drink. You don't have to be in agony."

"I'm fine."

"You're impossible."

She glared at him, but she couldn't commit to it. As soon as their eyes met, her glare softened to a smile. Her eyes began to well up.

"I still love you, though," she said.

"Love you too," he said with a wince.

"Just try a sip."

He shook his head. "I can't. It's not over yet. I still need to make sure you're safe."

"It is over. At least for now. Look around," Sasha said, gesturing to their placid surroundings. The tall pines around Gonzalo swayed in the wind. "Just calm down."

"I didn't survive this long out here by calming down," he said.

"Well, I survived this whole time too."

"I know."

"Do you? 'Cause you're not acting like it. I have it under control, Gonzalo."

"Say that again."

"No," she said with a smile she was trying to suppress.

"Come on, say it."

"I have it under control. What?"

"It's cute," he said.

"Shut up. I've been keeping it under control since I got out of McKinley. I know my way around. I know how to stay hidden. I've made a lot of friends out here in the zone who will help keep us safe. I know—"

"These are guy friends you've met?"

"Wha—? Some of them were guys, yeah."

"How friendly are we talking?"

"You better be joking. If you're not joking, that means that you did something."

Gonzalo put his hands over his head as if under arrest, and felt the pain surge in his stumps. "I'm joking, I'm joking."

"Good. Now will you take a sip already?"

"One sip."

"Sure. Fine. Go. While the wind is still blowing towards me."

Gonzalo sighed and lifted his gas mask just enough to expose his mouth. He placed the bottle to his lips and sipped. He lowered his mask back into place as he swallowed. It tasted just like Cream Soda. The effect was mild but took hold in seconds. He felt a tiny burst of happiness. His pain was still there, but it was in the background of his attention. For the first time, he noticed the magnificent beauty of the lake beside them. Berry bushes lined the shore. Slender pines were perfectly reflected in the flat water. Mountain peaks barely darker than the sky towered in the distance like gray guardians.

"Not bad, right?" Sasha said.

"Can't complain," Gonzalo said, and he carefully raised his

mask to take another sip. His pain receded to the point that he felt only dull aches. The safe future that Sasha promised was seeming more possible to him by the second. Why wouldn't it be? He didn't want to sell Sasha short. She had survived out here this whole time without him. Maybe he could just let her take the reins for awhile.

Gonzalo looked at his missing fingers. He'd actually forgotten they were gone for a moment. He'd prided himself on his strength for so long. He never thought he'd doubt the strength of his hands, but his injured hand felt weak. Destroyed. Practically useless. He looked at the Cream Soda frothing inside the bottle and thought of how much pain relief was in that liquid. He turned to Sasha.

"Sash. Are you sure you got this?"

She didn't get mock-angry at him like he thought she would. Maybe she could hear in his voice how serious he was. She met his gaze. "Everything will be fine, Gonz. You aren't doing this alone anymore. I'll take care of you."

Gonzalo almost wept. He hadn't realized how much he craved hearing someone tell him that.

"Well, here goes nothin' then," Gonzalo said and lifted his mask again. With the wind gusting toward Sasha, he tipped the bottle and drank. He kept swallowing until he'd downed all of it, then threw the bottle over his shoulder.

"Did you just drink the whole thing?!" Sasha said. "Oh, I can't wait to hang out with you."

Gonzalo laughed, and coughed a little, as he pulled his mask back on. Sasha was looking at him excitedly, like she expected him to explode at any second. He didn't feel some overwhelming sensation. But then he realized he didn't feel his pain whatsoever. He felt . . . good. Really good. He felt better than he had since . . . since he kissed Sasha that night in the quad.

He couldn't take his eyes off her as she finished pouring the gas and tossed the gas can in the back of the truck. She was stunning. He hadn't really looked at her until now. Not at all of her. And if he had, he hadn't been able to truly see her, because the beauty that he saw now made this whole long journey worthwhile.

"Hey, Sash."

"Yeah?"

"Wanna do it in the woods?"

She cracked up.

"Now you're talking," she said.

ACKNOWLEDGMENTS

We'd like to thank Alix Reid and the good folks at Carolrhoda Lab and Lerner Books for their vision and support; Kami Garcia for always having our back; our family and friends for their generosity and love; Andrea Cascardi for believing in this book when it was just a hunch of a story; Gillian King-Cargile and the incredible team at STEM Read for their tireless work and creativity; and Mollie Glick as well as everyone at Foundry Literary + Media for guidance every step of the way.